Realms of Shadow and Sun

Rachel Avery

Contents

Chapter One

T he dragon snarled and huffed under Renya's knees. She could feel the warmth radiating from the creature, feel the inhale and exhale of its lungs. She wrongly assumed dragons were reptilian and cold-blooded, but beyond the scales, nothing about this creature was amphibian-like. A pair of giant wings beat heavily, and Renya could hear them flapping against the air current as the large beast took her higher and higher into the cool, night air. The dragon dived a bit, and Renya felt her stomach lurch at the sensation. It was like hitting turbulence in an airplane, only this was not just a mixture of hot and cold air. It was hard to believe that a few hours ago she was in Grayden's arms, worrying about him seeing her thoughts, and now she was on the back of the fiercest creature she'd ever seen, being guided by the cruelest woman known to man.

Her thoughts went back to her last few moments with Grayden. She was brutally torn away from him before she could even make sure he was safe. The second she saw the knife plunge into his side, she knew she would do anything to spare him. She'd give up whatever she could in exchange for his life. Renya just hoped a healer was able to get to Grayden before he bled out on that field.

Cressida didn't say a word to Renya once they were airborne. She ignored her, not bothering to look back or acknowledge her presence. Renya was glad, wanting nothing to do with the monster. Her hand throbbed slightly where it was sliced open, and the sensation made her think about the blood promise she made. What did a promise like that entail? Was it reversible? There was no way she would willingly join the Shadow Queen's quest for domination without coercion. She would fight and sabotage the entire way.

Renya watched the features of the land grow smaller and smaller the higher they flew. She saw a shimmering lake housed deep within a crater, and an archipelago heading out to the sea in the west. Renya hadn't realized how vast this world was. She spent so little time in it, and now she was sure she would be locked up for the duration of her life. Without Grayden. She reached inside and tried to find him through their bond, but it was useless. She prayed it was because she was too far away, not because he was dead. They hadn't had the time to fully explore their bond and test its limitations. She couldn't imagine him dead, she couldn't think like that without completely breaking down. But either way, she would never see him again. Tears cascaded down her cheeks, and the windchill made them feel like icicles as they stung her skin.

The dragon was incredibly fast and powerful. Renya thought there were more dragons during the battle, but she only saw the one carrying her and Cressida towards the Shadow Realm. If the other dragons retreated back to the Shadow Realm, they did it under the cover of the trees.

The darkness of the lands ahead of them was like an omen foreshadowing what was to come. Sun and shadow touched each other, but there was nothing in between. The juxtaposition between the two realms was intense, and Renya realized instantly the lighter side of the divide was her home lands. Where she was born. Where she was once loved and comforted.

The dragon descended slightly as they approached the Shadow Realm territory, and the drop in altitude afforded her a closer glance at the realm that was hers by birthright. Everything below was bright and golden. From the pearly white buildings to the golden bricks, the entire area beneath her seemed to glisten. Ahead, in the center of the city, slightly raised, stood a majestic palace. It reminded Renya of the Taj Mahal, only more vibrant. Bits of the towers were destroyed, and the city nestled around the palace was deserted. It saddened Renya to see it that way; her first glimpse of her home was filled with emptiness and desertion. Grayden was so proud of his lands, and hers were desolate and abandoned.

Before Renya could commit the details of the city to memory, the dragon sped up and lost altitude rapidly. Renya squealed sharply at the descent, and she could hear Cressida laughing at her discomfort in front of her. The top of a dark forest came into view, and everything inside the line of trees was almost completely black. The only light came from the glow of the Sun Realm, which was hidden behind the overgrown foliage. The trees were tall and dense, their branches twisted and gnarled. The leaves were a deep green, but they were so dark they appeared black. The forest was silent, and the only sound Renya heard was the wind blowing through the trees. The area was so devoid of light that she couldn't fathom how the dragon was navigating through the trees. From the smell alone, Renya knew they were almost to the forest floor. The scent of pine needles wafted into her nose, and for a split second her mind transported her back to those nights with Grayden, when she lay in his arms, his masculine smell overwhelming her and making her feel safe and protected. She choked back a sob as the dragon finally reached solid ground.

A massive sound, like metal grinding on metal, came from up ahead and Renya saw a large tunnel in front of her, with torches illuminating the inside. Before the dragon could enter, Cressida slid off his back and gave him a pat on his large, scaled neck.

"Good boy, Brutus."

Renya swore she felt the dragon purr and vibrate underneath her body. She didn't have time to dwell on it before Cressida approached her. Barely glancing at Renya, she withdrew a knife that had been tied around her calf and sliced through the knots securing Renya's hands to the saddle. As soon as she was free, Renya pushed herself off the dragon and scurried as far away from Cressida as she could, bolting towards the midnight blackness of the forest.

Before she could make it even ten feet, she was jerked back, like an invisible cord pulling her back towards Cressida.

Cruel laughter bubbled up from Cressida's thin lips. "You made a promise in blood, princess," she sneered. "I don't need my magic to hold you here. But by all means, try to escape. I'll enjoy watching your spirit break and revel in the helplessness you'll soon feel."

Anger surged through Renya, and to her surprise, golden strands of magic cascaded from her fingertips. An ember separated itself from them, and fell to the ground, igniting a pile of dry pine needles and dead leaves. Cressida reached out with her dark tendrils of magic and extinguished the flames easily.

"So you've found out how to use my magic." She looked at Renya with disgust and anger.

"It's my magic," Renya said through clenched teeth. "You just tried to take it from me."

"Actually, it never belonged to you. You took it from me first, *daughter*."

Chapter Two

P ain sizzled throughout Grayden's entire body. His side felt like it was on fire and the hurt radiated all the way down to his feet. He kept his eyes shut, not wanting to acknowledge the inevitable. Once his eyelids opened, he would have to admit that he once again lost Renya. His Little Fawn. He scrunched up his eyes even tighter, feeling the moisture threatening to overflow and the pressure increasing along his brow.

"Prince Grayden?" a gentle voice asked.

He rolled to his uninjured side and hissed at the sudden pain from the slight movement. He finally opened his eyes, taking in his surroundings. A gauzy canopy blocked the view of the stone ceiling, and the scent of Renya's hair, washed with lavender soap, still lingered on the pillow next to him. Grayden was in the bedroom he and Renya shared at the Twilight Kingdom.

"Oh Gods, you're awake!" The soft voice came again, and this time he recognized it. "I need to let Dimitri know you're conscious," Julietta said.

Grayden didn't respond, and instead pushed himself up to a sitting position. He gasped, the pain excruciatingly raw and sharp. His hands gripped the down comforter as he breathed through the sensation.

"Grayden, no. You need to heal." Julietta put her hand on his bare shoulder and then instantly pulled it away. "Gods, you're burning up. I think your wound is infected."

He ignored her concern and attempted to swing his legs out of the bed. He was still in his trousers but his shirt and armor had been removed. His bare feet hit the floor and he glanced around, looking for his boots. Every single movement sent a searing jolt of anguish through his nerves. It felt like his lungs were in a vice. Grayden looked down and saw that his injured side was tightly wrapped with care.

Julietta stood next to the bed, a horrified look on her face. She was wearing a peach gown, having changed out of the nightgown she was wearing during the attack, and Grayden swallowed down the panic as he worried about the amount of time he was unconscious. Fates, his Renya. How did he let this happen? Feeling deep inside, he tried to sense her. He stilled his breathing, searching for her. There. She was there. Alive. He could feel her, but not with the same intensity as before. She must be a great distance away, he surmised, most likely already at the Shadow Realm, but at least she was alive.

Grayden tried to stand, but swayed unsteadily on his legs, his strong muscles failing him.

"You've lost a lot of blood, Grayden. You need to lie back down."

"No. I won't stop until I get her back," he growled.

If Julietta was shocked by his tone, she didn't show it. Instead, she lowered her voice and spoke softly to him.

"Your brother is on his way here now. He will help you get Renya back. But you can't do anything in the shape you are in."

"What plans have been made to retrieve my

mate?" He practically spit out the words, then felt instant guilt as Julietta stepped back, a glint of fear in her eyes. Grayden sighed, and then grimaced when he felt the pain again. Gods, he wasn't fit to launch any type of attack. He couldn't even stay on his feet. Nausea overtook him and he fell back to the mattress.

"I'm sorry, Julietta. I just...I need Renya." His voice was small and his anguish palpable.

Julietta walked towards the table near the fire, and brought back a tray with a bowl of broth. "My mother is talking with Gillbert and Orien to figure out what to do next. I know you need Renya, but our people are suffering. We've lost a third of our village, and there is no food and not much shelter. Times have been hard for a while, but the dragons and Shadow Realm soldiers made quick work of the village. Everything was ransacked."

Once again, guilt flushed in his cheeks and around his neck. Of course, their village was all but destroyed. He was surprised that this room seemed to be unscathed, and looked around for damage. Julietta caught his eye, seeming to understand.

"The north half of the castle is untouched. Once the Shadow Queen got—got what she came for, they immediately retreated."

Grayden heard the hesitation in Julietta's voice. She was trying hard not to say Renya's name, as if it would pain Grayden even further.

His head swam and he was having trouble focusing. He saw the look of concern on Julietta's face, before her features faded and everything went black.

∞

The next time he awoke, Dimitri was at his side. His rough hands fiddled with the bandage around Grayden's torso.

"Ah, you're awake. I'm afraid you're battling a nasty infection in that wound. I've tried to draw it out using a poultice, and it seems to be working, albeit slowly."

This time, the nausea and dizziness wasn't as strong. It still hurt to sit up, but Grayden managed to do it without whimpering in pain. He studied Dimitri, glad to see their healer survived the battle unscathed.

"We'll get her back."

Grayden said nothing. He felt empty inside, the pain of Renya's absence weighing on his soul. Without her, he was nothing. Had nothing. Cared about nothing.

Dimitri accepted Grayden's silence and examined him closely. He unwrapped the bandage and his eyes enlarged when he took in the gaping wound.

"That bad, huh?" Grayden said, his voice raspy.

Dimitri sighed, and moved towards the edge of the bed to grab several bottles from his bag. "It's still horribly infected." He opened a jar full of mint green paste and gently applied it to the wound.

It stung, but Grayden bit back the pain. A sting was nothing compared to the loss of Renya. "Well, Cressida kicked me several times there. I'm not surprised."

Dimitri kept silent and smeared the contents of another jar on the inside of a fresh bandage before wrapping it around Grayden's waist. Before he could secure it, the door to the room flew open.

"Grayden, are you okay?" Phillippe rushed over to his brother, concern clouding his features. There were dark circles under his mocha-colored eyes, and his jaw was covered in coarse stubble.

Grayden managed to sit up. "No, I'm not okay. Renya is gone and I'm too weak to do a damn thing about it."

Dimitri finished securing the bandage and swiftly gathered up his supplies, backing out of the room so Phillippe and Grayden could talk.

"We'll get her back, brother."

"You know what? You're the second person to say that to me within the past half hour, yet no one has offered up a single plan." Grayden clenched his jaw tightly.

"Whoa there, calm down. I care about Renya too. But we have a multitude of problems we're facing. The entire village outside is a war zone. People are displaced, there's no food or clean water, and the dead haven't even been recovered from where they fell. The second I got here, I dispatched as many of our soldiers as I could spare to help restore the city and at least stabilize things here."

Grayden knew his brother was right, but every single instinct told him that none of it mattered. The only thing in this entire world that carried any sort of weight was the connection he shared with his mate. He looked away, ashamed at his behavior but overwhelmed with the aching need inside him to get her back.

Phillippe looked down at his brother and sighed. "I can't imagine how difficult this must be. Fated bonds are so rare, it's hard for any of us to imagine how you feel. But we will get her back. Can you still feel her?"

Grayden closed his eyes and reached for her down their bond. She was there, but rather than the fiery inferno he usually felt, it was like a dim candle about to be extinguished. "She's there...but faint."

"You know she's alive. That's more than any of us would get if we lost our loved ones. You need to focus on that blessing."

Grayden nodded, but his insides were still knotted and he felt perspiration wet his forehead. He wasn't sure if it was from the fever or the turmoil in his mind. "How is our sister?"

Phillippe looked down at the stone floor and shifted his feet. "I haven't been able to see her yet. She'll only see Julietta. She won't let Dimitri give her anything to help ease her grief. I ran into Julietta on my way up here, and she said Selenia doesn't talk. She just stares into the fire and won't eat or drink."

Worry gripped Grayden's heart. Fates, everything was falling apart. Jurel was dead, Renya was gone, and nearly half the Twilight Kingdom was destroyed. He was also certain his magic was completely depleted. Grayden had pulled everything from inside of him on that hill to try and reach Cressida, but he wasn't able to bring forth even a spark.

Phillippe saw the look of despair on Grayden's face and clapped him on the back. "One thing at a time, Grayden. One thing at a time."

Chapter Three

For the third day in a row, Sion wondered if he should just kill Brandle in his sleep. Surely he could make it look like an accident? He could push him off a cliff, bury him alive in an avalanche...the list of punishments and death Sion wanted to grant him seemed never-ending. But as satisfying as orchestrating his death might be, he knew Grayden was still relying on him to play his part at Cressida's court.

Sion watched the fire, listening to Brandle snore in his tent. It surprised him that Brandle trusted him enough to sleep and let him keep watch. For his part, Sion slept with his fingers curled around his dagger, upright and ready to attack. He rarely slept more than a few minutes at a time, not trusting the queen's cousin for a moment.

He heard the old man cough, and went over to the tree he was bound to. Sion hated that this elderly man was forced to sleep upright in the ice, tied to the snow-laden tree, with nothing but the freezing ground under his thin, strange garb.

Sion looked at the man, taking in his torn shirt and shiney shoes. The strange footwear was black and had laces, but they were low, not fit for the Snow Lands at all. His glasses were broken, and one edge dangled lower than the other. His eyes, however, were a piercing blue. Sion couldn't fathom why this human man was important to the Shadow Queen. Perhaps he was banished to the human realm? When Sion and Brandle went through the portal and found the man, bent down and inspecting a long row of books, he went without a fight. Almost as though he was expecting them, his cerulean eyes twinkled in amusement before he was frozen with Brandle's magic and forced into their world.

The man rubbed his hands together and blew on them, trying to keep warm. The golden buttons that kept his sleeves together gleamed in the light of the fire. Sion looked back, making sure Brandle was still snoring, before he spoke.

"I'm sorry about this. I wish I could let you go and return you to your world."

The old man just looked at Sion, his mouth twitching as if he possessed a secret that Sion couldn't possibly understand.

"Trust me. I'm right where I want to be." He studied Sion, his silver hair damp against his scalp, the snowflakes melting and dripping alongside his face.

Sighing, Sion reached into the bag he wore on his shoulder and produced a few traveling cakes. He knelt down and handed them to the man, and he grabbed them, shoveling them down quickly.

"Do you have a name?"

He swallowed hard, then produced another sly grin. "Cyrus."

Sion rocked on his heels before standing and moving back to the fire. He grabbed a pot and began filling it with snow and herbs.

"Well Cyrus, what does the Shadow Queen want with you? What importance do you hold for her that she sent us all the way to the human realm to retrieve you?"

"Oh trust me, I'm important to her. At one time, I was the most important person to her."

Sion snorted, finding that hard to believe. And yet...it was a strange request, traveling through the portal to kidnap an aging human male. There was some kind of connection there, as impossible as it seemed.

Cyrus began coughing again, a dry rattle creeping up from his lungs. Sion turned his attention back to the pot he placed in the fire. The soft citrus smell dissipated through the air, and Sion heard the old man sigh.

"I haven't smelled crimling tea in almost twenty-five years."

Sion's suspicions were indeed correct. This man wasn't just a human. He was Fae, and glamoured like Renya was. For whatever reason, he was either banished or hiding in the human realm.

Sion grabbed the pot and poured the contents into a silver mug and brought it over to his prisoner. If Brandle had his way, the poor man would be starved and beaten. But that wasn't who Sion was. He passed the tea over to Cyrus, and the man's blue eyes sparkled knowingly.

"You're not really hers, are you?"

Sion kept his face neutral. How could this man guess his duplicity so easily?

A slight chuckle came from the elderly man. "You're a Ruffio, aren't you? From the Snow Lands?"

Sion's eyes widened and he felt his neck perspire as he glanced over at the tent, praying to the Gods that Brandle was still asleep. His boisterous snores escaped the thick canvas of the tent, and Sion's shoulders relaxed.

"I guessed right, didn't I? I knew your father a bit. You look exactly like him. Anyone from the Snow Lands and a descendant of Markus Ruffio would never betray their own."

Sion didn't dare speak of his double-role, but didn't argue with this stranger either. He let the silence linger as Cyrus finished his tea.

"How is King Efferon?" He asked the question so nonchalantly that Sion was shook for a moment. It was odd that this man, whom they found organizing books, knew of the late king.

"He passed away about five years ago. The queen as well." Sion spoke the words with heavy sadness. Grayden's parents had always been kind to him and his family. King Efferon was even his godfather.

"Both? What happened?"

"A sickness. None such that had ever been seen before. Healers were called from every corner of our world, but none could save them."

Cyrus frowned. "A sickness, you say? Did anyone else become ill?"

Sion frowned. No, no one had. The Snowden children were kept away, but the healers and servants hadn't gotten sick either.

"Not a sickness, my boy. I bet they were poisoned."

Sion felt dizzy, the blood rushing to his head and then pooling in his cheeks. Fates, murdered? Why hadn't anyone looked into this possibility? He thought back to those bleak days after the king and queen's death, days in which he tried to keep Grayden from falling apart at the seams. Sion had dunked his friend's head in the horse's water trough to sober him up enough to attend the funeral. Grayden took the loss of both parents incredibly hard, and then being thrust into the role of ruler added even more pressure. Tumwalt and Almory were bustling around trying to prepare Grayden and plan for the future. Was it possible they overlooked the true cause of their deaths?

Cyrus looked at Sion, his eyes full of sympathy as the young man tried to take in this revelation.

"Who is ruling the Snow Lands now? If I recall correctly, the eldest Snowden child had no magic. The other was practically a babe in leading strings."

"Phillippe, the eldest, possesses no magic. The younger, Grayden, now leads the lands." Sion tried to keep his voice neutral, but had trouble keeping the pride out of his voice when he mentioned his best friend.

"And it's him you serve, isn't it?"

Sion nodded, just the quickest jolt of his head.

"Ah, I see. Tell me, what has Cressida been up to? Besides her plans for total domination, that is."

"She's managed to bring dragons into this world."

It was Cyrus's turn to become unhinged. "She didn't?"

"I'm afraid so. Three, soon to be four. She's practically unstoppable." Sion took the mug back from Cyrus and began packing up his bag. He looked at the horizon, just as a tiny sliver of sun climbed into the sky.

"Four dragons? I just—I can't believe she would go that far."

"You have no idea how far her depravity goes," Sion retorted, thinking of the bite marks on his shoulder.

Cyrus opened his mouth to respond, but stopped when they heard rustling coming from Brandle's tent. Sion quickly moved away from Cyrus and back towards the fire.

Brandle crawled out of the tent, his usually neat beard disheveled. His robes were wrinkled, and he looked annoyed.

"Sleep well, Brandle?" Sion was all but smirking. It was amusing to see how hard the outdoor travel was on Brandle. Obviously he enjoyed the finer things in life a little too much.

Brandle scowled at Sion, then glanced at Cyrus. "Sion, get him up. I want to be back at the Shadow Realm by this evening. I refuse to spend another night in that tent."

Sion ignored Brandle and took his time packing up his tent and supplies before securing it to the horse. While they were able to use magic to transport themselves for some of the journey, neither possessed enough magic to transport their prisoner back to the cliff high above the Shadow Realm valley.

Sion walked over to Cyrus, snow crunching underfoot. He cut through the ropes binding him to the tree, and Cyrus pushed himself off of the frigid ground. Sion felt guilty as Cyrus struggled on his frozen legs. He came over and helped the elderly man onto his horse, before Brandle came behind and secured him to the saddle. Sion grabbed another rope, and the prisoner's horse was tied to his horse. Brandle extinguished the fire with a flick of his dark tendril of magic, and then climbed onto his own horse's back before strutting ahead.

Cyrus sat regally on the back of the horse, as if he

had been riding all of his life, gearing up for the voyage ahead.

The closer they got to the Shadow Realm, the heavier Sion's chest became. Every step of the horse's hooves brought him closer to Cressida's clutches, and her bed. As soon as the snow started to thin, he knew it was only a matter of time before she could sink her teeth into him. Both literally and figuratively, he thought with a shudder.

They left the icy brightness of the Snow Lands and entered into the darkened forest of the Shadow Realm. Sion rode through this forest many times, but the dead and decaying trees always left him with the feeling that he was being watched. Every crackle of a branch made him turn, every rustling leaf made his heart race.

Finally, they left the forest behind and stood at the base of the cliff. Sion glanced back at Cyrus, and saw steady resolve in his expression.

Brandle looked at Sion and Cyrus then bristled. "I'm going to use magic, you can use the spiral staircase with the human," he sneered. He let the black mist cover his body before it funneled and he disappeared. Sion sighed. For the first time in days, he was free of Brandle's stares and insults. His oily presence slickened every moment of the journey. Even returning home to the Snow Lands was tainted by Brandle's irritation over every snow drift.

Sion dismounted and untied Cyrus from the saddle. Two men, wearing the same golden garb Sion wore, came forward and took the horses.

In the short time it took Sion to reach the entry to the spiral staircase, he was physically sick from dread. Cyrus stretched and grunted next to him, his muscles aching from the journey. His hands were still bound, and guilt ate away at Sion's insides. Checking to make sure that no one was around, he untied the older man.

Cyrus looked up, surprised.

"Go, quickly. Back to the Snow Lands. Our people will take you in."

Cyrus stood there, unmoving.

"Did you hear me? You need to move fast!"

"I'm right where I want to be, trust me, my boy. Now that I'm here, I can almost feel her. This is a reunion I'm looking forward to."

Sion's mouth went slack as he tried to take in the man's meaning. What person in their right mind would want to be reunited with Cressida? Sion would give anything to be out of her clutches and free to live his own life.

"If I can't convince you to go, I have no choice but to bring you before the queen. I don't know why she desires you so, but the fact that she made us cross into the human realm to find you means you are instrumental to her schemes. She won't let you live. Once she gets what she wants, she'll discard you." Sion tightened his fists unconsciously, nails digging into his palms.

"Don't concern yourself with my welfare. I can look out for myself." Cyrus rolled his stiff shoulders and neck. "Just bring me to her."

Sion stood at the base of the turret that led to the palace, perched precariously on the mountainside. Using the little magic Cressida afforded him, he blasted out a string of black mist that twisted and twirled in the air before forming the shape of a door on the side of the turret. Sion reached out with the borrowed magic, pushing against the bricks as they slid back and a passageway emerged. He sighed, the dread making his stomach churn.

If the appearance of the doorway surprised Cyrus, he didn't show it. Instead, he marched in ahead of Sion, his rope bindings trailing loosely.

The smell of moss and damp earth hit Sion's nose. What used to be a good smell, the scent of the forest after a rainstorm, now made him nauseated. Standing in the middle of the circular chamber, he let a little more magic flow and the torches lining the wet walls lit, their dull glow matching the look in Sion's eyes. Cyrus looked around, almost reminiscing, as if he remembered this place from his past. Before Sion could ask him about it, he moved his foot to the first stone slab step, his shiny shoes clacking against the rock.

"Up we go."

Sion followed behind, surprised at the agility of the older man. He seemed to be in amazing shape despite his silver hair and wrinkled skin.

The spiral passageway went up and up, like a giant beanstalk soaring upwards to the clouds. Even Sion was huffing towards the end, and Cyrus stopped to catch his breath a few times before they reached the landing.

The passageway opened up into a dome-shaped space, with open-air windows at the top. Cyrus looked resolute as Sion pressed open the marble door leading into the palace. He followed Sion across the marble tiles, taking in the ivory pillars that didn't provide any protection from the valley below. Every walkway was exposed, with no walls to break the wind. Whenever Sion walked them, he felt like he was walking a tightrope, his position in the air as precarious as his position in Cressida's court. The walkways twisted and turned, forming a giant labyrinth across the sky. After navigating the maze, they reached the last sky bridge leading to the throne room.

Sion grabbed the ropes binding Cyrus and tightened them, then forced him behind to assume the role of prisoner. They crossed over into the throne room, where Brandle stood regally, as if he was the one who should be ensconced on the black mist throne. Sion moved towards the center of the room, wind tickling his hair but providing a cooling breeze. He wanted to shed his thick fur, but he stood stalwartly until he felt the wind in the room dash and funnel in front of the throne, where Cressida's dark shape began to take form.

The mist evaporated and Cressida stood in front of Sion and Cyrus, smirking. Her long hunter-green dress dragged the floor, and an embroidered serpent with jeweled eyes wrapped around her torso like a belt. Her eyelids were painted green to match her dress, and large, gold cobra-shaped earrings hung from her earlobes. She twisted in the spot, her high heels clicking on the floor.

Sion bowed his head, not eager to meet her cruel eyes. But he detected movement out of the corner of his eye as Cyrus stood a little taller.

"So...it's been a long time," Cyrus said, staring Cressida down.

Cressida pursed her lips and moved to stand in front of Cyrus on the dais circling her throne. She peered down at him, and Sion could feel the malice radiate from her body.

Finally, she spoke. "Hiding in the human realm? I should have guessed it before. You always had a soft spot for those weaklings."

Cyrus shrugged, arms still bound in front of him. "It was better than being in the same world as you."

Cressida hissed, and back-handed Cyrus. He turned his head with the impact, but didn't make a sound. He faced forward again, calm despite the storm rising in front of him.

"Brandle, take him away. See that he's placed in the south wing, farthest from my chambers. I don't want him anywhere near me. Bind him, with both ropes and magic. And if he fights...well, feel free to get creative. Just don't kill him. That pleasure will go to me."

Brandle nodded, and his dark magic encompassed himself and Cyrus, and then they both disappeared from the throne room.

Cressida stepped down from the dais, pushing past Sion and heading out of the throne room. Sion was just about to let out a sigh of relief when she turned back towards him.

"You are no longer permitted to leave the palace, for any reason. Your sole purpose in this realm is to serve me."

The bile hit Sion's mouth and for the thousandth time since he joined her court, he wished the Fates would grant him the sweet release of death.

Chapter Four

R enya stared blankly out the window, her mind whirling as she tried to find a way out of this predicament. She'd done nothing but sob since Cressida's guards shoved her in this room. Her body ached from trembling, and she wanted nothing more than to collapse on the bed behind her and sleep away all her troubles. She could no longer sense Grayden, and the tension and worry she felt made her head pound. She didn't know if it was the distance, or if he was unconscious...or dead. He was bleeding so profusely when she left him on that hill, with destruction and carnage surrounding him.

And then there was the revelation from Cressida. Her mother? How could that be possible? The very notion frightened Renya down to her core. How could that cruel, sadistic witch be her mother? She must be lying. It had to be some kind of plot or play for power. There was no way that she could be a product of that evil woman. And yet...the Shadow Queen seemed to know Aunt Agatha immediately at the Sunset Land. Recognized her...even feared her. *Was it true*?

Renya was broken. Her entire life was a lie. First her heritage and lineage, and this newest revelation? She wanted to do nothing more than crawl up into a ball and disappear.

Another tear leaked from her eye, and Renya

didn't even bother to wipe it away. She watched it drip down onto the marble vanity in front of her, pooling against the cold surface. The separation from Grayden was unbearable. She now understood his frantic behavior to get to her after their bond developed. It was like a piece of her soul was gone, locked away in a vault and inaccessible.

A knock on the door drew her out of her misery for a split second. She rose up and moved to the corner of the room, horrified that it might be the Shadow Queen, yet wanting to interrogate her about her outlandish claim.

Instead, an older woman entered the room almost bashfully. Her hair was auburn but streaked with silver, and she had a sweet looking face, with soft eyes and a mouth that was pulled up into a tentative smile. Renya couldn't believe someone so kind-looking was here in this palace of hell.

The woman walked towards Renya slowly, balancing a polished wooden tray in her hands. She placed the tray on top of the vanity Renya was sitting at and then wiped her hands on her crisp cream-colored apron. She turned to leave the room.

"Wait!" Renya called, even though she was unsure of what she wanted from her.

The woman turned around, looking at Renya expectedly. Renya thought fast, sizing the woman up. She looked friendly, but perhaps it was a trap. Yet...there was something about her eyes that made Renya think she might be sympathetic to her plight.

"What's your name?"

The woman smoothed her hair off her forehead, looking at Renya before quickly bowing her head.

"Margot, your highness."

"Please, just call me Renya."

Margot looked at Renya quickly, before darting her eyes back down respectfully. "As you wish, Renya." Before Renya could open her mouth to ask another question, Margot zipped out of the room, shutting the door behind her softly.

Renya sighed as she looked at the tray on the vanity. There was a pink teapot steaming from the spout, and a teacup with a lemon slice at the bottom. A few slices of cheese rested next to it, along with some bread and sausage. She assessed the food, trying to determine if there was any chance it might be poisoned. It was doubtful, especially since Cressida could have killed her back at the Twilight Kingdom. No...she had a purpose for her, Renya was sure of it.

She sat back down at the vanity and poured herself a cup of tea. She wasn't thirsty or hungry, but she knew if she didn't eat or drink she'd lose her strength, and then she would never find a way back to Grayden.

She finished off a piece of bread while she took in the measure of the room. The guards locked the door as soon as they shoved her in the bedchamber, and Renya had been sitting numbly looking out the window for several hours. But now she surveyed the room, eager to find a way to escape or something to help her get free.

The mahogany bed was rather simple, with tall posters and red gauzy curtains wrapped around the canopy. A few blood red roses sat in a vase on the nightstand, and a small fire burned in a hearth on the opposite side of the room. Just off the corner was a tiny bathroom, with a small copper tub. Renya's heart sank as she thought back to all the teasing Grayden did, joking about the size of their bathtub at the lodge. It seemed like a million years ago that she sat on his lap in the tub while he washed her hair.

Another sob threatened to overtake her, but she swallowed it as best she could. If she wanted to survive, she needed to be stoic and strategic. No matter how much she wanted to dissolve into a puddle of tears, it wouldn't get her anywhere. She must put everything she had into getting back to Grayden.

How could she break the blood promise? There had to be a way. She felt for her magic and it hummed underneath her skin, but as soon as she drew it forth, she pulled it back in. She still had no idea how to really use it, let alone break a spell. And was it really her magic? Or was it Cressida's, like she claimed?

Her temple throbbed, and she felt a migraine forming. She had done nothing but cry and stare out the window since she was forced into this room, but Renya was still exhausted. Finally, she crawled into the bed, fully clothed, and waited for sleep to take her.

∞

When she opened her eyes again, it was morning, although the shadows persisted through the entire day. The only way Renya knew she slept through the night was by the arrival of chirping birds. She took a deep breath, immediately feeling for Grayden. After several failed attempts, she gave up, trying hard not to meltdown before the day even got started. She told herself the distance was the reason she could no longer feel him.

Before she could crawl out of bed, there was a

quiet knock at the door and Margot waltzed into the room with another tray and a gown over her arm.

Renya tried again to strike up a conversation while Margot arranged her breakfast tray on the vanity.

"Tell me about yourself, Margot."

Margot dropped her eyes and was silent. Renya sighed, moving to the vanity to examine her tray, noticing that instead of a meal, it just held a teapot and teacup.

Margot began pulling back the sheets on her bed, making it. Just as she began fluffing the pillows, she stopped and stood up straight.

"I have a son. He is a soldier for this realm. He was there that night."

Renya looked at her, perplexed by her meaning.

Margot continued. "When you were taken to the Sunset Lands by Brandle. He saw how much Prince Snowden loves you and how hard he fought for you. He wishes he served another kingdom. But as long as I'm in this palace, he has to be loyal."

Renya moved over to Margot, clasping her hands in hers before giving her a tentative smile. Perhaps she had a friend here after all.

∞

Renya entered the dining room, her stomach in knots and her appetite nonexistent. Like most of the palace, it was an open-air room. Oval-shaped and decorated with ivory pillars and hanging lights, it was actually very pretty. Renya was surprised to see a thing of beauty in Cressida's court.

The table was ivory, matching the pillars, and the chairs were delicate woven white iron. Margot motioned to a spot at the head of the table, and Renya sat. As soon as she was settled, Margot left the room, and Renya was sad to see her go. She was afraid to be alone with the Shadow Queen.

There was no one else in the room, and Renya waited at least five minutes. Finally, just as she was getting ready to leave and try to find her way back to her room, Cressida arrived, the black funnel cloud dispersing as fast as it appeared.

This time, she was wearing a deep indigo dress that matched her violet eyes. Tiny amethyst jewels sparkled along the neckline and the waist of the gown. Instead of a crown, she wore a silver band across her forehead, with a giant stone hanging halfway down to her eyebrows. She sat, making a big show of adjusting her full skirt before glaring across the table at Renya.

Renya glared back, seething in anger. The longer she went without detecting Grayden through their bond, the madder and more hostile she became.

Cressida finally broached the silence. "Since you've stolen my magic, and I'm no longer able to get it back, I'm going to train you to be my weapon."

"It's my magic. It's always been mine." Renya twisted her engagement ring nervously as she talked, before hiding her hands underneath the table to conceal it.

Cressida's eyes narrowed, staring at Renya, as if taking in her features for the first time. Renya did the same, looking for some sort of familial connection. She didn't detect any kind of similarities. While the Shadow Queen was dark and sinister, Renya was golden and bold. It was like oil and vinegar. They would never mix or come together.

"I'm a descendant of the Shadow Realm, but was also born with the powers of the sun. Light and dark, I controlled them both. But with your birth, I lost the powers of the sun and they passed to you."

Renya was taken aback. Her powers were golden and warm, much like the sun. She remembered the first time she reached out with them to Grayden, and the heat that flushed his handsome face. Surely, that was just a coincidence? She was born of the Sun Realm, after all.

"You aren't my mother."

Cressida snorted derisively. "I wish it wasn't true either. I wanted a strong, competent heir. Not some weak girl fawning over a hunk of meat like a vapid idiot."

Renya's face burned from the insult. "You're just jealous that Grayden wanted me, not some old hag."

Cressida stood and moved over to Renya in a flash. She grabbed Renya's hand, twisting it in her tight grip. Before Renya could react, Cressida wrenched the snowflake ring from her finger.

"No!"

But it was too late. Eyes glowing, Cressida held the ring up, allowing the stones to sparkle in the light before throwing it over the edge of the cliff and into the dark forest below.

A sob escaped Renya as she bolted to the side of the room, frantically looking down into the canopy of trees in vain for the little piece she had left of Grayden. When she finally realized it was gone for good, she sunk down to the floor and let the tears flow.

"See? Weak and pathetic."

Rage quickly replaced the anguish Renya felt and

she lashed out with her magic, golden beams aiming right at Cressida. But instead of making contact, they parted around her and disappeared.

"Stupid girl. You made a blood promise to me. Do you honestly think you can harm me? You'll do everything I say, and if you attempt to resist, I'll find your pathetic mate and end him. That was a warning. Insult me or disobey me, and there will be consequences. Dire consequences."

With a flash of black mist, Cressida was gone, and Renya stared at the horizon in front of her, wondering if she would ever find a way back to Grayden.

Chapter Five

C ressida left her bedchambers, locking the door securely behind her to keep Sion from sneaking off. He was her property, and she refused to give him any more autonomy. He would be right where she wanted him, when she wanted him. She was starting to have the feeling that he wasn't completely loyal to her. Ever since the cave-in at the Tidal beach, he seemed distracted. No matter. She would get to the bottom of it. Brandle had been instructed to monitor his every move.

She walked through the empty palace, a sense of peace washing over her. Everything was coming together. She had the girl in her captivity, and not only was she forced to assist and obey, she was miserable. Cressida was pleased the wretched girl was in pain, gleeful that it was now her daughter's turn to feel the despair of having a piece of her missing.

Cressida reflected back to the moment when she birthed the girl. She was happy, proud even, to bear her mate a beautiful daughter. When the babe came out fair and with golden hair, it was obvious she took after her father. But the second the cord was cut, part of Cressida's magic was severed, and it became clear who possessed it. But her mate didn't care. Once his blue eyes met the matching ones his daughter had, he fell hard. He swaddled the girl close to his chest, cooing and whispering her name over and over with reverence.

When he passed her to Cressida, she took the infant, eager to look at the daughter she grew in her belly those long months. But when she peered down into her tiny face, she felt...nothing. No connection. No maternal instincts. She felt resentful of this squirming creature who took her magic and captured her mate's attention so easily.

Cressida shook her head, clearing the memory away, as it tried to settle on her like a heavy fog. She moved quicker, leaving the ghost of the past in her wake.

She dismissed the guards as soon as she arrived in the dungeon. She didn't need the maids or soldiers gossiping.

He was chained in a cell in the corner of the room, lying against the wall with his eyes closed. The second she entered, he opened one eye, as if he was just hovering between wakefulness and sleep.

"I see the human realm aged you, just like it did Agatha. I wouldn't even recognize you."

Cyrus didn't acknowledge her comment.

"So, you teamed up with my sister? My own sister? To take away my daughter?"

Cyrus finally looked at her, his face calm. "What do you want me to say? The second you read that prophecy, we knew she wasn't safe from you. Your power had gone to your head, and you already resented her for taking some of it from you at her birth. Our daughter deserved better. She deserves everything."

"I wouldn't have hurt her."

"You could barely look at her. Instead of nursing her, being a mother to her, you locked yourself up in the library, pouring over scrolls and tomes, looking for ways to reclaim your own power. You didn't care that she needed you. You didn't care if she was hungry, or hurt or—"

"I still don't care."

Cyrus closed his eyes. "I wish I never would have been fated to you."

Cressida made a move as if to strike him, but then stepped back. "You betrayed me. And it will be the last thing you think about when I end you."

Cyrus scoffed. "I'm not afraid of my death. The only death I'm afraid of is the one that will come to our daughter—by her own mother's hand."

Cressida sneered, and her eyes flashed red. "Believe it or not, I won't be killing her. She's promised to me—a blood promise. She'll fight my cause, with absolutely no chance of freedom."

For the first time since arriving at her palace, Cyrus's eyes held a glimpse of fear. He swallowed hard, not wanting to meet her cruel and hollow eyes. "How did you coerce her into making a blood promise to you?"

"It was easy," Cressida said, licking her lips. "I just threatened someone she cared about."

"Agatha?"

A titter of laughter escaped from Cressida's throat. "You fool. You have no idea what has happened in this world. You took our daughter and ran away to the human world, hiding in that pathetic little shop of yours, peddling books to humans. You know nothing about her, even though you shared a world."

Cyrus looked puzzled.

"Our daughter...has a mate."

Chapter Six

G rayden stood in front of the house, or rather, what was left of it. He grasped the shovel at his side and dug into the debris, shifting it and attempting to clear a path. The thatched roof was set ablaze during the attack, and the remnants of the ceiling caved in. Grayden winced, the pain in his side still intense, but he continued shoveling aside wood until he made it inside the structure.

The devastation was heartbreaking. Ash and soot covered every piece of broken furniture in the house. Ceramic bowls and plates were crushed underfoot, and a little doll made up of navy yarn was partially buried in the corner under straw. Luckily, the family made it out unscathed, and were sheltered in the tents Phillippe brought with him from the training camp.

Grayden had been working hard all day, pulling out anything salvageable from the homes along the eastern side of the village, working quietly and quickly. No one seemed to notice him.

He continued to clean up the debris, but the job was mindless and didn't hold his attention. Although Charly and Phillippe suggested he help out to take his mind off of Renya, it wasn't working.

Every fiber of his being told him to throw down his shovel, leap onto his horse and ride until he got to the Shadow Realm and rescued Renya. He didn't want to stop until she was in his arms again. The adrenaline he felt pumping through his veins made him panicky and jumpy at all times. After he spent an entire day pacing and yelling at anyone who came near him, Dimitri and Phillippe suggested that he find something productive to do with his energy while they came up with a plan to get Renya back.

While his muscles might be busy, he couldn't help but let his mind wander to his last moments with Renya. He was devastated the second she promised to join Cressida. He would have rather died than see her in Cressida's clutches. But Renya was stubborn to a fault, and chose his life over her freedom.

He could still feel her, subtle but pulsing gently within him. It was reassuring to know she was alive, but knowing she was out there without him was unbearable.

Grayden moved farther into the dilapidated structure, pushing aside more boards and looking for anything salvageable. He moved towards the back of the house and then outside into the garden. He needed air... and he needed Renya.

A soft mewl caught his attention, and he looked down. Underneath the grass and scorched pieces of cedar, he saw the briefest movement. He got down on his knees, his trousers sinking into the soft mud. He moved aside the bits of trash and rubbage, and uncovered a soft nest made up of pieces of stolen fabrics and grasses. A pure white kitten was in the middle of the nest, its eyes unopened and tiny mouth crying.

He reached down and pulled out the kitten, surprised to see another directly under it. This one was brown and orange, and it looked cold and near death. He quickly scooped them up and tucked them into his tunic. Grayden moved back towards the street, looking for someone to pass the kittens off to while he continued his manual labor. With no success, he walked back to the castle, in search of the kitchen. After following a few maids down some corridors and probably frightening them, he finally followed one to the right spot. He entered the kitchen, looking around. A young boy stood near the fireplace, and Grayden got his attention.

"Could you bring me some warm milk? And heat up some towels and bring them to my room?"

The boy nodded, looking at Grayden curiously. Grayden tipped his tunic down and allowed the boy to see the kittens. He smiled immediately, and began rooting around the cupboards.

Grayden left the kitchen, carrying the kittens gently into the room he had shared with Renya. It was hard to spend time there, with the ghost of her memory haunting him. More nights than not, he fell asleep in other places within the castle. After a night of particularly heavy drinking, he woke up upon Kalora's throne with no memory of how he got there. After that, he decided to limit his consumption, no matter how much it helped to numb his pain.

He moved into the room, and found a towel from the bathroom. Removing the kittens from his tunic, he placed the white one on the bed and started rubbing the brown and orange one. Grayden kept trying to stimulate the kitten, to bring it back to life. Just as he was about to give up, he saw it open one eye and let out a pathetic meow. His heart lightened for a split second, and then he heard a knock at the door.

"Come in," he said, wrapping the two kittens up in the towel.

Selenia entered the room, her eyes still hollow. She was holding the warm towels and a teapot. She glanced around the room, and her eyes focused when she saw Grayden with the kittens.

"Grayden, what..."

"I found them outside in some of the rubble. I should have given them to someone else to take care of when I got back to the castle but...something made me want to bring them up here."

Selenia moved slowly to the bed, taking in the two kittens. "I went for a walk in the hall and I saw a boy bringing these up here. I told him I would take them. I was curious as to what you were doing."

It was the most words Selenia had spoken in three days. Perhaps bringing the kittens back here was the right thing, he thought.

Grayden brought the bundle near the fire and sat on the chair. He patted the vacant seat next to him, and Selenia came over carrying the teapot and towels. Wordlessly, he handed Selenia the orange and brown kitten and held the white himself. He dipped his pinkie finger in the teapot of warm milk and encouraged the kitten to drink. When that didn't work, he grabbed a hand towel from the bathroom and dipped the corner of it in the milk. Finally, the kitten began sucking, its eyes slowly closing.

Grayden and Selenia sat there a long time, feeding the kittens and not speaking. They both understood each other's pain, but didn't acknowledge it.

Finally, Selenia broke the silence. "How are we

going to get Renya back? I'm surprised you haven't ridden out already."

Grayden stroked the sleeping kitten in his lap. "I want to, trust me. I've gotten on my horse so many times only to ride back to the stables. To be honest, I don't know how I can get her back. I have no power left, and I'm no match for the Shadow Queen. It only took her a split second to immobilize me. I knew it was a suicide mission, but I only did it to try and save Renya. But in the end, Cressida got her anyway."

"Grayden, it's not your fault. How could you defeat Cressida without any magic? We are at an unfair advantage."

"It's not your fault about Jurel, either."

Selenia's lip trembled and she looked away, but not before Grayden saw the tears streaming down her face. "Yes, it is. If I would have forgiven him, he never would have stuck around. He never would have..." She stopped, unable to vocalize Jurel's death.

"My sweet one, he would have stayed no matter what. Even if you forgave him and took him back, I would have asked him to stay and accompany us back to the camp. Either way, he would have met his end."

"I shouldn't have said those things to him. My last words were in anger." Selenia wiped her eyes, her voice trembling.

"Me too, dear one. My last words were in anger as well. But, he knew we loved him. I'm sure of it."

Selenia nodded, but Grayden knew she still felt immense guilt. He did as well. He had banished Jurel to their winter camp, permanently. He felt shame, angry with how he reacted. But they couldn't change the past. Jurel was dead, and Renya was held against her will in the Shadow Realm.

Chapter Seven

I t was hard to even look at her. Every time she spoke, Renya wanted to flinch and look away. How had she pledged herself to this monster?

"Pay attention. Our magic works on impulse. None of that 'quieting the mind.' You have to want it. You need a reason to bring it forth."

Renya wanted to protest. But every time she tried to resist Cressida, her body burned and she lost control of herself. Whatever magic was woven into the blood promise was strong. Renya forced herself not to comply, to disobey, but she couldn't manage more than a few seconds of hesitation before her body snapped to attention. Even now, she tried to hold off, but the sweat started at her hairline and she felt sick for the three seconds she managed to force herself still.

"Now!" Cressida bellowed, and Renya acted on instinct, the bright golden strands of her magic bursting forth and rocketing towards Cressida.

The Shadow Queen blocked the rays with a lazy flick of her wrist, and a shield of black mist deflected the heat of Renya's magic.

"See? Instinct," she spat.

Renya glanced at the clock suspended between the two ivory pillars. She'd been working with Cressida for an hour already. Her body was tight and exhausted, both from using her magic and trying to defy Cressida at every chance she got. But at this point, she was starting to realize it was useless.

Just as she was about to ask to be dismissed and go back to her chamber, her jaw dropped.

Sion strolled into the throne room, with a piece of parchment in his hand. Renya wished she could meet his eye, beg him to help her out of this horrid predicament, but she knew she couldn't blow his cover. Instead, she watched him walk gracefully over to the Shadow Queen's side, speaking in a low tone and handing her the paper he carried.

Cressida grabbed the paper and read it, her eyes darting over the script. While she was reading, Sion gave Renya a meaningful look. Renya attempted to figure out what he was trying to tell her, but the second Cressida balled up the parchment in her hands, Sion dropped his eyes.

"Well, princess. It seems your mate survived. I was hoping he'd perish from his wounds, but it seems like I'll have to separate you two another way."

Renya's heart raced faster. Surely, there wasn't a way to separate them? Fated matings were sacred and eternal. Could she do such a thing?

Without glancing at Renya, Cressida swept out of the room, calling over her shoulder. "You're dismissed. Head back to your room, immediately. Sion, go back to my chambers. I'll be with you shortly. I have business to attend to."

Sion crossed in front of Renya, and in a split second, Renya's eye caught a tiny scrap of parchment floating to the floor in front of her. She placed her slippered foot on top of it and slowly pulled it towards her, eyes darting to ensure Cressida didn't see the movement. Thankfully, the Shadow Queen's back was turned, and she was already halfway across the sky bridge.

Sion left the throne room in a flash, no doubt heading to his own personal hell that was Cressida's room.

Alone, Renya bent and quickly grasped the paper, knowing that if she strayed too long, she'd be forced to comply by the blood promise. She thrust the paper into the bodice of her gown and quickly walked to her room.

The second she burst through the door, she pulled out the sliver of paper and unfolded it.

Tonight at dusk. Leave your window unlocked.

Renya's heart leapt and gratitude washed over her. Sion was going to help her. She was so thankful to have an ally here, even if she couldn't speak directly to him in anyone's presence.

Perhaps Sion had a plan to get her back to Grayden or had uncovered a way to break her promise to Cressida. Perhaps he would come bearing news of Grayden. She knew he was alive, Cressida's revelation was no surprise to Renya. She could still feel him at times. It wasn't like before, when she could feel him the same way she felt her own pulse, but whenever his emotions were strong she could sense them. She felt him the second he woke up and processed her loss every morning. It was equally as painful for her, and it sometimes woke her up from her own sleep.

She sat on the bed and tried to reach for him again. She would take anything, just a whisper of his voice or a flash of his face. Renya sat there, unmoving as the minutes flew by.

Before long, Margot arrived and brought her evening meal. Renya wasn't exactly being starved, but it was a far cry from the luxury she experienced in the other kingdoms. It felt like she was back traveling again, with just a few protein-packed items to sustain her. After the spread she saw at her breakfast with Cressida, she knew it was a statement. If Renya could be civil to Cressida, she would be allowed to take her meals in the dining room with a magnificent buffet.

Renya would sooner starve.

She untied the front of her gown and took a quick bath, eager to be rid of the sweat clinging to her scalp and back. She dried off, braided her hair and then slipped on the simple nightgown Margot left.

Renya unlocked the window and then pushed a large chest in front of the door to her room, blocking the entrance. If anyone tried to enter the room with Sion present, there would be some warning.

A soft bird call startled her, and she glanced at the window just in time to see Sion climb through. He was wearing his usual golden robes, but his dark skin was marred with several scratches along his cheek and temple. His robes were wrinkled and he was barefoot, and with a sinking pit in her stomach, Renya realized he came straight from Cressida's bed. Her face fell and she hung her head low. She might be Cressida's prisoner, but it was nothing like the evil hold she had over Sion's soul. She ached for him, but had no idea how to possibly console him.

Sion stood there for a second, awkwardly looking at Renya, before she rushed over and threw her arms around him. He stumbled a bit, surprised by the affection, but then patted her on the back.

"Renya...how are you?"

Renya stepped out of the embrace and sat on the bed. She motioned to the chair at the vanity and Sion pulled it out quietly and sat, before sighing heavily.

"I'm okay...a bit shook up. And hurting—every minute I'm away from Grayden is painful." Her eyes watered, but she kept her tears back, knowing that Sion was no doubt suffering as well.

"I'll try to get you back to him, however I can. But unfortunately, the queen has severely limited the freedom granted to me since your arrival. It's almost as though she senses where my true loyalties lie. But if she did, I can't imagine she'd let me live. Perhaps she just wants to keep your existence a secret."

"Is it true?" Renya asked, her voice small and wavering with dread. "Is she...my mother?"

Sion's brow wrinkled and he shifted uncomfortably on the stool. "While I don't know for certain, it's...very plausible. It makes sense that someone would hide you from her in the human world if she was after your power, but to go after her own daughter? Yet...her depravity knows no limits..."

"Sion, I'm so sorry. To act in the capacity you must—"

"Don't fret over me, Renya. I serve both you and Grayden faithfully, and it is my sworn duty to do what I must."

"Still—"

"I'm happy to serve my future queen. At least, I am assuming...?"

Renya rubbed the spot where her ring previously sat. Sion watched her and met her face, confused by her motion.

"Yes. Grayden asked me to marry him. But my ring—Cressida took it and threw it out over the valley."

"I'm so sorry, Renya. I imagine finding out her daughter is fated to someone whom she once desired has unhinged her. Even more than normal."

Renya hadn't thought about that perspective before and blanched.

Sion gave her a sad smile. "That's what I live with everyday."

Renya walked over to him and gave his shoulder a squeeze in acknowledgment.

"So...any idea on how to get us out of this mess?"

"You need to learn all you can, Renya. I know you're bound to her, so you can't leave. But you can learn and conquer your magic. Grayden will find someway to break the magic holding you here...but once that's done, you need to be able to survive. You're going to need to do what I do—make yourself useful to her." He grimaced before continuing. "Make her believe you are the daughter she's always wanted. Be her heir—at least on the outside and then fight her with everything you have on the inside."

Renya sat back down and smoothed her nightgown. "How do I do that?"

"You'll find a way. You're clever and quick-thinking. Maybe once you've earned her trust, you'll find some kind of weakness. But seriously, take advantage of anything she's willing to teach you."

Renya nodded. "Thanks, Sion. Do you think you could get a message to Grayden?"

"I'll try the best I can—Cressida is asleep and drank heavily before bed so I'm hoping she won't notice my absence. I'll try to get a hawk out. What do you want me to tell him?"

Renya hesitated for a second. What could she possibly say to him? "Tell him...tell him to trust me. To wait. And that I'm okay. And...that I love him." She flushed a bit, but Sion didn't seem embarrassed about her declaration.

"I will, Renya. Hopefully we'll talk again soon. Leave your window unlocked in the evenings and I'll try to visit when I can. Good luck."

Sion gave her a quick embrace, and then pushed himself through the window, his golden robes blowing gently in the night air before he disappeared.

Chapter Eight

"**A**bsolutely not," Grayden growled, his irritation evident. "I will not wait any longer to rescue Renya. I'm healed now—I'll go alone if I have to."

"Grayden, be reasonable," Phillippe pleaded, his dark eyes narrowed. "We'll need every soldier available to us if we want to have any real chance of defeating the Shadow Queen. If we separate our resources now, our Snow Land soldiers will be killed. We need to solidify all of our armies and make one targeted attack. We can't risk the men."

Grayden glanced around the table, fuming. How could they expect him to wait to rescue Renya? Every second they were apart was excruciating for him. There was so much to be done before they amassed the forces from the other kingdoms. Tristan and Esmeralda were still negotiating with the Spring Lands, and the Twilight Kingdom was trying to recoup the losses they endured. It would take weeks—if not months—to launch a full attack on the Shadow Realm.

Kalora seemed sympathetic, but she too nodded in agreement. "I know how hard this is, but we can't afford to lose any men—not if we want to have a chance at vanquishing her once and for all."

Grayden launched to his feet, seething in anger. He grabbed the dagger from his boot and threw it at the middle of the table, piercing the thick wood by several inches. He stormed out of the room, leaving the rest of the attendees stunned into silence.

His boots thumped noisily against the stone floor, and he headed towards his chambers. Grayden just started to climb the staircase when Selenia appeared at the top.

"Brother, yelling and threatening won't get Renya back any faster."

Grayden exhaled and continued up the stairs. He brushed past his sister and opened the door to his room. Selenia followed him inside, not waiting for an invitation. She took a seat beside the fireplace and looked at Grayden meaningfully.

He sighed and sat, looking at his boots while the fire crackled and hissed.

"I just don't know what to do without her," he said, his voice hardly above a whisper.

"I know. I feel the same way about—I just, I understand. But Grayden, she's alive. She's resourceful and brave. She'll be okay."

Grayden's face turned crimson and he instantly felt embarrassment over his tantrum. Renya was alive and he had proof—he felt a flash of anger through their bond this morning. Selenia had to come to terms with the fact that Jurel was gone. They'd sent his body back to the Snow Lands so he could be laid to rest with his father. Selenia had cried and tried to accompany his body, but Grayden would take no more risks where her safety was concerned. He was needed here, and he would trust no one else with her safety.

"How are you doing, Selenia?"

She shrugged, avoiding his gaze and looking into the fire. The snow-white kitten was curled up in front of it, sleeping soundly. Selenia changed the subject.

"Have you named her yet?"

Grayden looked at the sleeping kitten. "Sunshine, I think."

Selenia scowled. "Grayden, that kitten is whiter than Almory's beard. Sunshine? Really?"

He looked down at his boots again. The leather was starting to scuff and peel. He would need to replace them soon. "It was Renya's nickname. Her aunt called her that."

Instantly, a blush of guilt crept up into Selenia's cheeks. "Of course—I'm sorry."

Grayden shook off her apology. "What are you going to name yours?"

"It's a he, and his name is Puffin."

Grayden realized the connection instantly. Jurel's animal guardian was an arctic puffin.

Just as Grayden was about to comment, there was a knock on the door.

"Enter," Grayden said, not taking his eyes off of Selenia.

The door cracked open, and Julietta peeked her head in. "Are you busy?"

"No," Selenia answered, and Julietta waltzed into the room.

Julietta was more pale than normal, Grayden realized. Her eyes were exuberant though, and shining excitedly.

"I have some good news," she gasped, her violet gown swishing around her ankles as she looked closer at the pair. She held a heavy tome in her hands, the cover ancient and weathered. "I think I've found something useful in breaking the blood promise."

Grayden's eyes widened, hope seizing his heart. "Really?"

She nodded eagerly. "This book references the breaking of spells. It says here that 'spells broken under the light will always come to right.'"

Grayden and Selenia looked at her, confused. Then, Selenia's mouth dropped. "The Sun Realm?"

"I think so. I think it's referencing one of the missing Sun Realm Scrolls. The prophecy is only part of them. They also contain the secrets to powerful magic. Mother said that they were lost, but I think—"

"We leave at once," Grayden announced, already slinging his sword over his shoulder. "I'll take any chance. If these scrolls still exist, I will find them."

Chapter Nine

T his time, Renya focused. Her hatred of Cressida was still deeply ingrained in every soul-shattering breath she took, but she used her fury to fuel her magic.

Several days had passed since Sion suggested taking advantage of Cressida's teachings, and Renya felt more and more confident in her magical abilities. However, her relationship with Cressida was nothing but bitterness and intense detestation. Every lesson was a stand-off, and while Renya couldn't technically disobey her, she found it easier and easier to bend the rules of what she could get away with.

"I'm not seeing control," Cressida insulted, after Renya missed hitting an elaborate urn with her powers. "I want to see you aim and hit something for once."

Instead of aiming for the urn, Renya released her magic in Cressida's direction, and it shot against her chest. While it wasn't a powerful enough blast to seriously harm her, it was enough to surprise her and knock her backwards. She landed with a harsh thump against the cold marble flooring.

Renya suppressed a laugh, enjoying the way Cressida's phrasing allowed her to act against her, especially since that wasn't the Shadow Queen's intention. But in the end, it just put Cressida in a sour mood.

She picked herself up and glared at Renya, and

for a few seconds, Renya thought she might turn on her and use her black magic against her. But instead, Cressida just looked at her, eyes unblinking. Renya could feel the undercurrent of hostility raging silently in the room.

"If only your pathetic mate could see you now," Cressida jeered. "Too bad he has no power left. He's weak and useless. I'd hate to be fated to such a waste."

Renya ignored the insult. Even without magic, Grayden was powerful.

"It's too bad you'll never see him again. I might not be able to kill him directly, but there are ways to be rid of him."

This time, Renya's face turned red. Without thinking, she sent a huge burst of magic towards Cressida, golden and hot. But this time, the Shadow Queen was prepared. She sent up a misty shield, and the magic bounced off and hit Renya squarely in the chest. She gasped, the pain and heat of her own magic intense and aching. She felt herself fall back to the floor, sprawled out and unable to catch her breath. She lay there, trying to comprehend what happened. Cressida strutted over and looked down at her, contempt in her gaze.

"See? You're pathetic. Your mate is pathetic, your control over your magic is pathetic, and you are useless to me." She kicked Renya sharply in the side with the toe of her boot and then marched out of the room.

Renya didn't pick herself up. She was so tired of fighting, so tired of pushing herself to learn all she could from Cressida.

The longer she lay there, the easier the tears flowed. Hot and salty, they trickled down her cheeks before pooling at the back of her neck. She stayed there, exhausted and in tears, for almost a half hour before she heard the door open.

"Miss Renya! What happened?" Margot swept into the room, her apron starched and her hair in a tight bun. She hurried to where Renya lay, and knelt down beside her.

Renya wiped the tears from her cheeks and allowed Margot to help her up to a sitting position. Margot pulled out a handkerchief from her apron pocket and handed it to Renya. There was a delicate blue flower embroidered on it, along with Margot's name. Renya accepted it and wiped her tears.

"It'll be okay," Margot said, patting Renya's knee gently.

Renya breathed deeply, her chest still aching from the impact of her own magic. "I don't think I'll ever be okay again," she said, looking into Margot's sympathetic eyes. "I'll never be able to match her magic."

"You're not alone, Miss Renya. I'm sure your prince is out there, on his way to come get you."

Renya didn't have the heart to tell her that it didn't matter, that she was stuck here. Unless Grayden was able to defeat Cressida once and for all, she was bound by her blood promise. As much as she believed in Grayden, she knew the odds were heavily stacked against him. She didn't even know if he was healed, or if there were any lingering issues from his injuries. Cressida's dragons destroyed most of the Twilight Kingdom, and Renya saw so many fallen soldiers on the battlefield as she flew above the carnage on the back of the dragon. She knew any resources available were already thinned considerably.

Renya allowed Margot to pull her up, and she swayed on her feet the second she was upright. Margot helped catch her, and Renya leaned on her as they made their way back towards Renya's room.

Margot opened the door and helped Renya to the bed. She sank deeply on the mattress, the wind still knocked out of her. Margot removed her shoes and tucked her gently into the bed.

"Thank you, Margot," Renya said, slinking back against the pillow, her body tired of fighting.

"I'm rooting for you, Renya," she said, as she shut the door quietly behind her.

Chapter Ten

S ion's heart beat faster. Brandle stood next to Cressida, his lips curled into a gleeful grin. Brandle's appearance alone made Sion's brow sweat and perspiration trickle down his back. Whatever reason he was summoned for, it was something that made Brandle ecstatic.

Which meant trouble for Sion.

Renya stood at Cressida's left, obviously held there by the Shadow Queen's magic. Her eyes were frantic and desperate, another sign that what was going to transpire was deadly.

"How can I serve you, my queen?" he said, keeping his voice calm and steady despite the erratic palpation of his heart.

"That's the thing, Sion," Cressida said, her voice steady and unwavering. "I think you serve others, not just me."

This was it, Sion thought. He knew his treachery would eventually be uncovered. Fates, he only wished he could have done more. Found some kind of weakness, some useful information on how to defeat her.

He stayed silent, knowing there were no words to appease her. He knew she would grow tired of him and find a way to dispose of him. His only regret was that he wouldn't be able to take her down with him.

Cressida withdrew her milky white hand and pulled a piece of parchment from between her cleavage. Sion was grateful he'd never have to see her uncovered chest again. His charade was over, his own personal torment almost ended.

"Brandle noticed you heading towards the falconry a few nights ago. He followed you. Can you guess what he saw?"

Sion remained quiet. He kept his head bowed, wondering how his death would play out. He hoped it would be quick and dignified. He hated to imagine her toying with him, like she often did. She enjoyed playing with her prey before she consumed them.

"You don't know? Or you don't care to deny it?"

Again, he kept his tongue in-check. He wanted to lash out, to have the final word, but he was tired. Tired of this role, exhausted from the mental toll he paid. Pained from the emotional turmoil. He was glad it was over. Thrilled for the end to be here. He'd see his father again. It would all be okay. He said a silent prayer to the Fates. Let his death accomplish something. Fuel a fire within his lands to avenge his passing.

Cressida tapped her talon-like nails against the throne, enjoying Sion being in the hot seat. Brandle watched his queen, also entertained by Sion's predicament.

The wind ruffled Sion's robes, the cold oddly comforting. He looked at Renya, not wanting to incriminate her further, but he recognized the parchment Cressida held and knew Renya was just as much on trial as he was. He closed his eyes, bracing for what was coming. He saw it play out so many times, and had seen so much death in this room. He wondered how his own ending would come. Would she blast him with her magic? Slit his throat? Either way, his body would end up in the ravine below, carelessly tossed aside like so many others before him.

"Fine. Refuse to speak. It's obvious to me that you are working for my daughter's mate—that foolish boy. As if he stands a chance against me."

This time, Sion's pent up frustration and anger got the best of him. "Are you jealous that I serve him, or just jealous that he prefers your daughter over you?"

Pain hit him as a blast of magic collided with his chest. This was what he wanted. If he angered her, she couldn't draw out his death. But suddenly, the agony stopped and he heard a soft cry.

Renya had thrown herself in front of Cressida's path and was now twisting and writhing in torment. Cressida instantly stopped when she realized her target changed. Sion panted heavily, trying to recover from the piercing pain flowing through his body. He watched Renya do the same, her face pale but determination set in her eyes. It was now clear to Sion that either Cressida's magic was fading, or Renya was now too powerful to be controlled at the same time as Sion. Either way, it was a good sign.

The Shadow Queen strode towards Renya and yanked her roughly to her feet. "What are you doing, girl? His punishment doesn't concern you!"

Renya lifted up her chin, her gray gown trailing behind her. Despite the plain clothing Cressida forced her into, Sion couldn't deny her beauty. He understood Grayden's fascination with her. Her golden hair tumbled down her shoulders, the locks thick and shining. Unlike her mother, Renya didn't paint her lips or rouge her cheeks. Her natural grace was evident in the way she moved, her tone of voice, and her expressions. But right now, her brow was deeply furrowed in anger.

Sion was free again, unbound from Cressida's hold. He debated jumping off the edge of the cliff, ending it before Cressida could torture him to death. But as he looked on, Cressida struggling to overpower Renya once more, he paused.

Renya was flailing her arms in a cruel imitation of a marionette doll, arms moving uncoordinatedly. A bead of perspiration dripped down her wrinkled forehead, deep in concentration. A flash of surprise, then horror, and then something else—almost pride? —crossed the Shadow Queen's face. Sion knew Renya couldn't outright attack Cressida while the blood promise remained in place, but she was still fighting against both the magic of the promise and the magic Cressida was using. He beamed with pride, even though Renya's training was not his doing.

"Stop fighting me!" Cressida bellowed.

"Leave him be! Spare him, and I will never fight against you again. I'll cooperate in all ways!"

"Another blood promise then?" Cressida's thin eyebrow arched towards the open ceiling, clouds dancing above. "For your loyalty and unwavering cooperation?"

"No, Renya!" Sion screamed against the wind. There was no way he would ever allow Renya to make a blood promise for his life. Her loyalty to Cressida was too big of a price for anything. Seeing no other option before him, he ran towards the edge of the room, preparing to dive headfirst to his own death.

He was halted mid-jump by Brandle's magic. Frozen in midair, he hung, arms flung forward and dangling over the cliff.

"Orders, my queen?" Brandle's tone was downright cheerful and Sion wished for nothing more than to be free of this spectacle.

"A blood promise can only be given freely. I cannot force the girl's loyalty in any other way. I'll spare his life in exchange for your fidelity."

Sion knew he should feel relief, suspended in the air but knowing his life was safe, but he also understood the Shadow Queen's treachery. Death was truly the only way out.

"Do you agree, girl?"

Renya held her chin high, a single tear sliding down her cheek. "Yes. I'll make another promise."

Cressida's villainous laugh carried with the wind. Sion hung over the ravine, listening with foreboding as Renya once again made a blood promise to the savage queen to save a life.

"Now, release him," Renya commanded, her voice surprisingly calm.

Sion easily predicted the queen's reaction.

"Release him? You little fool. You may have spared his mortal life, but there is no way he'll ever be free of me."

Chapter Eleven

"I'm coming with you." Selenia threw her leg over her mount, her ruby cape trailing behind her.

"Absolutely not. I forbid it." Grayden pulled on his leather riding gloves and grabbed the reins tightly in his hands.

Selenia ignored him and clicked her tongue, forcing her mare, Honor, into a steady gait.

"Phillippe, back me up here!" Grayden yelled over his shoulder as he forced Damion into a quicker pace to catch up with his headstrong sister.

Phillippe just laughed, urging Nectaria ahead as well, shouting at Grayden's back. "She's not going to stay put, brother. You might as well resign yourself to the fact that your rescue mission includes one more."

Grayden frowned as he watched Selenia glance back at him, a smirk of triumph proudly crossing her face. He struggled internally about including her. Although his quest to retrieve Renya would no doubt be dangerous, it was the first time he saw a spark in Selenia's eyes since the passing of Jurel. Finally, he gave a curt nod and Selenia gave him a half grin. His heart leapt at the look. Although a month had passed since Jurel's death, Selenia still took to wandering the halls of the castle, absentmindedly stroking the walls and looking off into space. It deeply concerned Grayden, but he didn't know how to offer her comfort when he himself could barely keep it together.

"You are to follow my orders, exactly as I give them," he warned, as Selenia slowed down her pace.

She stuck her tongue out at him then looked ahead into the dark forest.

Grayden followed her gaze. He could see nothing but the outline of trees ahead. It would be a long ride to the Sun Realm, but he was determined to get there as quickly as he could. There must be some clue, some instruction on how to break the blood promise that Renya made to Cressida. Julietta's words gave him hope that such a thing was possible. If he could rescue Renya and break the blood promise, they could potentially have a fighting chance of beating Cressida for good. Surely Renya might have picked up some secret knowledge about her, some way to defeat Cressida? If not, perhaps Sion had.

For the first time since he woke up in their room alone, he felt the tiny flutter of hope stir within his chest.

Selenia slowed further, and Grayden finally caught up with her. "Which way, brother?" she asked, as Honor stomped at the ground impatiently.

Grayden eyed the forest. It had been many years since he rode this far west, through the thick, dimly lit woods on the outskirts of the Twilight Kingdom. Luckily, Phillippe had been through here last year. Grayden looked back at him, and he nodded.

"A little lost, there? I thought you were our fearless leader?" Phillippe chuckled as he edged past Grayden.

Grayden didn't laugh, but gave Phillippe a warning glance.

"Okay, okay. Sorry. I'll take the lead."

Phillippe led them along a small trail towards the right side of the forest. Grayden and Selenia followed, riding single file as the trees became denser and overgrown.

"Are you sure this is right?" Grayden watched as the path closed in even more.

Phillippe gave a snort. "Do you want to lead? By all means, go ahead."

Grayden shut his mouth and gnashed his teeth together. He knew he was being overbearing and controlling, but he couldn't stop worrying every minute that Renya was out of his reach.

"The trail is overgrown. No one has ventured into the Sun Realm for quite some time. I only know the way because Father took me on the eastern route to the Spring Lands, and we passed it along the mountain ridge. It's beautiful, but...eerie, in a way. Everything is opulent and gorgeous, but there's a quiet surrounding the entire desert. I'm not exactly looking forward to venturing inside the city walls..."

"I appreciate you coming with me. I couldn't take our army, but you're the next best thing."

"She's your mate, Grayden. She's part of our family. Of course I'll do whatever I can to get her back to us."

"Me too, Grayden," Selenia added.

Emotion welled up in Grayden's throat at his sibling's words.

The trio rode farther into the forest, silent except for the occasional broken branch or bird taking flight. When it started to get so dark that Grayden couldn't see his horse's head in front of him, he stopped the group.

"Let's rest here until daybreak."

Phillippe dismounted and helped Selenia down. She smoothed her skirt and began unpacking the sleeping roll on Honor's back.

Grayden watched her fiddle with the ties and then she moved over to aid Phillippe in removing the tent. She helped him pull it off and began assisting him with setting it up. She'd changed in the last month since they left the lodge. It saddened Grayden a bit, knowing Jurel's death was most likely the culprit. He hated to see his sister lose the exuberance for life she possessed.

Grayden dragged over some fallen logs and made a pit for the fire. He hunted around the area looking for some firewood, but moved farther into the thickening edge of the forest to find some drier wood. He didn't want the fire to smoke and give their location away. That was all he needed, an ambush of Cressida's soldiers before they even left the Twilight Kingdom territory.

A sharp snap of a twig abruptly ended his thoughts. He pulled his knife from his boot quickly and crouched down low.

A deep, screeching laugh came from behind a tall, moss-covered tree. "Hiding won't prevent me from knowing you, Grayden Snowden."

"Show yourself! Who are you and how do you know my name?"

A figure slowly emerged from behind the tree, the darkness partially obscuring its features. The mysterious apparition was definitely not Fae, and resembled no creature Grayden had seen before. As it moved into the moonlight, he could tell that it was shrouded in a green mist, and the creature's skin was a mottled gray, reminiscent of the underbelly of a pale fish. It opened its mouth wide, and rows of sharp, pointed teeth cracked into a grotesque smile.

"I know many things, Grayden Snowden. And how I know things is not for you to know." It gave another cruel smile and Grayden pulled his sword off of his back. Before he could unsheath it, he was frozen in place.

"My magic may be weaker than in the past, but it's still a great deal stronger than yours," the figure taunted, creeping towards Grayden. He couldn't see where the creature's feet hit the ground, and he had a sickening suspicion that it was floating through the air.

Grayden heard rustling behind him, and he knew Phillippe was approaching. He tried to shout a warning, but his paralyzation was full-body. He couldn't even move his lips.

He felt Phillippe brush against him, sword drawn, before he too was frozen. A few seconds later, Selenia emerged and was caught in the creature's hold as well.

"Ah, it's all three Snowden siblings. I was hoping I'd get the chance to meet you. Your father was an interesting character, so I've been longing to meet his offspring."

Grayden was shocked to his core. This creature met his father? His father obviously lived past the encounter, so Grayden was instantly confused as to the beast's intentions.

He watched Selenia struggle against her invisible bonds, and he was shocked when he saw her move her fingers and open her mouth.

"A powerful one, we have here. Yet you don't use your magic, princess. You could control it, you know. I could tell you how."

Selenia managed to free herself completely. "I don't know who or what you are, but I don't need any help from you."

"You might change your mind, one day. You're young, after all...and I know everything that lies ahead of you."

Selenia looked at Grayden and Phillippe. "Let my brothers go!"

"I will...for a trade. A small trade, and you shall all go on your way."

Grayden was released from his bonds instantly. He heard a soft thump as Phillippe fell on his knees next to him, frozen in mid-leap.

"Don't make any kind of trade, Selenia!" Phillippe scrambled to his feet and put himself in front of his sister and the taunting figure. "She's a Murcurial!"

Grayden and Selenia looked puzzled. The Murcurial laughed. The rags it wore shifted as her diaphragm moved up and down with her movements.

"Phillippe Snowden knows of me, he does? If I could blush, I would."

Phillippe didn't respond to the Murcurial, but looked at his siblings carefully. "They are tricksters who try to change your destiny!"

"Only partially right, Phillippe Snowden. Know your future, I do. It's you who decides whether or not to try and change it."

The Murcurial moved slightly towards Selenia, and Grayden instantly shielded his sister. The Murcurial laughed again. "Missing your mate, Grayden Snowden? Would you like to know if you're reunited? If the pretty Sun Princess will ever be your bride?"

Grayden's eyes widened. The offer was incredibly tempting; his desperation for Renya clouded all aspects of his judgment.

"Grayden, don't listen to her. Their riddles will drive you mad, trying to find meaning in the ramblings." Phillippe once again tried to put himself between the Murcurial and his brother and sister.

"You will enjoy the feeling of power, Phillippe Snowden. But you'll have to choose. Would you rather love, or magic? For you shall not have both."

"Stop it! I'll not hear my fortune!" Phillippe lunged at the Murcurial, but the second he made contact at the spot where she was hovering, she disappeared.

"Selenia Snowden…you grieve for the wrong man. The one you are meant for is in pain, yet instead of caring for him, your heart is torn for another. Silly girl. You know nothing of true pain and true love." The Murcurial reappeared behind Selenia, snatching at her cloak. Selenia screeched and tried to push her off.

"I just want your pretty mantle. Then leave you alone I will."

"Why should we believe you?" Grayden demanded, his sword drawn and pointed straight at the Murcurial. The Murcurial stared down the sword, her lashless eyes black and unblinking.

"Your mate carries a secret. One she has not told you, one she might not even know herself. Would you like to know if she'll live to reveal it?"

Before Grayden could answer, Selenia unclasped the arctic fox pin holding her cloak together and threw it at the Murcurial's feet. "Here, begone! Leave us be and speak no more!"

The Murcurial glanced at the offering, then bent to retrieve the cloak. Her boney fingers extended from the rags she wore, and Grayden felt slightly sick as he looked at flesh rotting off the bone. "Many thanks, Selenia Snowden. We'll meet again, you know. Next time, it will be you who seeks me out. Bring me a handsome payment and I'll serve you well."

"Never," Selenia spat out through clenched teeth. She moved farther back into the canopy of trees, as far away from the creature as she could get.

With another manacle laugh, the Murcurial slank back into the forest, a cloud of mist surrounding her. After a few seconds, she had completely disappeared.

Grayden let out a shaky breath. What did the Murcurial mean? A secret Renya was keeping from him?

Phillippe approached Grayden and rested his hand lightly on his shoulder. "Don't worry about it, Grayden. Murcurials love to entertain and frighten us with their fanciful talks of the future. Father said they downright lie just for the fun of it."

Grayden nodded, but he still couldn't push the worry from his mind. Selenia came to his other side, shaken up from the encounter as well.

"Do you think there's any truth in her words? Do they ever tell the truth?" She was shivering, partly in fear, and partly from her missing cloak. Grayden pulled off his fur and wrapped it around her slender shoulders.

Phillippe scratched his jaw, a full beard covering his face. "It's hard to say, but you mustn't dwell on what she said. That way lies madness. Fae have gone crazy trying to discern meanings in their protestations. Just forget what you heard."

Selenia nodded, but Grayden could tell she was focusing on the Murcurial's words as much as he was.

"Why did she want Selenia's cloak?" Grayden asked.

"I have no idea. I don't think they weave spells or any dark magic. Perhaps she just liked it?"

Selenia shuddered. "Let's get out of here. I can still sense her presence. It feels like...rot and decay. I can almost smell it."

Grayden picked up the pile of wood he started to gather and then put his other arm around Selenia and guided her back to the camp. Phillippe followed behind in silence. None of the siblings spoke, each deep in thought, contemplating the confessions of the Murcurial.

Chapter Twelve

T he dungeon was a far deal better than sleeping in Cressida's bed every night, Sion decided. It was wet, cramped and musty, but anything was better than being between Cressida's legs.

His cell faced the dungeon door, so he could see the comings and goings of the guards serving Cressida. He knew many were only loyal to her out of fear, and he hoped to work that fact to his advantage somehow. Sion was sure he'd eventually be able to bribe or talk his way out. He'd torture Cressida until she broke the blood promises, grab Renya, and they would flee together. They could take shelter in the fallen Sun Realm or head to the Spring Lands, seeking shelter and safe passage there. He'd get a letter to Grayden, and—

"Sion?"

A rough voice came from the cell to Sion's left.

"Cyrus?"

The old man coughed and wheezed. "How are you doing, my boy?"

Sion approached the bars of his cell, trying to catch a glimpse of the old man. From the rounded angle of the dungeon, he could just make out the elderly gentleman leaning against the wall of his own cell.

"I've only been in here an hour, so I'm more concerned with how you are doing."

Cyrus laughed, and the sound was so hearty that

Sion instantly doubted the old man's age. "I've been sleeping, conserving my energy. I told you, I'm right where I want to be. Where I need to be."

"Why on earth do you want to be her prisoner?"

Silence.

Sion decided that Cyrus wasn't going to answer, when he suddenly spoke low. "I don't have much choice, but I do believe you'll do what you can for my Renya."

My Renya? No—it couldn't be—

Cyrus continued. "Renya is...my daughter."

Sion laughed, hardly believing what he was hearing. This old man, who spent his time in the human world—then it clicked. He did spend his life in the human realm—guarding over the very portal Renya fell through.

"You mean—"

"Yes, my boy. I was once Fated to your queen."

Sion felt sick. And embarrassed. Not only had he slept with Renya's mother, but her father knew about it.

Cyrus seemed to read Sion's mind. He laughed, and the sound echoed through the stale air of the dungeon. "Don't worry about it, I don't care if you've made me a cuckold. I was able to sever my mating bond with Cressida a long time ago...once I found out that it was the only way to save my daughter."

"But—why are you here then? Why allow yourself to be captured? You know she'll want to kill you for what you've done."

"Trust me, my boy. She needs me. I'm critical to her plans. She wants her daughter's unquestioned loyalty—and there's one thing standing in the way from that. But with any luck, I'll be able to right a wrong and finally do something for my Renya."

Cyrus wasn't making any sense, but Sion didn't want to question him further. There was a plan in place, and someone else to look out for Renya besides him. He felt relieved, knowing he had an ally in this God's forsaken realm.

"What can I do to help you?" Sion leaned forward, lowering his voice. There were no other prisoners currently held in the dungeon, but he didn't trust Cressida not to have ways to listen in.

"We're going to free my daughter and get her safely to her mate—but first, the Shadow Queen needs me for a bit of magic. Once it's performed, she'll find out my betrayal. If I don't make it out, I need you to help Renya. Tell her—tell her that her father never stopped fighting for her."

"But the blood promises—"

"Let me worry about that. Trust me, I'm right where I need to be to set things right. Just promise me, you'll look after my Renya if I don't make it out of here?"

"I've been looking after her since I saw her wearing my best friend's pin."

Cyrus nodded. "I'm trusting you, my boy. Don't let me down."

A large creaking noise came from the doorway, and Sion quickly pushed himself back against the wall of his cell. Cressida strode into the dungeon, her eyes squinting in the near darkness of the chamber.

Sion watched her glance between the two cells, and he could see her internal struggle as she attempted to decide which former lover she wanted to toy with first. She marched towards Sion, choosing the most recent betrayal.

She stood directly in front of him, her black dress

blending in with the darkness of the dungeon. Tiny bits of onyx, sewn into concentric circles sparkled on the skirts from the sole torch on the wall. Sion feigned disinterest. He knew she could hurt him, bring him to the edge of death, but she couldn't push it past that. The blood promise Renya made saved his mortal body, at least.

"Oh, sweet Sion, how I hate to see you restrained...at least, in these conditions. I'd much rather you'd be chained to my bed." She adapted the saccharine tone she liked to use when she was antagonizing her prey. "I'm sure you'll come to regret your betrayal quickly. The dungeon isn't any place for a man with your...talents."

Sion swore he saw a grin flash across Cyrus's face. He couldn't fathom how Renya's father could find this situation humorous. Perhaps he was slightly unhinged? His ex-mate was deranged, so why not him too?

"My 'talents' are no longer yours to control."

Cressida scoffed. "I can make you do anything I want, my dear Sion. I just can't kill you. But don't fear, I no longer desire you. How could I, when you've aligned yourself with the losing side?"

A chuckle came from Cyrus's cell. "The only losing side is whichever one you're on, Cressy."

Sion watched the hatred flash in Cressida's eyes. "Don't you dare call me that," she hissed, her breathing so irregular that Sion could hear her gasp for air.

"So you didn't let your former lover call you by your little nickname, Cressy? It sounds to me like your relationship was purely physical."

This time, Cressida lashed out. Her black magic crept into Cyrus's cell and wrapped around his neck cruelly.

Cyrus sputtered and coughed, but Cressida didn't let up. His eyes became wide and his face started to turn red. As if in a trance, Cressida tightened her hold.

"Stop!" Sion shook the bars, helpless in the cell and against the Shadow Queen's magic.

Cressida suddenly released Cyrus, and he crumpled to the ground, massaging his neck and breathing deeply.

"You fool. You want me to kill you? I won't. I still need you."

"Ahhh, you're in the market for a new lover now? I admit, our time together was pleasurable, if not short."

Cressida fumed, but Sion could tell she was trying hard not to lash out again. Whatever she wanted Cyrus for, it was incredibly important. She watched Cyrus for several seconds, before turning back to Sion.

"I'll deal with you later. Let's just say, we are going to have some fun, seeing how far I can push you without ending your life."

Sion didn't even react. The second Renya made her promise, he knew this was to be his fate.

Cressida turned on her heels and flicked her fingers. The bars around Cyrus's cell disappeared, and he was instantly bound by her magic. She dragged him out of the cell, not caring as he stumbled behind her.

"Come, you old fool. It's time for you and your precious daughter to have a reunion."

Chapter Thirteen

R enya paced in the throne room. She had no idea why Cressida summoned her. They'd already had a magic lesson that morning, and the dislike and tension in the room was so palpable that the Shadow Queen stormed out after fifteen minutes into the lesson.

The clock chimed, and Renya sighed. She smoothed the rough dress she wore, and played with the aragonite necklace at her neck. At least Cressida hadn't taken that from her. Renya rubbed her thumb over ring finger, her heart breaking over the loss of her ring. Not only was it another link to Grayden, but it was his mother's. Her eyes burned and she tried not to think of the lost family heirloom.

She heard footsteps approaching the throne room from the sky bridge. Her thoughts turned to the last time she had been in this room. Her pulse thundered with worry and fear for Sion. She'd gladly make as many promises as she needed to in order to save the people she cared about. She only hoped he'd find a way out of her clutches. But at least his life was saved.

Brandle strolled into the room, his chest puffed out. Ever since Sion's betrayal was revealed, Brandle's arrogance only grew.

"Our queen will be here shortly," he announced, taking his usual place next to the throne.

Renya ignored him. Instead, she took a moment to try and feel Grayden through their bond. She detected a bit of fear and worry from him earlier, and it scared her. She searched, but she couldn't feel him. It seemed she could only sense him during times of great emotion. But even though she felt his turmoil, she was glad for the knowledge that he was still alive.

After a few more minutes, Renya heard the telltale sound of Cressida's ridiculous shoes against the glass of the sky bridge. Renya turned her eyes to the bridge and saw her mother begin to cross, but someone else quickly caught her eye.

The Shadow Queen was dragging an elderly man behind her. He was clearly in rough shape, tired and pale. Cressida was obviously binding him with her magic, as he stumbled and struggled in her wake.

Renya wasn't sure what was going on. Why would Cressida care about an old man? He didn't even look Fae, in fact, he looked...human.

Renya stared, and a memory pulled itself into the forefront, like a parched man crawling towards a desert mirage. As the man came closer, Renya took in his sparkling blue eyes and his filthy, yet elegant suit. It was the man from the bookshop. The owner. What was he doing here?

Then, another memory, long forgotten, reached the surface of her consciousness. Those same blue eyes, looking down on her from above. Younger, more vibrant, but the same. Renya struggled against the realization, not believing what was in front of her.

Cressida reached the edge of the bridge, and strutted towards her throne. The man followed behind, still stumbling. She sat, and the man was finally released from his bonds.

Blue eyes met blue eyes. Renya's head started to pound, and she felt dizzy. This couldn't be true. This man, he was important. A part of her. She could feel it. And then she knew, knew with a startling certainty. This man was her father. She knew it like she knew the sky was blue or that Grayden was her soul mate.

The second Renya correctly guessed his identity, the man smiled. A sweet, fatherly grin crossed his face. Renya watched as he struggled, moving his arms as if to sweep her up in his.

Renya was so tired, so confused, and so broken in that moment that she wanted nothing more than to rush into his arms and collapse, desperately seeking some kind of parental comfort.

Cressida no doubt sensed the raw exchange of looks between the two. Not a word was spoken, but the air was charged with unbridled emotion.

Finally, the man spoke. "My Sunshine. My dear, sweet Renya."

Tears sprung in Renya's eyes and her heart hammered in her chest. She felt like every breath she took might shatter her lungs.

"Well, isn't this touching," Cressida mocked, looking at father and daughter with a disgusted look. "It's clear who you take after. I hoped to have a daughter worthy of me, but you are just as worthless and weak as your father."

"Love isn't a weakness. You'll never understand its true power." The man spoke freely, and Renya was shocked at how he mouthed off to Cressida without fear of retaliation. This man seemed so gentle, so caring and warm, that Renya couldn't believe how he could have possibly been involved with the Shadow Queen.

"We'll see about that. Did you wonder why I brought you here, Cyrus? It wasn't to have this touching reunion with your daughter."

Cyrus. Her father's name was Cyrus. Renya felt pieces of her soul click together. She had a father. And he seemed to hate her mother as much as she did.

"I have a hunch. And I won't do it."

"Oh yes, you will. If you don't, the girl possesses no usefulness to me. I'll kill her right in front of you, and then kill you next. And once she's dead, the blood promises are broken and I'll kill her mate, and her little friend Sion for good measure."

Renya paled. What did the Shadow Queen want her father to do? What could be worse than being pledged to Cressida?

"I won't break her bond. They are sacred."

"You had no problem breaking ours," Cressida retorted.

"It was the only way to keep her safe from you. I'll admit, I never expected to have to hide our child from you. But I knew, the second you discovered those prophecies, you'd stop at nothing to take her power and prevent her from overthrowing you."

"Too bad it did you no good. You only delayed the inevitable."

"I won't break our daughter's fated bond. I refuse."

As his words and meaning hit Renya's brain, she started to shake. Violent tremors coursed through her body and fear, unlike anything she felt before, overtook her.

Suddenly, clearer than she had ever heard it,

came Grayden's voice in her head.

Renya? Renya, what's wrong?

It only lasted a split second, and she tried to feel for him, to respond back, but he was gone. She choked through a sob, relieved to hear Grayden but terrified about what Cressida was threatening. Surely her own father wouldn't do that? What would happen to her and Grayden if their bond was broken? Would she still love him? Would he love her? Would they never be able to love again?

"You'll do it. That blasted bond is the only thing keeping her from fully submitting to me. If you don't break it, I will kill her. She's no use to me if she's constantly plotting to get back to her pathetic prince."

Renya began hyperventilating as she saw her father's face fall.

"If I do this, you must free me and Sion. Allow us to go to the human realm in peace."

Cressida laughed shrilly. "That won't be happening. You are in no place to negotiate. It's simple. Break her bond, or everyone she loves, including you, dies."

Cyrus looked at Renya, his eyes pleading. "My daughter, please forgive me for this. I have no choice. This isn't the destiny I would have chosen for you. I tried my hardest to protect you, I even watched you from afar. When you were attacked, I was there. I couldn't stop the gossip, but I could ensure you remained untouched by evil. I watched over you the best I could, my Sunshine...I love you."

Renya thought she was going to collapse. Her head swirled and for a moment, her entire mind went blank. These revelations, combined with the fear of being severed from Grayden, was too much.

Before she could say anything, she was tightly bound by Cressida's magic. She fought as hard as she could against the misty bonds, but her mind was so blocked that she couldn't even bring her magic forth.

She looked at Cyrus, her eyes pleading. Sadness, mixed with resolve, was evident in his expression. Hot tears trailed down her cheeks, and the fury welled up within her.

"Do it, and do it now. If you hesitate, I'll fling her off the cliff this second."

Cyrus approached Renya, his arms outreached. Renya watched him approach, and it was like everything was happening in slow motion. He put his hands on her shoulders, and then looked into her eyes. She could see the emotion there, and she knew, with intense clarity, that he loved her. For just a few seconds, with his hands surrounding her, she felt safe and protected.

Then pain, unlike any she experienced, coursed through her as she felt her father's magic enter her. Red hot and radiating, it was more painful than falling through the portal or having her magic unlocked back on the beach in the Tidal Kingdom.

"I'm so sorry, my dear Renya," Cyrus said, and Renya closed her eyes against the burning sensation. It felt like all of her blood was boiling in her body, cooking her from the inside out. She cried out loudly, the pain overwhelming her.

Cyrus moved his hands from her shoulders and moved them up to the sides of her head. The pain instantly stopped. He leaned in and whispered gently to her, pushing her braid over her shoulder like Grayden had done so many times before.

"Trust me, my dove. All will be right."

Then, a blinding light flashed through the room, and Renya was unbound.

"Is it done?" Cressida asked gleefully.

"Yes. Our daughter will never know love again. Are you happy?" Cyrus glared at Cressida. "I've broken her bond, desecrated something sacred for the second time in my life. Because of you."

Cressida's eyes gleamed and she looked giddy. Cyrus backed away from Renya slowly, his eyes downcast and full of regret. He wiped his hands on his suit pants, as if disgusted with himself.

"I suggest you let her rest before you put her through anything else," Cyrus said, motioning towards Renya. "That magic comes with a cost, and she'll be weak the rest of the day."

"Fine, whatever. Go to your room, girl. We'll start a new chapter tomorrow. Now that you are no longer fated, you'll have no choice but to fully commit to me."

Chapter Fourteen

H e felt her, he was sure of it. One minute, he was riding, trying to gauge how much farther until they left the protective canopy of the Twilight Kingdom forest, then a blast of deep emotional pain surged through him. He felt dizzy, and he actually thought he might pass out from the intensity of feeling that overcame him. He swayed on top of Damion before he caught himself and readjusted his balance.

Selenia's sharp eyes missed nothing. "Grayden, what's wrong?"

"I think–actually, I'm positive–I felt Renya."

"That's wonderful. You haven't been feeling her much, have you?" She spurred Honor on to catch up with him.

"She's hurting." He couldn't keep the grief and apprehension out of his tone.

Selenia's face fell. "Grayden–I'm sure she's okay."

He hung his head low, unable to answer her. He kept his eyes ahead on the bright light just outside the line of trees.

Phillippe caught up and studied them both. "What's going on?"

Selenia jumped in, saving Grayden the pain of responding. "Grayden could feel Renya, and she's in trouble."

"Grayden, we'll get her back. I know it," Phillippe

said, trying to reassure Grayden as much as he could.

"She's my entire life," Grayden said, in a small voice, hardly audible over the hoofbeats of the horses.

"We know, Grayden. She's a big part of our lives now too." Selenia pushed her ringlets back over her shoulder and looked grimly ahead.

No one said anything until they reached the edge of the forest, knowing the pain Grayden was in was uncategorizable.

As they approached the Sun Realm, the temperatures increased and the horses, equipped and adapted for the Snow Lands, started to struggle in the intense heat. Selenia had shrugged off Grayden's fur and her gloves were long gone. Grayden's shirt clung to his back, and Phillippe removed his altogether. Their pace slowed significantly as the sweltering heat wore them down.

The trees thinned, and soon the forest floor transitioned from soft, earthy-smelling dirt to coarse sand. A vast desert appeared before them, hot and unforgiving.

"A desert? Phillippe, where are you leading us?" Grayden grumbled while unbuttoning another button on his tunic. It was the first word he'd uttered in an hour.

"This is the fastest way to the Sun Realm. We could have come through the southern border, but you have to go around Gradis Lake in order to get there. It's an easier route, but it would add at least three days to our journey." Phillippe dismounted and walked along his horse for a bit, grabbing his water pouch and drinking deeply.

Grayden nodded, and dismounted as well. He

pulled a few small traveling cakes out of one of the saddle bags and passed them to his siblings. Selenia nibbled at hers, while Phillippe inhaled his without chewing. Grayden passed his rations to Phillippe, his appetite long gone. He accepted it hesitantly, worry etched along his forehead.

"Have either of you been close to the Sun Realm?" Selenia asked.

"No," Phillippe answered. "But Father saw it up close in his youth. He said that it's beautiful–but at the same time, incredibly...chilling."

"Chilling?" Selenia asked.

"He said that parts of it are destroyed, but other areas are completely untouched, as if any second someone is coming back to claim it."

"Do you think we'll find any clues as to how to defeat Cressida?"

Grayden looked at Selenia. "That doesn't matter. All that matters is freeing Renya from the blood magic."

"Grayden," Phillippe warned, "if there's any clues there as to how to beat her, we need to look. Getting Renya back, only to have Cressida take her again or destroy our entire kingdom, isn't much better. Renya would want us to search for anything in their archives that could potentially help us and our world."

Grayden knew his brother was right. He wasn't usually so self-serving, so selfish. But now that he was fated, everything else seemed to fade into the background. Food had no taste, and no amount of fireale could numb his pain. Colors were dull and sounds were nothing but noise. Loving Renya fundamentally changed him.

As they carried on, he found himself following

Phillippe absentmindedly, thinking about the first time Renya traveled with him on horseback. She tried to hold herself away from his body, but she fell asleep quickly and relaxed against his chest. He remembered the smell of her hair and the softness of her body. Then there was that moment at the inn, where she gaped at his shirtless body, warmed by the fire. He smiled briefly, thinking about the pink in her cheeks when she was embarrassed.

The trek through the desert was rough. They watered the horses right before leaving the borders of the Twilight Kingdom, but there wasn't a stream or pond in sight. Nothing but scorching sand lay ahead of them, the heat rising up and obscuring the horizon. Grayden looked at Selenia, her lips parched and her back slouched. She didn't complain, but he could tell this journey was arduous for her.

Phillippe, on the other hand, ventured so much through their world that he was immune to the elements, seemingly unbothered by the humid desert air once he removed his shirt. Every once in a while he'd shake the sand out of his short hair, but he kept riding without complaining, like the dutiful soldier he was.

Grayden was no stranger to the harsh and extreme climates that made up their world either, but between his injury and the fact that he hadn't had a decent nights' sleep since he woke up alone in their shared bed, he was seriously impaired. He wasn't the strong soldier he usually was. However, nothing, not exhaustion or injury, would convince him to stop moving forward.

At the hottest part of the day, Phillippe broke the silence.

"I think we need to camp now, and move again when the sun starts to set."

Grayden looked around, trying to see if there was any natural shelter. The tents would bake them to death in the intense sun. A little to the west, he saw a large outcropping of rocks. He nudged Phillippe and pointed, and Phillippe nodded.

"That'll work well. If we rest for a few hours, and travel through the evening, we could be at the Sun Realm before the next sunrise."

The outcropping Grayden spotted was actually a cave, hollowed out against a small, rocky hill. It was just big enough for them to spread out their sleeping rolls.

Grayden rubbed down the horses and gave them a bit of water from their stores to try and get them through the next few hours. Selenia and Phillippe rested easily, but Grayden sat at the cave entrance, looking out at the vast expanse before him. Somewhere out there, just beyond the rolling hills of sand, was Renya's birthplace. The place she should have called home, if she had grown up here. He wondered what their lives would be like if she hadn't been taken to the human world. Would they have found each other as soon as they came of age? Would he have been drawn to the Sun Realm, his heart searching for her across this very desert? Perhaps his mother and father would have met Renya before they passed, and given their blessing of their marriage.

It was a nice dream, but there was no use dwelling on it. His parents were dead, and Renya was a prisoner. He sighed, wishing for the thousandth time that Renya was beside him, sharing his sleeping roll. But instead, he stared at the horizon and drifted off with his back against the hard, rocky wall in front of the cave.

Phillippe shook him awake, and Grayden could instantly feel the heat pulsating from his skin.

"What the hell were you thinking? Falling asleep in the direct sun like that? You're burnt to a crisp." Phillippe took his water skin and poured some water over Grayden's head, dampening his hair and cooling his sizzling forehead.

"I must have dozed off," Grayden responded, standing up on stiff legs. "I closed my eyes for just a second."

Phillippe tried to hide his annoyance. "Look, I know this is hard for you, but you need to focus. You need to concentrate on our end goal here. If you don't drink, sleep, eat and *think*, you won't be alive long enough to save Renya. Enough is enough. Selenia lost Jurel, and she's handling her grief much better than you are, and your mate is still alive."

Grayden's face reddened even more. Selenia had every right to be grief-stricken, but it was he who slowed them down.

"Selenia wasn't mated to Jurel, but you're right. That's no excuse. I'm sorry, Phillippe."

"Don't apologize. Just look after yourself. Focus on what we need to do. We need to find the magical archives as quickly as we can when we get to the Sun Realm castle, and you need to have all of your faculties about you to do that. You know I'm not bookish, and I've spent most of my life outdoors, under the sky. You're the one who was holed up in Father's library."

Grayden pushed back his hair and nodded his understanding. He was in desperate need of a haircut and a shave. At this point, Renya would hardly recognize him.

He loaded up the horses while Phillippe went to wake Selenia. When she came over to help with her horse, Grayden noticed her eyes were puffy and swollen. She'd obviously been crying, but he didn't need to ask why. He hadn't even fully processed Jurel's death yet, he'd been too focused on getting Renya back. He put his arm around Selenia's shoulder and gave her a slight squeeze. She looked up at him, eyes watering.

"It'll be okay, my dear one," he said, patting her on the back. She nodded, and then squared her shoulders in resolve.

"Let's go get the answers we need to get Renya back," she said.

∞

Phillippe was right. The Sun Realm was breathtakingly beautiful, Grayden thought, as they approached the gate into the city. The realm was right at the foot of the desert, but it appeared so suddenly, and so brightly that Grayden thought it was a mirage at first.

A golden, ornate gate towered above, with angelic figures spiraling up the sides of the columns. The entire kingdom was enveloped in a tall, limestone wall protecting the city from the harsh elements of the desert. Spikes made out of gold lined the tops of the walls, and more carvings, some of animals, some of angels, decorated the wall.

"Oh my," Selenia said, stepping back to take in the magnificent structure in front of them. "That's... really something."

Grayden was equally impressed. It suddenly hit him that he was outside Renya's lands, her birthright.

It was night and day different from his. Everything in the Snow Lands were covered in a soft, delicate blanket of sparkling snow. Here, the gleaming sun bathed everything in a warm glow. They couldn't be more different from each other.

"Well, are we just going to stare, or find a way in?" Phillippe teased, walking directly up to the gate and giving it a big shake.

Unsurprisingly, the gate didn't yield to Phillippe's half-hearted attempt.

"You really thought that would work?" Grayden said, an eyebrow raised in Phillippe's direction.

"You never know," Phillippe retorted, shrugging his strong and broad shoulders.

Grayden surveyed the gate and surrounding wall. There must be another way in. He started walking the perimeter of the wall, and Phillippe, knowing what his brother was thinking, started in the opposite direction.

Selenia walked back to the horses, leading them over to a small stream that was flowing out of a small gate through the wall.

"Grayden!" she yelled excitedly. "Come here!"

Grayden ran back towards her, instantly alarmed. "What is it?"

"I think I found a way in," she said, pointing at the gate. It was partly rusted and crumbling.

"Good work, Selenia. Phillippe, come here. We need your strength."

Within minutes, Phillippe and Grayden had worked the gate off the hinges, allowing for a small passage through the wall.

"I'll go first," Grayden said.

"Selenia in the middle, and I'll go last," Phillippe agreed as Grayden took off his boots and removed his shirt and then threw them over the wall.

He heard Selenia gasp behind him, and he realized this was the first time she saw his wound. It was healed, but the scar left behind was deep and an angry red.

"It's okay, Selenia. I'm healed," he said, while wading through the stream. He dipped below the surface of the water, swimming under the gate. He appeared quickly on the other side and then looked around him. The source of the stream was a serene lake, lined with palm trees and soft grasses.

Selenia emerged on the other side of the gate, swimming to the side of the bank. "Wow, it's gorgeous here. We'll need to find a way to get the horses in so they can graze."

Grayden looked around. They seemed to be in some kind of garden area, with greenery surrounding the entire lake, and lush flowers blooming. The most fragrant smell lofted towards his nose, and he inhaled deeply. The floral scent reminded him of Renya's skin, during those tender nights that they fell asleep wrapped in each other's arms. He quickly shook the memory away, determined to focus on the task ahead of him.

"Oh Fates," came Phillippe's voice as he emerged from below the surface of the lake. "That's really something."

Grayden dragged himself to the bank where Selenia sat, attempting to wring the water out of her skirts. He looked around for his boots and shirt, and found his boots just alongside the bank. His tunic, however, was floating in the water. He grabbed it, and joined Selenia in trying to wring out their wet clothing.

Phillippe trudged up to the bank, removing his boots and dumping out the water from them.

"I'm going to head back towards the gate and see if I can find a way to get the horses in. I left them tied to a small palm tree, but they won't stay put for long," Phillippe said. He stomped off, leaving a trail of dripping water behind him.

Grayden held out his hand to Selenia and helped pull her up off the bank. Another thick stone wall separated the lake and trees from the heart of the city. But this time the gate was unlocked. Grayden pushed against the iron barrier, and he and Selenia moved farther into the city.

"Do you think Renya has memories of this place?" Selenia asked as they entered the city.

"I'm not sure," he said, his eyes quickly surveying the town.

Opulent, grand buildings greeted them as they emerged from the garden. Everything seemed to be made from either a creamy-colored marble or was gilded. Grayden found it incredibly strange that the city hadn't been looted long ago. He stopped to admire a particularly handsome building, with images of different fruits and vegetables carved on the stone door, entombed in a golden finish. He went to open the door, and a blast of heat hit him squarely in the chest.

"Grayden!" Selenia exclaimed, rushing to her brother's side. "What happened?"

Grayden rubbed his chest and stood farther back from the door. "It seems as though there's some kind of protective spell upon these buildings," Grayden said.

"That explains why it's been untouched for so long. There's still some kind of magic defending this place.

"Do you think we'll be able to get into the palace?" Selenia asked, frowning.

"I don't know, Selenia." Grayden swallowed down the rising panic threatening to overwhelm him. What if they couldn't even get into the palace to find the scrolls? Before he could investigate the magic surrounding the building, he heard the tell-tale sound of Damion's neigh and turned around to see Phillippe leading all three of the horses in the direction of the garden lake.

Grayden examined the next building along the street. He peered inside the windows and found an ordinary home. There was a parlor, with cushions spread along the floor, and doors leading off to other rooms of the home. A fine sitar sat in the corner, and he could just make out some sheet music on the floor next to it. It did indeed appear as if the residents just disappeared. There was no sign of any kind of struggle on the streets and no damage done to the buildings. They were just…empty.

As he took in more of the city, he couldn't help but feel like someone was watching him. He turned around several times, expecting to see Selenia or Phillippe behind him, but they were both back at the lake, caring for the horses.

The unease followed him and grew more intense the farther he moved into the city. Finally, he decided to wait until Phillippe and Selenia were done with the horses. He couldn't shake the feeling that he was walking into an ambush, even though none came.

As he was heading back towards the lake, he

swore he saw a girl's face in the window of the vacant house he passed earlier. But when he looked again, the face was gone. He shook his head to try and clear his vision. His eyes must be playing tricks on him.

He approached the bank and watched as Phillippe and Selenia brushed down the horses and unloaded them.

"I thought we'd camp here tonight," Phillippe said, unrolling the sleeping rolls. "The horses can graze on the grass, and it's close enough to the palace that we can spend most of the evening investigating."

Grayden moved over and started to tend to Damion. The horses were in rough shape after the desert, Grayden noted. They weren't used to the warm climate and instead, were bred and adapted for high altitudes and cold weather. As much as he hated to delay, it was a good idea to rest here overnight and most likely the next night, too.

"Are you ready?" Grayden asked, once the animals were properly seen to.

Phillippe slung his broadsword over his back and Selenia grabbed a saddle bag and threw it over her shoulder.

"What's that for?" Phillippe asked.

"You think we've come all this way and we aren't bringing the scrolls and books with us?"

"Ah, good point," he said, as he started up the path.

They walked silently for a while, and Grayden still felt the sensation of eyes on him.

"Do you feel that?" Phillippe asked Grayden, his voice low so as not to worry Selenia.

"The feeling that we're being watched? Yes,

but I've seen no one or any activity." Grayden didn't mention the little girl he thought he saw. It seemed so improbable that anyone would be left in this abandoned kingdom. It was rumored to have fallen many, many years before. He wasn't even sure how Renya's ancestry was possible. He assumed that a tiny faction might have escaped and survived, hidden in another kingdom under false heritage.

A chilling thought suddenly entered his mind. What if it wasn't true? What if the Sun Realm hadn't fallen, and it had been inhabited when Renya's parents lived? If so, where was everyone now?

Phillippe gripped the hilt of his sword as they walked through the city, prepared in case the slightest noise or rustle came. Grayden followed up from behind, putting Selenia in the middle.

They moved through the city quickly, but every once in a while they stopped to observe a shop or building. Selenia gasped as she saw a clothier shop, brocades, silks and satins filling up the window in front. She looked longingly at the door and then down at her stained dress, still partially damp despite the heat.

Even Phillippe stopped as they passed a swordsmith's shop, with all kinds of swords and knives displayed proudly in the window. An intricate and ornate chess set caught Grayden's attention as they passed by a silversmith's workshop.

The marble streets twisted and turned, like a maze around the palace. It appeared to be built in the center of the town on a gentle hill. Every time they thought they were getting closer, the path they chose would take them in a different direction.

"We should have left a trail of breadcrumbs,"

Selenia mumbled, stopping to adjust the pack she carried. "How much farther do you think?"

"I think we're almost there," Grayden said, noticing how the streets seemed to narrow.

They turned a corner, and suddenly found themselves in an enormous courtyard. The area reminded Grayden of the spokes of a wheel, with different paths leading out in all directions into the city. The courtyard was round, with a large circular path connecting all the others together.

The palace was huge. Turrets jutted out from every corner, towering above. It was made of the same limestone material like the walls protecting the city, but even more carvings adorned every surface. There was gold everywhere Grayden looked, and he once again marveled that the city and its structures hadn't been looted.

"It looks undisturbed and perfect," Selenia commented.

"Not quite." Phillippe pointed to the eastern side of one tower. The entire surface of the tower was blackened, and pieces of rubble lined the ground under it. Easily half of the tower was missing, open and exposed to the elements.

"I wonder what happened there," Selenia said, glancing above and walking carefully around the rubble.

Grayden had an unnatural feeling the longer he looked at the spot. It was as if something significant happened there, something he should know. Almost as though he was there before, it felt oddly...familiar. Perhaps he had heard it described or seen it in a book? But even as he searched for the memory, he knew that wasn't it.

"Well, what are we waiting for?" Phillippe moved towards the large gate. Grayden's fears about the palace being impenetrable were unfounded; the gate was wide open and they moved through it with no resistance. Easily the height of more than two men, the gate was huge and heavy. Had it been closed, Grayden wasn't sure how they would have managed it. It would have taken half a dozen men to move it even a fraction.

Beyond the gate was a small corridor, with a fountain in the middle. A golden eagle, perched on a branch, was prominently depicted, carved into the marble of the fountain. Water trickled down the branch and tree, falling into a reservoir.

More paths led to different parts of the palace, branching off in several directions.

"Which way?" Selenia asked.

Grayden didn't answer, but his feet carried him towards the eastern tower. He couldn't explain why, but he needed to see what transpired there.

Wordlessly, Phillippe and Selenia followed him through a passageway and up a spiraling staircase. Like most of the tower, the staircase was crumbling and they watched their footing carefully the higher they got. Burgundy tapestries lined the walls of the tower, with large valkyries decorating them. In the oldest of Fae languages, the motto "the sun shall never set," was proudly displayed on them.

Ironic, Grayden thought, as they continued their way up the dilapidated tower. The closer Grayden got to the top, the harder his heart started beating and he felt his palms moisten.

He finally reached the landing, which opened up

into a large suite of rooms. His boots thumped on the marble tile as he moved past the dark wood paneling and into the room on the far left. He stopped dead in his tracks when he saw what was before him.

The circular room was painted a majestic midnight blue, with glittering images of the sun peppering the walls. A mural of a sunrise hung over a handsomely carved crib. Baby items were strewn about the room, and he saw tiny little clothes, blankets, and broken furniture. A lone baby bonnet, caked with dust, rested right next to his boot.

His heart knew what this was before his mind could catch up. He felt her here, felt the ghost of her presence in this nursery.

This was Renya's childhood room.

Chapter Fifteen

R enya sat on the floor with her back against the bed frame, sobs echoing off of the walls of her chamber. She couldn't believe that her own father was alive.Not only that, he took away the one thing she had left. Her bond with Grayden.

The second her father performed his magic, it was like a part of her died. The knowledge that her fated mate was no longer connected to her broke her all over again.

She cried ugly, loud tears until her nose ran all down her face. She used her sleeve to dry her face, not caring about ruining the simple dress she wore. As she rolled up her sleeve, she caught a glimpse of her mating mark. The sparkling snowflake was there, as brilliant as ever. Confusion whirled around in her brain. Shouldn't her mark be gone if her bond was broken? Cressida didn't bear a mark after splitting from her father, so if her connection to Grayden was really severed, shouldn't her mark be gone too?

She traced the snowflake with her finger, and she swore she could feel Grayden, just beyond her reach. She wasn't sure if her mind was playing tricks on her, or if she could really feel him.

A quick rapt against her window drew her attention away from her wrist. She picked herself up off the cold floor and couldn't believe it when she saw Sion's face peering back at her. Renya quickly undid the lock and swung the window open.

Sion hoisted himself up into her room, looking so much worse than she had ever seen him. He had large, open gashes bleeding on his chest, and his feet were completely bare and filthy.

"Sion, how are you here?" Renya asked, flabbergasted at his sudden appearance.

"Hold on Renya," Sion said, as he turned back to the window. Another face appeared, and Renya watched in disbelief as her father was assisted into the room by Sion.

Cyrus dropped to the floor and stood in front of Renya. He was incredibly pale, and he looked almost like a ghost. Renya stared at him, unsure of how she should act or even how she felt.

"Sunshine. I'm so sorry," the old man said. "I never meant for it to be this way."

The anger Renya had been carrying finally unleashed itself. "You mean you didn't mean to break my bond? The one thing I had left? The thing that I cared about more than anything in this world? You robbed me of my mate, my future husband! He means more to me than you ever will."

Cyrus stared back at Renya, confusion wrinkling his brow. "My darling daughter, I would never break your fated bond. Do you know just how sacred those are? When I broke mine to your mother, there were deep consequences and dark magic to pay. But I did it for you, my dear girl. To keep you safe. I would never rob you of the man you love."

Renya's voice caught in her throat. "But...I felt something break," she said in a small voice.

"I did sever a connection, but it wasn't your fated bond."

Sion cleared his throat. "Enough of these riddles. What did you do?" He looked at Cyrus expectantly.

"I broke her blood promises. She's no longer bound to her mother. She's free. The dark magic binding the promises were rooted in deception and coercion, even if Cressida didn't believe it. A blood promise made under those circumstances can be broken with magic."

Renya's eyes widened. She couldn't believe it. She was free? Just five minutes ago, she thought everything was taken from her and no hope remained. Now, she was free to return to Grayden. "You mean I can leave?"

Cyrus frowned. "You can, my daughter. But I would beg you to stay."

"To stay? Why on earth would I stay here, with that monster?"

Cyrus looked at Renya, and she felt as if he was sizing her up for the first time. "Your mother is strong. She has amassed more power than I ever believed she could. Not only that, but she has managed to bring dragons into this world. You find yourself at a crossroads, my darling girl. You can leave, and return to your prince. Or, you could stay and earn your mother's trust. Be useful to her. She believes that you are no longer fated, and that you are bloodsworn to be loyal and obedient. There might be a way to use that to your advantage and potentially save us all."

"So she's really my mother?" Renya asked in a small voice.

"She is, I'm afraid. She wasn't always this way, my dear child. She could love, once. She loved me. And she loved you, in her own way. But she was so fearful of being weak, of losing her magic, that she became blinded by power. She allowed it to blacken her soul, to transform her into what she is today. I saw the signs, as soon as you were born. We uncovered a prophecy, buried deep within our forgotten libraries underneath our palace. It foretold of a light bringer, who would bring back magic. When Cressida found it, she brought seer after seer to our home. She became obsessed with finding the meaning behind it. She neglected you and me. Finally, one seer told her that you would take her power and her life. Your aunt overheard the conversation, and she and I devised a plan to take you to the human world and hide you there."

"Aunt Agatha is really my aunt then? Your sister?"

"She's your aunt, but not my sister. She was born of shadow."

Renya gulped. All this time, her aunt kept the truth from her. Cressida and Agatha were sisters. She felt a headache coming on, and her brain felt like it was going to burst with all the revelations.

"So you are really my father then," Renya said, looking at Cyrus as if for the first time.

"I am. I loved your mother, but what I felt for you...I can't even describe it. When I had to choose between you two, I chose you. I broke my bond with Cressida to keep you safe and hidden. I couldn't take a chance of her finding me or sensing where I was. And I paid dearly for it. I lost my magic for several years, and was stuck in the human world for longer than I intended. But I never stopped watching you, never stopped protecting you. When you moved to Seattle, right across the street from the portal, I knew that it was time for you to return. Just as I suspected, you were drawn to the portal. At the time, I thought it must have been the prophecy drawing you home. But now, I think it was your bond, bringing you to the man who would replace me as your protector."

Renya stood there, unsure of how she felt. She believed this man, believed that he was her father. But she was confused, and angry at being lied to for her entire life. Even when Aunt Agatha came to save her, she still withheld the whole truth from her.

"What about my aunt? Where is she?" Renya asked, panicky. If Cyrus was at the bookstore, shouldn't he know where she was? Despite the fact that her aunt had lied to her numerous times, she still needed her safe.

"I'm sorry Renya, I think the Shadow Queen bound her to another world. But don't fret, Sion and I are going to head back through the portal and try to recover her. Her power is unmatched, and she's vital to helping us defeat Cressida."

"Back through the portal?" Sion asked, glancing at Cyrus.

"Yes, I'd like to head home to the Sun Realm, and then search for Agatha in the portal corridor. I know it's a lot to ask, especially for how much you've been through here."

Sion gulped, obviously uncomfortable with Cyrus knowing how much he'd been doing here. Renya's eyes became wide again, putting together the fact that her friend had been sleeping with her mother, and her father knew about it.

"I'll go," Sion said quickly, looking between Renya and Cyrus. "Anything is better than being her plaything." He looked at Cyrus and blushed. "Sorry," he added.

Cyrus brushed off the apology. "I'm thankful for you, Sion. You know the Snow Lands well, and you've been through the portal once before."

"So, you're leaving? Now?" Renya asked.

Cyrus nodded. "We need to leave before she realizes we've escaped. Hopefully we'll get a good head start." He wiped his hands on his suit pants. He was dirty and covered in grime, no doubt from spending his days and nights in the dungeon.

"So...will you stay?"

Renya's heart sank. She wanted Grayden, needed him. Her body ached to be next to him. She envisioned their reunion, the happiness that would radiate from his face when they were finally brought back together. She imagined sleeping on his warm and muscular chest, his calloused fingers softly tracing small circles on her arms after making love. The scene she painted in her mind was so vivid, so wonderfully warm, that she almost refused right away. But the longer she thought, she knew the future she pictured for them would never exist as long as Cressida did. With despair in her heart and heaviness in her chest, she agreed. "I'll stay as long as it takes for her to trust me."

"You are truly my daughter. So brave and beautiful. I only hope this mate of yours is good enough for you."

It felt odd, so strange to be in Cressida's palace, talking with her father about her future husband.

"He's the best man I've ever known," Renya said, red creeping up her cheeks.

"He really is," Sion added.

Cyrus looked satisfied with their answer, and moved back towards the window. "Sion, we better get going. The magic I used to free us will linger and leave a trace. I'm afraid she'll find us sooner rather than later, and I'm weak from breaking the blood promises."

Sion moved towards the window, then paused before heading back over to the center of the room. He gave Renya a firm embrace, and kneeled before her. "You might not be crowned yet, but you're my queen all the same."

Cyrus looked on proudly, as if watching his daughter earn the respect of her subjects delighted him.

"Goodbye, Renya," Cyrus said, preparing to climb out the window.

"Wait," Renya said, as she came closer. Cyrus stood upright in front of her, and surprise crossed his face as she moved into his arms.

This man was a stranger, someone she had known less than a day, but she couldn't send him away without acknowledging the sacrifices he made for her. It was clear they were done out of love. But as he put his arms around her, Renya was shocked to feel a sense of completeness as her father embraced her back.

She pulled away, noting the tears that threatened to fall from her father's eyes.

"Take care, my Renya. My Light Bringer. I named you that because the second you came into this world and I held you in my arms, you became the light that ruled my life."

Chapter Sixteen

G rayden moved over to the broken crib, looking at the miniature valkyries carved into the back. There were little suns too, and the bedding and blankets were a creamy butter-yellow. He ran his hand along the side of it, and could almost feel traces of his mate.

Phillippe and Selenia entered behind him, both looking baffled at Grayden's fascination with the room.

"Grayden, shouldn't we go look for the archives?" Phillippe asked. He moved closer to where Grayden stood, as if trying to figure out what was going through his brother's head.

"I think...I think this was Renya's nursery," he said quietly, turning around to take the rest of the room in. Part of the circular wall was destroyed, and rubble littered the plush rugs covering the stone floor. A layer of dust was thick on all the surfaces, but he could tell from the care that had been put into decorating the room, Renya was loved. A small painting of an elkten was on the wall, which both excited and mystified him. Why was his animal guardian depicted in her room? Was it a coincidence? Or perhaps fate?

"How do you know?" Selenia asked, disbelief etched on her face.

"I just do," he said, looking at the mural above the cradle once again. Suns and stars flickered against the light, almost as if they were moving.

He moved away from the cradle and he heard a slight crack when he brought his foot down. He bent over and picked up a heart-shaped necklace. He rubbed his fingers over the smooth gold surface and turned it over. There was an engraving, and in fancy text, he could just make out the inscription:

To Cressida, Love Cyrus and Renya

Both horror and bewilderment flooded all of Grayden's senses. Everything around him seemed to stand still as he stared at the back of the necklace. His throat felt dry and his insides turned. It couldn't be.

Selenia came up behind Grayden and looked over his shoulder.

"What in the Gods' names?" she exclaimed, glancing at the necklace and then Grayden's face. "That can't be..."

Grayden turned over the necklace again and realized it had a small hinge on the side. He opened it, and found a miniature portrait. A woman, holding a newborn, stared back at him. He recognized the violet eyes and dark hair at once. It was Cressida. And there was no doubt that the blue-eyed babe sitting on her lap was his mate.

He blanched, almost feeling ill. How could his sweet, brave, intelligent Renya come from such a monster? And who was Cyrus? Her father?

His eyes frantically darted across the room, looking for other clues. Besides some carved toys and a chest filled with elaborate gowns and linens, which he suspected were to be part of Renya's trousseau one day, he found nothing else to answer the millions of questions that bombarded his mind.

"What does this mean?" Phillippe asked, looking at the necklace and then around the room. "Is Renya... really the Shadow Queen's daughter?"

Grayden nodded, his throat dry and his chest tight. It didn't change how he felt about Renya, but it did significantly change the war they were about to face. Fates, how could he have not put it together? He remembered the surprise he felt when Agatha let Cressida live, even though her magic was strong and Cressida had none at the Sunset Lands. He thought back and pictured Agatha's magic, black and misty. The twin of Cressida's. Her sister. Agatha must have sensed the danger Cressida posed to her own daughter, and hid her away in the human world. It wasn't just because of the prophecy. It was because Renya's own mother would harm her. And where was Renya's father? Dead? It was clear that something happened here in this room. Another memory hit him and like a flash, and he remembered the nightmare Renya had. She was warm and happy, and then darkness appeared. Was she witness to whatever took place? As an infant, did those memories stay with her?

"That's...intense," Phillippe commented, looking awkwardly at Grayden. "And...didn't Cressida want you at one time? The mother of your mate? That's just... wow."

Grayden ignored him, already aware of the implications. He closed his hand over the locket, and tucked it into his tunic. He wasn't sure why, but he needed to take it with him. Perhaps to provide proof to Renya...his stomach lurched again. How could he tell Renya? She would be horrified at the revelation.

"I think we should go," Selenia said, backing

away towards the door. "This room feels like...like we shouldn't be here."

"I agree," Phillippe said, grasping Grayden by the arm. "Come on, Brother. Let's go find the archives."

Locating the lost library proved to be more difficult than they could have fathomed. They explored every tower, searching every room. The palace boasted a golden music room, filled with many different types of instruments, a drawing room with a large palm tree growing straight out of the ground and through a large opening in the ceiling above, and even a pond full of strange fish that they had to cross over by stepping on flat rocks strategically placed in a path from one side of the room to the other. They even looked in the kitchen and the store room, and were perplexed to find fresh vegetables still in the cellar.

"Do you think there's some sort of spell on this room, keeping the produce fresh?" Selenia asked her brothers.

Phillippe scratched his jaw, and Grayden examined the room closer.

"I'm not sure, but I'm getting the feeling that perhaps this city isn't abandoned after all," Grayden said, looking at the soot in the fireplace. He walked over and poked at the ashes with a fire poker. Sure enough, he uncovered some hot coals.

"Grayden..." Phillippe warned, noting the recently extinguished fire.

"I know...someone is here, or has been here very recently."

"Let's keep moving, and quickly," Selenia said, hitching her bag up over her shoulder.

They exited the kitchen and then went through

another corridor until they came to a dead end. There was a plain stone wall in front of them.

"A dead end. Let's turn around and head out. We've searched everywhere," Phillippe said.

"Wait!" Selenia whispered, moving closer to the wall. "Can't you hear that?"

"Hear what?" Grayden asked.

"There's a draft, or wind blowing through the edges of the corner of the wall." She kneeled down on the floor and put her ear against the stone. "I'm sure of it!"

Grayden reached down and put his hand along the seam of the wall. "I feel it," he said, the cooler air hitting his hand. "There's a secret passageway here."

"Move back," Phillippe said, pulling out his broadsword. He forced the sharp blade into the corner and pushed. The wall in front of them moved an inch, sliding seamlessly into a hollow opening on the other side.

"Help me!" Phillippe said excitedly, pushing on the blade even harder.

Grayden grasped the edges of the wall and pushed, and another few inches disappeared. Phillippe threw his weight against his blade, and Grayden pushed as hard as he could. Another six inches of wall slid into the other side .

"I think that's as far as it goes," Grayden said. "Did you bring a torch?" he asked Selenia.

"Of course," she said, and removed a long wrapped piece of wood from the pack she carried. Grayden grabbed it and struck a piece of flint from his pocket onto the torch. It burst into flames and he held it in front of the passageway.

"I'll go first. Selenia, you next, and then Phillippe, you take the rear."

Phillippe let out a chuckle at Grayden's phrasing, but was given a stern look from his brother in return. "Sorry," he said sheepishly, before getting behind Selenia.

Grayden turned sideways and pushed himself through the narrow opening in the wall. It was tight, but he just managed to squeeze through. He lifted the torch and looked around. A long staircase was in front of him, with no landing below in sight. He sighed as Selenia pushed herself through the wall easily.

"What do you think is down there?" she asked Grayden.

"Hopefully the answers we've all been looking for," Grayden said.

"Ummmm...we have a problem," Phillippe called, his voice muffled. Selenia and Grayden turned back to see Phillippe, or rather, half of Phillippe, wedged in between the walls.

Larger in the chest and a bit stockier than Grayden, it was clear that no amount of wiggling would allow Phillippe to clear the door. Finally, after a few minutes they gave up.

"I'll just guard out here, I guess," Phillippe said, pushing himself back into the corridor.

Grayden nodded, and he moved quietly and quickly down the stairs, with Selenia following behind him.

The stairs seemed to go on and on, twisting and spiraling down beneath the palace. The farther down they got, the colder it became. Selenia began shaking almost immediately, and even Grayden was chilled in his damp shirt. Finally, after almost a half hour, the stairs abruptly ended in front of a massive wooden door. Ancient in appearance, and etched with runes, it was firmly locked.

"What should we do?" Selenia asked.

Before Grayden could respond, the door swung wide open.

Chapter Seventeen

R enya woke up with renewed determination. She would get Cressida to trust her, and somehow learn how to defeat her. She must have some kind of weakness or fear they could exploit.

Renya washed in the small copper tub and got dressed quickly. Margot appeared with her breakfast tray, and Renya didn't waste any time in scarfing everything down. She'd definitely need her strength if she was going to try and become the ally and heir Cressida sought.

"Anything else, Miss Renya?" Margot asked.

"Actually...I need some make-up."

"Make-up? Margot looked at Renya, confused.

Renya held out her arm, and her mating mark sparkled in the light. Margot gasped as she took in the meaning.

"You're fated to your prince?"

"Yes, but Cressida thinks she's broken my bond. I need your help in covering it up."

Margot disappeared, and then came back a few minutes later with a light colored powder. She helped Renya apply it, adding several layers until she was satisfied that it wouldn't rub off.

"Thank you, Margot. I know I can trust you." Margot smiled and backed out of the room.

Renya fixed her hair and took a few deep breaths

before leaving the room. Her chambers were like a small sanctuary in the palace, and every time she left them she feared what would happen. At least Cressida never came in here, always sending someone to fetch Renya. Other than their training sessions, Renya hardly saw her.

She walked to the throne room, where Cressida was already waiting for her. Usually, she was late and made Renya wait for her, so instantly Renya was on edge.

Cressida's face was ashen, and her entire body seemed to hum with untamed magic.

Renya approached her, but was careful to stay several feet in front of her. Usually she'd stare Cressida down, but she remembered her promise to her father and dipped her head downward respectfully.

Cressida walked over to Renya, and wrenched her chin up.

"It appears my prisoners are gone," she hissed at Renya. "I'm assuming you played some kind of part in their escape?"

Renya's heart beat faster. She looked into Cressida's violet eyes, trying to think quickly.

"Which prisoners?" she asked, dropping her eyes demurely.

"Don't play dumb with me, girl!"

"I couldn't betray you if I wanted to. I'm bound to you now, and I promised not to fight. I pledged my loyalty to you."

Cressida relaxed instantly, remembering the blood promises. She let go of Renya's chin, her nails leaving small marks against Renya's skin.

"Sion and Cyrus are gone. If you know anything,

I command you to tell me." Cressida moved to her throne and sat down.

Renya kept her face blank and emotionless. "I don't know anything. I was in my room all night. As far as I'm concerned, I don't care what happens to them. Sion clearly left to save his own hide, and I have no allegiance to a man that would abandon his only daughter in the human world."

Cressida's eyes flashed to Renya's, no doubt looking for sincerity on her face. She must have been pleased with what she saw. "You don't wish to know more of your precious father?"

Renya treaded carefully. She knew too much flattery would make Cressida suspicious, but she had to act like her mating bond was broken and she was still bound in loyalty.

"No. I suffered in the human world. I was... attacked. I had no magic, and part of me was missing. My father—if you can even call him that—ripped me from my rightful place in this world."

Cressida pursed her lips, and Renya hoped she hadn't taken it too far.

"Magic should never be locked away," Cressida agreed, tapping her nails against the throne. Renya noticed that it was a habit for her. "We are nothing without our magic."

"It was horrible in the human realm. I never felt like myself until you freed the magic inside of me."

Surprisingly, Cressida nodded. "I understand that. Let's get training. I still have much to teach you, daughter."

∞

Their practice session lasted much longer than usual. Cressida was still harsh, but at times, she was more patient with Renya.

"To weave magic, you need more than just your thoughts. Your magic is the magic of the Sun Realm, so your powers will always prefer the light."

Renya looked at her, confused. "What does that mean?"

"There's light and dark magic. Not in the sense you're thinking, of evil and good magic. But dark magic tends to be more earthbound. It uses the forces in the ground and darkness of night. My magic is far more powerful here in the Shadow Realm. Yours is more powerful in kingdoms and lands where the sun plays a dominant role. The Sun Realm, obviously. The Tidal Kingdom. The Spring Lands."

Renya chewed the inside of her cheek thoughtfully. It was only a day since she pledged to get closer to Cressida, and she already pieced together some valuable information.

"What other types of magic are there?" Renya asked. She wanted to directly ask about Grayden's magic, but she didn't dare. As far as Cressida was concerned, Grayden no longer held any claim over Renya's heart.

"There was earth and fire, but that magic has all but disappeared."

"What happened to the Sun Realm?"

Cressida shot her a warning look, and Renya halted her questioning quickly.

"I want to show you how to properly shield yourself," Cressida said, changing the subject.

Renya braced herself, knowing that Cressida had

no qualms about hitting her with her magic at full force. Renya quickly let her magic flow, and tried to imagine a web of her magic around her, like Kalora had tried to teach her at the Twilight Kingdom.

As soon as Cressida unleashed her magic, Renya got flustered and dropped her shield. She closed her eyes and braced herself for the impact, but it never came. When she opened her eyes, she saw Cressida pulling her magic back into herself. Renya tried to hide her surprise. Perhaps Cyrus was right, and Cressida would start to trust Renya.

"Perhaps it's best if we took a break. You're obviously worn out."

Renya nodded and tugged at her sleeve. She was perspiring heavily from the warmth of her magic, and she was nervous that too much moisture would cause the make-up covering her mating mark to melt.

"Come. I want to show you something." Cressida moved towards Renya, and grabbed her hand. Renya wanted to pull back, disgusted by her hard, boney fingers, but she didn't even have time to react before Cressida spun and her dark magic transported them.

It was a strange sensation, almost as if Renya's belly button was being pulled towards her back while she was whirling quickly. It only lasted a second, but it was jarring.

When the world stopped spinning, Renya looked around. She was in a damp, darkly lit room with a massive door in front of her. A pulsating sensation radiated from the door, and Renya realized it was enforced by magic.

"Where are we?" she asked Cressida.

"You'll see soon enough," she replied, as she

unlocked the magic encasing the door with a flick of her fingers.

Cressida moved through the door and Renya followed behind, entering a long, dank passage. The walls were wet and dripping, and puddles of muddy water lined the stone walkway. Renya skirted around them and shivered as they walked farther down the path.

"Perhaps we'll need to have some warmer clothing made for you," Cressida said, watching Renya's teeth chatter.

Renya didn't say anything, but her spirit lightened slightly. She couldn't care less about what she was wearing, but Cressida's offer was another step in the right direction. Perhaps this would be easier than she thought.

"Is my Aunt Agatha really your sister?" Renya asked, trying to make conversation as they continued down the narrow path.

Cressida pursed her lips, and Renya wondered if she made a mistake bringing her up.

"Yes. How did you know that?"

Renya didn't miss a beat. "Her magic...it's dark like yours."

"Smart girl," Cressida said, looking intensely at Renya. "Yes, and she betrayed me."

Renya didn't apologize, but she didn't defend her aunt either. "It was really miserable in the human world. I was isolated, and I felt like a part of me was missing."

Cressida looked at her, and Renya thought for a second she detected a tiny amount of pity on her mother's face. "That's how I felt when you took my magic."

"I never asked for it," Renya said cautiously.

Cressida sighed and continued moving forward through the passageway, ducking her head as a large stalagmite protruded from the ceiling.

"Watch your head," she warned Renya.

Renya tried another approach. "When I was in the human realm, a man attacked me. I got away, but it ruined my life. I lost my job, my friends and had to move away. If my magic wouldn't have been locked inside of me, it could have ended differently."

Cressida stopped in her tracks, her shoulders slightly hunched. She didn't turn around, but continued walking. Renya wondered if she was gaining any sympathy from her mother. Surely, no mother could bear to hear that her child was attacked?

After a few more minutes, Cressida turned back to Renya. "Men can't be trusted," she said, her indigo eyes flashing. "They'll betray you as soon as they get a better offer. Be glad you don't have to worry about having a mate anymore."

Renya struggled to keep the disgust off her face. There was no one in this world that she trusted more than Grayden. "At least I don't have to worry about that," Renya agreed, but the lie tasted like ash in her mouth.

Cressida looked pleased. Before Renya could say anything else, they turned the corner and entered a large antechamber. Two guards stood in front of a huge, heavy door. Renya could smell rotting flesh and could hear roars. The hair rose on the back of her neck, and for a second, she thought about turning and running.

This was where Cressida kept her dragons.

The guards opened the enormous doors, and Cressida slipped inside. "Come," she ordered Renya.

She stepped inside hesitantly, not sure why Cressida would bring her here. Renya's eyes were as big as a dinner plate as she took in the sight before her.

Four dragons were encased in a large glass cage. She instantly recognized the reddish-colored one with the orange eyes that carried her into this realm. He wasn't the largest, though. As Renya carefully skirted alongside the wall, as far away from the glass dome as she could, another dragon, this one even larger and with fuchsia scales, snorted into the air. Renya's legs shook at the sound, and she was instantly transported back to the night she was separated from Grayden. She held her breath and then inhaled deeply, trying to fight down the rising panic. Cressida moved forward, closer to the encasement, and beckoned Renya to follow.

"Brutus, Belinia and Berline," she said proudly, pointing to each as she named them. Berline was a bit smaller than Brutus, with teal scales that shimmered under the glow from the torches.

Behind the juvenile, a tiny dragon, about the size of a miniature pony, poked its head out.

Renya let out a gasp, hardly believing her eyes. The littlest dragon crept closer to her, swishing its tail and keeping its pink eyes locked on Renya. Unlike the other dragons, it walked on all fours and reminded Renya of a tall alligator. Its scales were a midnight blue, and it didn't have wings.

Cressida gestured towards the smallest dragon. "She just hatched two days ago."

The dragon finally approached the glass, and peered at Renya intently. Renya hesitantly touched her hand to the glass, and the dragon snorted and then made a deep noise that Renya swore was akin to purring.

"She likes you," Cressida said, astonishment heavy in her tone.

Renya stood there, mesmerized by the baby dragon. The creature continued to pace in front of the glass, keeping her eyes locked on Renya. "Does she have a name?"

"No, not yet." A voice came from the far corner of the enclosure. Renya jumped at the male's voice, while Cressida just groaned.

An elderly man appeared as if from nowhere, walking towards the spot where Renya stood.

"Who do we have here?" he asked in a gravelly voice. Renya took in his appearance and surmised that he wasn't from the Sun Realm. His attire was completely foreign, different and more primitive than anything she saw during her time here.

"She's none of your concern, Travers." Cressida's tone was harsh and contained an air of finality, as if any further questions about Renya would not be tolerated.

Travers glanced at Renya again, but quickly looked at the baby dragon.

"Well, whoever you are, it appears as if she's quite taken with you." He flicked a dirty thumb towards the smallest dragon, who was prancing around the edges of the glass enclosure, trying to get Renya's attention.

Cressida watched the dragon, her eyes narrowing, but then turned thoughtful. She turned and looked at Renya, then back at Travers. "Do you think she'd permit her to approach?"

Travers nodded. "She already looks like she's

trying to bond."

"Renya, come here," Cressida said. It was the first time she'd ever addressed Renya by her name. It sounded strange coming from Cressida's mouth, although Renya knew there must have been a time when she heard it frequently. She reached inside, trying to find some memory of this woman, but nothing came. She only saw the piercing blue eyes of her father that were identical to hers.

Obediently, Renya walked over to Cressida. "It seems as though this baby dragon is trying to bond with you. Do you know what that means?"

Renya shook her head, still surprised at the civil tone Cressida used. She was so used to hearing her saccharine voice, insults rolling off of her tongue.

"When dragons are young, they are able to imprint. Some imprint on their parents, some siblings. And sometimes, other creatures. Brutus, as you might have noticed, has imprinted on me," Cressida explained. "I'm interested to know if this small female will imprint on you."

Renya bit her lip. She was intrigued, and did want to see the little dragon up close. But the other dragons were incredibly frightening. "How does it work?"

"You'll need to enter the enclosure and walk up to her slowly. You'll know instantly if she imprints on you."

It was just as Renya feared. She'd have to get in the glass cage with the other dragons. Renya hesitated, but then squared her shoulders. She must continue to impress Cressida. This would be a perfect way to show her mother just how brave and valuable she could be to her.

Cressida instantly acknowledged Renya's resolve with a small nod. "Good. I knew you would be unafraid."

With Traver's assistance, Renya entered the dragon's territory slowly through a small, hinged opening in the glass. The dirt floor was soft underneath her feet, and she moved along the edge of the glass wall, taking small, tentative steps.

Brutus, Cressida's bound dragon, glanced at her lazily before looking directly at Cressida. The Shadow Queen gave a quick jerk of her jaw and Brutus ignored Renya, and then snorted into the air and made a loud, visceral roar. The other two adult dragons looked at him, and then went back to what they were doing.

Renya walked slowly over to the pink-eyed dragon, her pulse thumping and her heart hammering like it might burst through her chest. The other dragons continued to ignore her, but the littlest instantly took notice. She didn't take her eyes off of Renya.

Unsure of what to do, Renya approached her and slowly reached her hand out. The dragon looked at her, unblinking and then cocked her head, the way a well-trained dog might. Then, without warning, she pushed her snout underneath Renya's outstretched hand and purred contentedly.

Surprised, Renya stroked the dragon's nose, its small scales still pliable, unlike the older dragons. A smile crept up on her face and the dragon nuzzled Renya's hand, emitting a happy, chirpy sound.

"That's it!" Cressida said excitedly, her voice slightly muffled through the glass.

Travers clapped his hands, watching the scene before him. "You've done it!"

Renya continued to pet the dragon, feeling an attachment to the creature instantly. Upon closer inspection, she noticed tiny wing buds jetting out from her back.

"She's a beauty," Renya said, admiring the creature.

"Then that's what we shall name her," Cressida responded. "Her name is Beauty."

Chapter Eighteen

"**W**ho are you?" Grayden demanded, staring down at the tiny woman standing in the doorway.

"You break into our realm, invade our palace, and then have the nerve to ask who I am?"

The woman was remarkably old, older than Almory, older than anyone Grayden met before. Her curly hair fell past her shoulders, and it was so white that it almost seemed to absorb the light from the chamber behind her. She was dressed in a simple, flowing white dress. Her face was so wrinkled that she looked like she was in a constant state of confusion, with her forehead scrunched up and her eyes pulled back. Her skin was almost as pale as her hair, and Grayden figured that she must hardly ever leave the indoors. She carried a short staff with a gaudy sun emblazoned on the top, and a giant ruby in the center of the sun. Her eyes were a piercing gray, and she looked at Grayden and Selenia as if she could see all the way into their very souls.

"I'm here seeking knowledge about breaking a blood promise," Grayden said, putting himself in front of Selenia. "I'm Prince Grayden from the Snow Lands."

The old woman glanced behind his back at Selenia. "And who is this?"

"My sister," Grayden responded, shielding

Selenia further.

"You can calm down, I'm not going to hurt her," the old woman wheezed, her voice crackly as if she had a perpetual case of pneumonia. "Come inside," she said, and turned her back to them and walked into the chamber.

As soon as they entered the room, the door shut behind them with a loud boom. Grayden turned and instantly noticed there was no handle or knob on the door. He fought down the panic he felt, ignoring the hair that stood up on the back of his neck as he worried that this was some kind of trap.

He looked around the dimly lit room, searching for something, anything that would signal he was in the right place. That he had finally made a step in the right direction, one tiny moment closer to breaking the blood promise and freeing Renya from...her mother. However, as he took in the small chamber, with nothing more than a short bookcase alongside one of the walls, his hope fell. This was the ancient library of the Sun Realm? The place where magic from the old Gods was kept and protected?

Selenia caught his eye, and he could tell she too was not impressed at the sight before her. Aside from the wooden bookcase, there was an oak desk with a large, open book on it, as well as a quill. Another door, slightly smaller than the one they entered through but no less grand, stood next to the bookshelf.

The woman finally spoke. "You say you seek ancient knowledge?" she said, looking directly at Grayden.

"I seek a spell to break a promise my mate made."

She let out a shrill laugh, which echoed in the

empty room, bouncing off the bare walls.

"You foolish boy, do you think it's so easy to break a fated bond? It's hard to do and requires a sacrifice. One that you are unable to pay."

Grayden didn't ask for her to elaborate her meaning. "I would never break my bond," he said, trying not to raise his voice at the anger he felt at the mere suggestion. "I wish to free my mate from a blood promise she pledged to another."

The woman looked over at the bookcase for a split second, but it was enough for Grayden to catch the look. There was knowledge there, important knowledge.

"Why do you think I could undo this promise? A blood promise is never meant to be broken. The very nature of a blood promise is that it can't be undone."

Grayden lifted his chin. "This promise was nobly made, and my mate suffers because of it."

"Ahhhh...you want your mate back. All those who seek magic in this library are selfish and only travel here for their own wish-fulfillment. One of the many reasons why the rumor that the Sun Realm had fallen was spread. Representatives from every land from every corner of our world have been here, seeking our knowledge to better or enrich their own pathetic lives."

Selenia finally spoke up. "We need to break this bond to vanquish the Shadow Queen."

Another cackle came from the old woman. "A boy with no magic? And a girl who refuses to use hers? You think you can take down the Shadow Queen? Ha! Her ending has already been foretold, and it is not some silly love-sick prince who will bring it about."

"No," Grayden responded, his eyes beaming with

pride. "It's the Light Bringer. My mate."

Before the woman could respond, the earth underneath them began quaking, and a violent tremor knocked them all off their feet. As Grayden and Selenia picked themselves up off the ground, they noticed the woman was gone.

"Well, that could have gone better," Selenia said dishearteningly.

∞

Grayden's shoulder was in agony, but he wouldn't give up.

"Grayden, you're going to kill yourself," Selenia said, as he rushed the door again, trying to get it to open. He bounced off, hesitated for a second, then rammed it with his other shoulder. Nothing. It wouldn't budge.

Grayden stood back, rage rushing inside of him. He didn't come this far to get stuck in an underground chamber. Surely there must be a way out. He guessed the elderly woman left by magic, but there must be some other way. He stared at the door, then held out his hand, focusing as hard as he could. Nothing. Just as he suspected, he had no magic left.

"Selenia?" he asked, looking over at her. She was slumped against the wall, listening intently as if she could hear a way out. "I know you don't use your magic, but could you please try?"

Selenia looked at him sadly. "I already tried, Grayden. I don't know if this room is protected from outside magic, or if mine is gone as well." She sniffled, and a single tear dripped down her cheek. Grayden stopped ramming the wall and sank down to sit against the rough stone wall with his sister.

"I'm so sorry, Selenia," he said, putting an arm around her shoulders.

"I'm not upset about my magic, I'm just upset that I can't use it when I need it. Part of me felt comforted, knowing it was there, just in case. But I guess that's gone." She looked ahead, unseeing and with her arms wrapped around her knees.

"Not just that, but I'm sorry I ever brought you into this. When I found Renya again, I shouldn't have come back to the Snow Lands. I should have hidden her somewhere, taken her away where she couldn't be found. This is all my fault. I'm the reason Jurel is dead, I'm the reason we're trapped in here."

"Grayden, I think we would have ended up here, regardless of our choices."

Grayden leaned against the wall, the cold seeping into his muscles. His shoulder would be bruised for days, but the coolness of the wall brought him some relief. "You know, Renya said something like that."

"She did?"

"Yes, when we were at the Twilight Kingdom. She said the prophecy was proof she would vanquish the Shadow Queen, because it was foretold. It gave her strength and assurance, I think. She said she felt like every move she made was the right choice, leading her to do whatever she must do."

"She's very wise," Selenia said, and then she jerked her head up, listening. She sat up straighter, her eyes wide.

"What is it?"

"I can hear Phillippe," she said. "Hush!"

Grayden sat quietly, watching her facial

expression. She stood completely still, eyes closed. She finally opened her eyes, and looked at Grayden.

"He was talking with someone, but I couldn't make out anything."

"Maybe it was the woman that was in here?"

"Maybe," she answered, looking at Grayden. "But it sounded like it might have been a man."

Grayden frowned, hoping Phillippe was okay. Then, from across the room, a flash of gold shone and three figures slowly spun around, becoming more and more substantial by the second.

His jaw dropped. "Sion?"

Sion and Phillippe were standing in the room, along with a man that looked vaguely familiar. Another golden circle spun, and the elderly woman appeared again.

Grayden wasted no time before rushing up and giving Sion a hearty hug. He pulled back, looking into his friend's face for injury, before asking about Renya.

"She's fine, Grayden. Unharmed and becoming more and more powerful with her magic."

Relief poured over Grayden like rain during a thunderstorm. He released a loud breath, as if he hadn't properly breathed since Renya left him. "Really?"

"Yes, really."

Grayden eyed the other man beside Phillippe, trying to place him.

"Grayden, this is Cyrus," Sion said, gesturing to the man.

At once it clicked. The picture in the locket. The piercing blue eyes. He looked much older now, far older than he should, given Renya's age in the picture, but there was no doubt about it. This was Renya's father.

If he was with Sion, did that mean he had been in the Shadow Realm as well?

"I take it this is the man you serve?" Cyrus said, peering into Grayden's green eyes, taking the measure of him.

"He is. Cyrus, this is Grayden. Your daughter's... mate."

"And fiancé," Grayden added, growling slightly. He didn't want anyone else to forget it.

"A little possessive, are we?" Cyrus laughed as he clapped Grayden on the back. "I've been there!"

Grayden was momentarily taken aback, realizing that he was now in the presence of Renya's father. "I guess I should have asked you for her hand, and I would have, if I knew you existed. Does Renya know you're alive?"

"She does, my boy," Cyrus replied, holding out his hand to shake Grayden's. "And I did you a favor before leaving. I broke her blood promise."

"You broke the promise, and then left her there?" Grayden said, irritation and admonishment in his tone.

"Now wait just a second," Cyrus said, sensing that Grayden's temper was rising. "It was essential to our plan."

"I don't care a fuck about your plan!" Grayden roared, his fist itching to punch someone. "All I care about is my mate!"

Sion placed his hand on Grayden's arm, trying to calm him. "It was her choice, Grayden."

Grayden looked like he might strangle Sion or Cyrus, or maybe both of them.

Phillippe came to the other side of Grayden. "Brother, you must stay calm. Let them explain."

Grayden breathed deeply, trying to regulate his pounding heart and the red-hot rage that threatened to break itself loose.

"You're not catching him at the best time," Sion said to Cyrus. "He's usually much calmer."

"He freaks out wherever Renya is concerned," Selenia added. "You should have seen him when his head advisor accused Renya of witchcraft. You could hear him yell all the way to the Tidal Kingdom."

Grayden looked at them all helplessly. "I need to get her back."

Cyrus nodded. "You will. She's now free of the blood promises she made."

"Promises?"

Sion looked guilty. "She made another promise to save my life."

Grayden's jaw clenched and unclenched. He viewed Sion as a brother, and cared for him deeply. The fact that Renya made another blood promise to save his friend both touched and infuriated him.

"I've broken them both, so she's now free whenever she wants to leave."

"Then why is she still there?" Grayden asked, his voice still shaking with anger, but he was cooling down slowly.

"She opted to continue to be trained by Cressida. Renya knew the best chance we have to defeat her would be for her to gain Cressida's trust, learn her secrets and improve her own magic."

Grayden instantly knew Cyrus spoke the truth. That was exactly something Renya would do. Sacrifice herself for the people she loved. For the world she now belonged to.

"When can I rescue her?"

"Within the next two weeks. She's improved drastically in her magic, and given her cleverness and sweet disposition, I have no doubt she will be able to charm her mother quickly."

"I've no doubt about that," Grayden said, sighing deeply.

"So Renya knows? She knows of her heritage?" Selenia asked, watching the interaction, engrossed.

"She does. Cressida told her almost instantly after capturing her. She didn't believe it at first, but once Cyrus confirmed it..." Sion drifted off.

"How did you find out?" Cyrus asked, a slight frown on his face.

Grayden pulled out the locket from his tunic and handed it to Cyrus. Cyrus took it gently, a slightly pained, but sweetly reminiscent look on his face.

"Ahhh, yes. I'd long forgotten about this. There were some good memories, before she became obsessed with the prophecy."

"The Sun Realm scrolls?" Phillippe asked, crossing his arms across his chest, trying to follow along in the family drama unraveling before his eyes.

"Yes. I take it they were rediscovered after I left for the human realm?"

They all nodded.

"I see. We found them shortly after Renya's birth, here in our libraries." Cyrus gestured at the lone bookcase.

"That's...hardly a library, let alone libraries," Selenia said, looking towards the bookcase.

A shrill laugh came from the elderly woman's mouth. "That's just the index."

They all stared at the elderly woman, except for Cyrus, who started walking towards the bookcase.

"This is Libera," he said, acknowledging the old woman. "She's our head seer and the Keeper of the Knowledge."

"We've briefly met," Selenia grumbled, still irritated over their abandonment in the locked chamber.

Cyrus ignored Selenia's comment, humming to himself as he pulled out a book from the shelf. He handed it to Libera, who smiled widely as she accepted it. She ran a pale, wrinkled finger over the spine, and the door next to the bookcase started to sparkle and pulsate, almost as if it was moving incredibly fast while standing still. Suddenly, it stopped, and the door swung inward.

Cyrus stepped through the door, beckoning for them to follow him. Wordlessly, they entered the room, mouths agape. A huge, multistory chamber was laid out before them. Books and scrolls lined every inch of the room, with sliding ladders on every wall. A wrought-iron spiraling staircase stood in the middle of the room, leading up to the second and third stories.

"Whoa," Phillippe said, breaking the silence.

"What is this place?" Grayden asked.

"The great library of knowledge. Libera has been protecting it since we found it. It was long forgotten, but my grandfather stumbled across it while chasing a pig through the palace—long story—and it's taken years to categorize and organize the books." Cyrus strolled over to a shelf, picking up a set of scrolls.

"Is that what I think it is?" Grayden asked.

"Yes. The Sun Realm Scrolls. Once they were

found, Cressida became obsessed with them. It was what led me to sever our fated bond. There was a seer who deduced Renya would be the one to end Cressida, and I feared for her life. Her Aunt Agatha and I hid her away, as I'm sure you've figured out."

"You were fated? I thought fated bonds couldn't be broken?" Grayden asked.

"They shouldn't be, and I'm the first person I know who has attempted and succeeded," Cyrus said, looking at Grayden. "It cost me dearly, and I lost my magic for over twenty years, in which I was stuck in the human realm, aging rapidly. But it was worth it, to save my daughter."

"Do you know where Agatha is?" Grayden asked, knowing that Renya was incredibly worried about her aunt.

"I have a hunch that she's been bound to another realm in the portal corridor in the human world. Sion and I are going to go track her down."

"What about Renya? How do we get her back?" Selenia asked.

"We will need to pull her away from the Shadow Realm. She can't leave voluntarily, or at least, it can't seem that way. Cressida believes I severed Renya's mating bond. She also still thinks the blood promises remain intact. In order to keep her trusting Renya, we will need to make it seem like we are removing her against her will." Cyrus looked around the group, making sure everyone understood. "I'll go with you, to make it seem like I'm there to break the blood promise."

"Won't she try and get Renya back?" Phillippe asked.

"She will, but we'll head towards the Snow

Lands. Her magic will be weakest there, and I can place a protection spell on your lodge that will make it seem as though it's abandoned."

"Is that what you've done here?" Grayden remembered the small girl he thought he saw in the window.

"Yes. The Sun Realm never fell. It's been cloaked for many, many years." Cyrus looked pleased with himself, no doubt proud of the magic protecting his city. "Now that you know it's cloaked, the magic will break and you'll see the city as it truly is. Trust me, you'll never want to leave."

Chapter Nineteen

"**I**'m here, Little Fawn."

Renya opened her eyes, sitting up in her bed. Grayden stood before her, his eyes sparkling.

Without hesitating, Grayden pulled his shirt off, tossing it on the floor. He kneeled before Renya, slowly stroking her bare legs with his calloused hands. Renya whimpered as his wandering fingers pushed up her linen nightgown and reached her inner thighs.

"Did you miss me?" He moaned against her thigh before placing a tender kiss alongside her knee.

Renya nodded, so wrapped up in the way his hands felt against her skin that she couldn't talk. Grayden continued to tease her, and then lifted himself up slightly to tug her bottom lip into his mouth. She moaned, feeling the wetness grow between her legs.

Grayden helped her to lift her hips, and he pulled her undergarments down her legs before throwing them over his shoulder. Completely bare to him, he blew against the apex of her thighs, and her breathing hitched.

"Do you want me, Renya?" Without waiting for an answer, he pushed his trousers down his muscular legs, and then positioned himself between her hips. With a quick thrust, he was inside her, and she wanted to cry as soon as she felt him. He felt impossibly large, like their time apart made her forget just how much of a man he was. She stroked his hair as he whispered words of praise and declarations of love. His mouth moved to the hollow of her throat, and she gasped as his rough hand palmed her breast.

"Grayden..." she moaned, throwing her head back. Pleasure radiated throughout her body. It happened so fast, and she knew it was because it had been weeks since she'd had him. She felt her body coming back to life, felt the connection between them as she pulsed around him.

Renya panted as she came back down from her high, clutching at Grayden.

But there was nothing there.

She opened her eyes quickly, looking around the room, her heart racing and her sex throbbing. But there was no Grayden. She blushed, realizing what just transpired. It felt so real. It was real, she was almost certain.

As her breathing returned to normal, she walked to the window, ignoring the moisture between her legs, and looked out over the darkened valley. Her heart hurt, knowing that somewhere out there, Grayden was missing her as much as she missed him. Feeling defeated and slightly ashamed, she crawled back into her sheets, which were slick from her sweat, and tried to fall back asleep. However, the memory of Grayden's kiss swirled around in her head, and she tossed and turned the rest of the night.

∞

Beauty darted in between the trees, jumping over logs and dodging branches. Every time she leapt over a log, she would flap her tiny wings, achieving a small amount of airtime before she slammed back down to the ground. Renya was certain that if it wasn't for the fact that she was carrying her on her back, Beauty would be able to fly.

The forest was dark, and Renya could hardly see anything in front of her. But Beauty didn't hesitate, prancing happily and weaving in between the trees. Her scales were starting to harden, and Travers said that her wings would be full grown within the next month, and she would be able to take to the sky.

Renya didn't care about flying, she just enjoyed the time they spent together in the forest. With Cressida circling on Brutus, far above the canopy of trees, Renya felt free. The affection she got from Beauty helped to fill the aching hole in her heart, and the dragon seemed to understand Renya in ways that Cressida never could. She was certain Cressida now trusted her, believing Renya was fully under her control, but she still maintained her attitude of aloofness. Sometimes, her icy exterior would melt, and she'd treat Renya like a friend, but never a beloved daughter.

Still, it was a vast improvement to how she was initially treated. She was well fed, better dressed, and was more powerful in her magic than ever before. But at night, she'd lay in bed, her body still and the room quiet, and she'd picture Grayden's emerald eyes staring at her. Renya would imagine them together, him on top of her, kissing and caressing every inch of her. Those were the moments she lived for.

During the day, she had Beauty. At night, the memory of Grayden.

Beauty slowed as they approached a large pond.

Renya hadn't been this far into the forest before, but every day Cressida seemed to trust her more and more and allowed her more freedom.

Renya got off of Beauty, and watched her dance away to get a drink from the pond.

"Where are you?" Cressida bellowed from above, her view of Renya blocked by the thick foliage around the pond.

"Beauty is just drinking from the pond."

"Head back as soon as she's done. Can you find your way if I go on ahead?"

This was the most freedom Renya was ever allowed. Cressida must truly trust her, to leave her alone in the forest with Beauty. "Yes, I know the way back. I'll see you soon."

"You will join me for dinner this evening."

"Okay," Renya agreed, her eyes on Beauty. She hated the meals shared with Cressida, and they were happening more and more frequently. Several times a week her presence was required in the grand dining hall, and she was forced to make small talk with her mother. It wasn't all a waste, though. Occasionally Cressida would drop a useful tidbit here or there, and Renya added them to her mental arsenal to use against the Shadow Queen. She'd learned that Brutus's mate, Belinia, hated Cressida with a passion and refused to obey her. Cressida could no longer enter the glass enclosure, for fear that Belinia would attack her. Renya also noticed a large cut on Cressida's thigh. The ugly gash seemed to come and go, and Renya wasn't sure why it was there and other times, it disappeared. However, halfway through one meal, Renya dropped her fork and crawled under the table, and noticed it was there, even though it hadn't been there at the beginning of the meal. She deduced that Cressida was using her magic to conceal it. That fact alone kept Renya up at night, wondering why she would go through the effort to conceal a wound like that. Her mother was vain, yes. But it seemed like an awful amount of work to keep it hidden.

The sound of Brutus's wings flapping pulled her out of her thoughts, and she felt the gust of wind as he turned and headed back towards the palace, Cressida on his back.

Renya moved closer to Beauty, who had meandered over to the far side of the pond.

As she approached the dragon, she noticed her neck was starting to feel warm. The closer she got to Beauty, the hotter it began to feel. Bewildered, she reached to touch her neck, only to find that the heat was radiating from the aragonite necklace Esmeralda gave her in the Tidal Kingdom.

She carefully unclasped the necklace and looked at it. There, in the dark of the forest, the necklace glowed a deep amber. Renya dropped the necklace in surprise, watching as it hit the mossy earth beneath her feet. She picked it back up, unsure of what was happening.

Suddenly, she remembered Esmeralda's story about the necklace, and how their legends said that it helped a mother find her lost son. Excitedly, she moved towards Beauty, and watched the necklace grow brighter and brighter. She continued walking, and after about ten feet the color faded and the necklace lost its luster.

Was it broken? Or was it a trick of the light? It

couldn't be, because Renya felt the heat radiate from it before she saw the glowing beads.

Sighing, she balled it up in her hands and started back towards Beauty, worried if she dallied too long, Cressida would send Brandle to fetch her. The time she spent with Cressida's cousin, her second cousin, repulsed her.

The necklace warmed in her hand, and began to glow again. Beauty noticed the shining bauble, and sauntered over to Renya's side.

"What do you think is happening, Beauty?" Renya asked, stroking the dragon absentmindedly and looking around the bank of the pond.

Then she saw it. Resting in a pile of mud right in front of her, a few inches away from the bank. The snowflake diamonds glistened in the light emitted from the necklace, and Renya reached out with trembling fingers as she snatched her engagement ring from the muck.

Tears leaked out of her eyes as she wiped the mud off on her sleeve, seeing the gorgeous braided band emerge from the filth covering it.

"Oh Beauty!" Renya exclaimed, holding the ring close to her heart. "I never thought I'd see this again." She dried her eyes on her sleeve, and then tried to decide what to do with the ring. She couldn't wear it, that was for certain. Since Cressida believed her bond was broken, it wouldn't make any sense for her to still wear the ring of her former mate.

Renya threaded the ring through the beaded aragonite necklace, still clutched firmly in her hand. She did the clasp at her neck, and then tucked the ring securely down the front of her gown. As long as she didn't wear anything low cut, she could continue to wear Grayden's ring, close to her heart, where it belonged.

Chapter Twenty

Selenia walked through the bustling market, completely surprised by the stark contrast from before. Vendors were on every side of the street, peddling food and wares. The entire marketplace was cloaked in a rich and spicy aroma, warm and comforting to her nose.

She passed the same stores she saw on her way in, but this time she could see Fae inside, bartering and bickering, laughing and talking. Selenia couldn't believe all of this was hidden by a blanket of magic. Even the palace was inhabited, with maids and guards stationed at every post.

Her eyes caught on the dress store she admired from the street before, and she hesitated only a second before pushing the door open and walking inside. Silk and muslin, cotton and brocades lined the shelves, with mannequins every few feet, draped in beautiful gowns.

"Can I help you?" A sweet sounding voice piped up from behind a counter. The girl was around Selenia's age, maybe a bit younger, with an intricate braid trailing to her waist.

"These gowns are exquisite," Selenia complimented, her fingers running over the lace trim on the green silk dress on the mannequin nearest to her. "Do you make them?"

The girl blushed and shook her head. "I help with

the trim work. My mother is the real seamstress. Are you looking for anything in particular?"

"I need a new hat." The desert was harsh, and Selenia's nose was pink from the sun. She hoped a hat would help protect her better.

The girl nodded and led her over to a small display of hats. Selenia grabbed the first one she saw, a large-brimmed bonnet with a bow on the side. It wasn't what she usually preferred, but it should offer protection for her pale skin. The shop attendant grabbed the hat and boxed it up for Selenia while she rummaged through her pockets for some silver.

"Is there anything else I can help you with?"

"No, that's everything..." Selenia trailed off, her eye catching on a dress in the very back of the shop.

The gown was ivory white, with tiny peach-colored rosettes forming a strap up one shoulder. It had a sweetheart neckline with tiny pink gems outlining the bust. Embroidered flowers, in light pinks and various hues of pale orange cascaded down the bodice, leading to a set of full skirts. Selenia could just make out a peach petticoat underneath the dress.

She walked over to the mannequin, unable to take her eyes off of such a magnificent piece of craftsmanship. She lightly traced the tiny silk flowers at the waist, amazed at how intricate the sewing was.

The girl came over and stood next to Selenia. "It's one of a kind. A Sun Realm wedding dress. Are you getting married soon?"

Selenia inspected the full skirts before answering. "No. But I know someone who is."

∞

"I want to help." Selenia pushed out her lower lip and looked at her brother defiantly.

"No, Selenia. Not this time. Cyrus, Phillippe and I will rescue Renya. You and Sion will leave for the Snow Lands in the morning."

"But—"

"No buts," Grayden said sternly, pushing around the food on his plate with irritation.

"Selenia, I agree with Grayden. The Shadow Queen will be absolutely furious when we retrieve Renya. She'll attack us however she can, using whatever she can. I need you safe at the Snow Lands, far away from here." Phillippe looked at Selenia, pleading. "Please understand."

Selenia grumbled and continued eating. She stabbed a piece of chicken with her fork a bit too roughly, and her plate slid against the golden tablecloth.

Dinner at the Sun Realm was a lengthy event. Course after course came out, and Selenia had trouble staying interested in food that long. Maybe dessert, but definitely not all the dishes that came out of the kitchens.

"Do we have everything planned out?" Phillippe asked, downing an entire glass of wine in one sip. Selenia knew her eldest brother could handle his drink well. Unlike Grayden, he spent much of his time in the mountain camp, drinking with his men well into the early hours of the morning.

"I think so," Grayden said, hardly touching his food. Selenia knew he must be nervous, now that the moment he had been waiting for was almost here. The last month was excruciating for him. Well, for all of them, Selenia thought. Grayden without Renya was an absolute pain in the ass. He was short-tempered, incredibly quick to yell, and grumpy all of the time. Selenia was glad they would be rescuing Renya in just a few days' time. Any longer, and Selenia would have gone herself just to save them all from the annoyance of her brother's mood swings.

"Cyrus will use his magic to transport Phillippe and I to Renya's room in the castle. Cressida has magic protecting her entire castle, but Cyrus said he can break it.

Cyrus bobbed his head in agreement. "Her magic leaves a trace, and since I am familiar with it, I can undo it."

Grayden continued. "Once we have Renya we'll head to the Spring Lands at the border. They should provide us shelter. Then, we will all head back to the Snow Lands and Cyrus will perform the protective magic on the lodge. Once that's done, he and Sion will go back through the portal to try and locate Agatha. The rest of us will continue to plan and train."

"Why do I have to leave tonight then?" Selenia whined a bit, not eager to start the journey back.

"Because you need to take the horses back, and I don't want you or Sion anywhere near Cressida. Once she finds out the blood promises are broken, she will kill Sion on sight and use you as bait. Now, finish your dinner and go get ready."

Selenia slammed her fork down in annoyance. "Stop bossing me around," she threatened, storming out of the dining room. Before she reached the door, she decided to backhand Grayden on the back of his head. He jerked forward, but made no other response. Satisfied, Selenia left the room and made her way up the long staircase into the guest wing of the palace. Unlike the tower that contained Renya's room, the rest of the castle was in immaculate shape. Everything was dusted and polished, clean and orderly.

Selenia found her room and closed the door tightly. She didn't fear retaliation from Grayden; she knew she hadn't hit him hard enough to cause any sort of significant pain, but she wanted to be left alone with her thoughts.

It annoyed her to no end that Grayden thought he was responsible for her in all things. She was nineteen now, and fully capable of caring for herself and making her own decisions.

She collapsed on the soft bed, feeling the mattress sink down a bit with her weight. She stared up at the ceiling, and like most nights, she thought of Jurel. The days kept her busy enough that she didn't dwell on it all the time like she did at the Twilight Kingdom, but the nights were harder. Quietly tucked away, she remembered the look on his face, the one that haunted her dreams. His mouth slightly agape as his life's essence pooled behind his back. Selenia could still smell the blood, and sometimes it was so thick in her dreams that it choked her, and she woke up breathing hard, trying to pull air into her greedy lungs. If only there was a way to forget about him. A way to break the spell he had over her.

A knock on the door pulled her away from her thoughts. She opened the door, expecting to see Grayden. Instead, Phillippe stood there, bulky as ever, with a concerned look on his face.

"What do you want?" she said, a bit harsher than she meant to.

"Selenia, I just wanted to let you know that Grayden and I care about you deeply. We couldn't bear to see anything happen to you. We've already lost our parents, we can't lose each other too."

Selenia's face reddened slightly with shame and embarrassment. She knew her brothers considered themselves to be her caretakers. While they were overbearing at times, Selenia knew they had her best interests at heart.

She sighed deeply, wanting to collapse onto the bed and put this day behind her. "I understand. Tell Grayden I'm packing and I'll be ready to go in an hour."

Phillippe nodded and shut the door behind him. She could hear his boots thump against the hard floor as he stomped back to his room.

She glanced at the small traveling trunk she brought with her. She left most of her things at the Twilight Kingdom with Julietta, knowing that they'd be traveling light to the Sun Realm. It didn't take her long to toss in the few clothes she brought with her. She tucked in her cloak and gloves, knowing she'd need them once they crossed into the Snow Lands. Finally, she carefully placed Renya's wedding dress carefully inside the trunk. As soon as she was finished, she dressed in the lightest gown she could find, and headed downstairs, lugging the trunk behind her.

She found Grayden in the entrance hall, looking into the fountain absentmindedly. He didn't even see her approach.

"Are you okay, Grayden? I'm sorry I hit you."

He looked up at her, and Selenia could see the heaviness in his eyes. His thumb brushed against his wrist, and Selenia knew he was trying to feel Renya through his mating mark.

"I'm just...eager to get going. The closer I am to getting her back, the more nervous I get. I've also...been feeling her more."

"That's great, Grayden!"

But the look on his face was not one of happiness. "What is it?"

He sighed and rubbed the back of his neck. "She's...happy, at times. I'm not sure why or how, but there hasn't been as much sadness coming through. And a few nights ago, I woke up and I could feel her... release..." he trailed off and looked down, embarrassed.

Selenia understood his meaning, and while she wasn't exactly sure what transpired, she imagined that the physical loss of Renya was taking its toll on him.

"Do you want her to be miserable, Grayden?"

He looked at Selenia, struggling to vocalize his complex emotions. "No, of course not. But, Selenia... what if she wants to stay?"

"Stay? Grayden, of course she won't want to stay."

"Her mother...it's her family. She's always envied us for our family, and now she has one."

"You're right, Grayden. She does have a family. But it's us. You, me and Phillippe. We are Renya's family. She's just there, playing a role. As soon as she sees you, she'll run into your arms and it'll be like you've never been apart."

Grayden looked at her, emotion right underneath the surface. His eyes softened. "You're right, Selenia. I'm just being crazy..."

"No argument there." She playfully slugged him, and he chuckled.

"Do you have everything you need?"

Selenia patted her trunk. "Yes. I also wrote to Julietta to ask her to send the rest of our things home to the lodge. I included Renya's as well."

"That was thoughtful of you, dear one."

They both turned as they heard someone approaching from the other side of the room. Sion strode towards them, no longer in the flowing garb he arrived in. Instead, he was wearing loose-fitting pants and a shirt that was completely opened, but tied together with a cord of lace.

"Looking good there, Sion," Grayden teased.

"Cyrus gave me these. They are traditional Sun Realm clothing."

"I don't think I've ever...seen so much of you," Grayden continued, enjoying roasting his friend a bit.

Sion ignored him, and looked at Selenia. "Are you going to be comfortable in that?" He gestured to Selenia's riding outfit, which consisted of a long skirt and a silk top, buttoned all the way up the neck. Selenia loved the way that the hunter-green color complimented her hair, but agreed that it wasn't ideal.

"It's all I have," she said, pulling out the sun hat she purchased. "But I'll be fine."

Without another word, Sion headed out the door to the stables, where they had moved their horses.

Grayden looked down at Selenia. "Phillippe wanted to say goodbye, but he's with Cyrus in the armory, gathering up whatever weapons we'll need. I think goodbyes are hard for him too, but he won't admit it."

Selenia wrapped her arms around Grayden. "Goodbye, Brother. And good luck. Renya will be back where she belongs before you know it."

Chapter Twenty-One

S ion couldn't believe he was finally returning home to the Snow Lands. After he crossed back through the portal to return to the Shadow Realm, he thought he'd never see them again. He knew he had Renya to thank for his life, and he would never stop being indebted to her.

He lifted his face up to the sun, feeling the warmth hit his cheeks and brow. After spending so much time in the darkness of the Shadow Realm, the sun energized him and made him feel like a new man. Sion still had scars, both physical and mental, that would stay with him for the rest of his life. But riding on Phillippe's horse, Nectaria, with a slight breeze fluttering the open neckline of his tunic, felt like a rebirth.

"You better watch where you're going," Selenia said from slightly behind him.

They'd traveled into the night without stopping, and now it was almost midday. They hardly spoke, and Sion knew Selenia was lost in her own thoughts. He himself took Jurel's passing incredibly hard, but he didn't know how close Selenia and Jurel were until Grayden took him aside and provided him with the facts of Jurel's passing. Sion made sure to give Selenia space, also while protecting his best friend's little sister.

Selenia caught up to him, and he studied her

features. Although she wore a large hat to protect her fair complexion, it was clear that she was no longer the churlish girl he'd chased away with play swords and teased for most of his life. Her auburn ringlets hung prettily behind her shoulders, and her posture had changed. She carried herself with more grace, and took herself a little more seriously than she did before. Sion wasn't sure if it was the loss of youth or the loss of Jurel that changed her so significantly.

"Are we near where you made camp before?" Sion asked. They planned to rest during the most intense heat of the day, and then travel again during the cooler evening hours. Their route would take them past the Spring Lands into the Snow Lands. It was a much more direct route than heading back to the Twilight Kingdom and up the Mountain Pass.

Selenia looked around, her eyes shaded by her hat. "Yes, I think it's just behind this dune."

Sure enough, the small cave came into view. The pair dismounted and walked towards it, with all three horses trailing behind them.

"Wait, stop," Sion said as Selenia went to enter the cave.

"What's wrong?"

"Nothing, I hope. I just want to check it and make sure nothing is in there before you go in."

"It was fine earlier," she argued.

"Absolutely not. I will see you safely to the Snow Lands, Selenia."

Sion entered the cave and came back out almost immediately. "It's all clear."

"Told you," Selenia said under her breath. Sion just shook his head. That was the Selenia he remembered. Quick to argue, quick to anger, and even quicker to forgive. He ignored her comment and began to unpack the saddle bags. Selenia started to help, carrying a small trunk over to the cave.

As if in slow motion, he watched Selenia drop the trunk, close her eyes and then fall into the desert sand.

"Selenia!" he yelled, dropping the supplies he was carrying and rushing over to her. He felt her face, and noticed she was incredibly clammy and even paler than usual. He bent down and scooped her up, careful to support her head. Once he was inside the cave, he laid her down carefully on the floor.

"Selenia, wake up!" Sion patted her cheeks gently, and then ran to the horses to grab the water pouches. He hurried back to the cave, and felt her forehead again. She was sweating profusely and needed to cool down.

Gods, forgive me for this, he thought, as he undid the buttons at her collar. He continued unbuttoning until her silk shirt was completely open. He averted his eyes, trying hard not to notice the skimpy bralette she wore. He said a silent prayer, hoping that Grayden would never find out that he saw his sister in her undergarments.

He removed her shirt completely and soaked it in water from one of the water skins, and then began wiping her face gently with the damp shirt. "Selenia, come on. Wake up," he whispered gently. "Please!" He untied her sunhat and removed it. Her hair was silky smooth under his fingers, so different from Cressida's coarse hair.

Finally, one of her eyelids began to flutter. "Thank the Fates!" he exclaimed, relief flooding through him.

"What happened?" Selenia asked, her voice a dry whisper as she regained consciousness.

"You got overheated and fainted. You can't travel in those clothes, at least not through the desert."

She looked down, realizing she was exposed. Her hands went to cover herself, but Sion shook his head. "No time to be modest, Selenia. You need to cool down fast and drink. Now."

He pressed one of the water pouches to her lips and she drank greedily. After a few sips, he took it away from her.

"More," she said, her lips patched and cracked.

"I'm sorry, Selenia. You need to rehydrate slowly."

She nodded weakly and attempted to sit up, struggling.

"Stay here, I'll go get the sleeping rolls."

"Where am I going to go?" she teased, weakly, but with a slight smile.

Sion's breathing finally returned to normal. Grayden would have killed him if something happened to her. Fates, he would kill himself. Selenia was sweet and innocent, and needed to live a full life.

He grabbed the trunk she dropped, as well as the sleeping rolls. He brought them back to the cave, setting the trunk in the corner and unrolling the sleeping rolls. Once he was satisfied with their arrangement, he walked over to Selenia, and picked her up in his arms.

"Sion, I can walk!" she protested, but rested her head on his shoulder.

"I'm not going to take any chances with you," he said, and laid her down carefully on the bed roll. He grabbed the water skin and pressed it to her lips again, allowing her a few sips.

"How are you feeling?"

"I have a pretty bad headache, and my shoulder hurts from where I fell."

Sion frowned. "Let me look at your shoulder. It might need to be wrapped."

Selenia obeyed, and turned her back so Sion could examine her. He tried to be gentle, but she winced sharply as he palpated her shoulder.

"I'm so sorry, Selenia. I think it might be dislocated. I could pop it back into place, but with your fainting spell, I'm afraid it will be too painful and you'll lose consciousness again. I'd rather wait until we are home and have Almory or Dimitri look at it. They can give you something for the pain."

She nodded, trying to pull her shirt back on.

"It's too hot for that blouse, Selenia. Do you have anything else?"

"I have...a nightgown. It's in the trunk."

Sion wasted no time, and started rifling through her belongings. He pulled out a lightweight silk nightgown. It only had thin straps to hold it up, and Sion felt guilty that she'd have to be dressed so immodestly in front of him. But, survival was more important, he told himself.

As he pulled out the nightgown, he noticed a large, carefully wrapped package that fell to the bottom of the trunk.

"Selenia, what's this?"

She looked almost embarrassed. "It's...a wedding dress. When I bought my hat from the market in the Sun Realm, I saw it in the shop, and I knew it was meant for Renya."

Sion was speechless. He was away from the Snow Lands for so long, he forgot how selfless Selenia could be. He tucked the dress back carefully, and closed the lid to the trunk.

"Selenia, that was incredibly sweet of you."

She brushed off his praise. "As much as I like to give him a bad time, I love my brother. I know he'll love Renya in that dress, and I want her to feel like the princess she is when she marries him."

∞

Sion watched Selenia sleep, still concerned after her fainting spell. He stared as her chest rose and fell, her breathing slow and easy. Leaning against the wall of the cave, he closed his eyes for a little bit, trying to protect them from the dry heat of the desert.

"No! Please, no!"

Sobs came from the corner where Selenia slept. Sion opened his eyes and saw her thrashing and moaning.

"Gods, please don't!" Her entire body trembled. Without thinking, Sion pulled her onto his lap and held her close to his chest. His arms wrapped around her tightly so she wouldn't injure her shoulder any more than it already was.

"Shhh...it's okay, darling. It's just a bad dream." He stroked her hair, the silky strands feeling even softer than they were earlier. Her body was covered in a sheen of sweat, but he didn't care. He just continued to rock her, murmuring comforting words into the shell of her ear. Finally, she pulled herself out of the nightmare and looked around at the cave and where she sat on Sion's lap. She tried to push herself away, but Sion held on to her tightly.

"Stay here a moment longer, I don't want you to faint again, especially after you've worked yourself up into a sweat." At least, that was what he told Selenia. He surprised himself, enjoying the comfort her lithe body provided, resting easily on his lap. It had been so long since he'd had contact like this. Gentle and tender, easy and sweet. Cressida tortured every inch of him, and he forgot how good a woman's touch could be. He breathed in deeply, smelling the floral scent seeming to surround her, even in the dry and desolate desert.

Selenia held incredibly still, not responding to him, yet not fighting him either. Her injured shoulder was hanging limply.

"Sion?" she asked tentatively.

"I get nightmares too," he confessed, closing his eyes and pressing his forehead against hers. "The last six months have been...excruciating for me." He squeezed his eyes shut, trying hard not to relive them in his thoughts.

"Sion...what exactly occurred at the Shadow Realm?" Selenia pulled herself back, tears in her eyes from her nightmare, but concern for him in her gaze. He closed his eyes again, ashamed and unsure if this was something he wanted to share. Grayden and Renya knew, as well as Phillippe, but it appeared as if Selenia was sheltered from the truth.

He kept silent, his eyes open but downcast and focusing on her bare shoulder as he held her. Her nightgown's oversized neckline slipped down her upper arm, and without thinking, without realizing what he was doing, he placed a soft kiss there.

She looked at him, puzzled, but didn't push him

off. "Sion, tell me what happened to you." Her tone was soft, but commanding.

He sighed and held her closer, looking past her shoulders and at the wall of the cave. He couldn't make this kind of confession with her looking at him.

"While I was at the Shadow Realm, I became...a plaything of Cressida's. She used my body, tried to break my spirit and infiltrate my mind. Selenia, some of the things she did to me..." he trailed off, holding back the tears that threatened to fall. He never thought he would have to deal with the ramifications of what transpired in her realm. He thought he would die and never have to deal with the trauma of it. But seeing Selenia, shaking from her own nightmare, made him realize that they would never be free from the reach of Cressida. Even if she was defeated and put down, the invisible scars of her cruel reign would mar them forever.

"Oh, Sion..." Selenia pulled him closer to her, clinging to him with her uninjured arm. "I'm so sorry that happened to you."

He picked his head up and looked into her eyes. Sion never realized the depth they held, the raw emotion tucked just behind her playful banter. He saw pain there, not just for herself, but for him too. As if his body had a mind of its own, he pressed his lips gently to hers.

She inhaled deeply, shocked by his actions, but then tentatively moved her mouth with his. Her kiss was shy and inexperienced, but that made it all the sweeter for Sion. After the bleakness and evil he was surrounded with, her goodness and innocence seemed like a fresh wind, blown in from the pure, crisp air of the Snow Lands.

He parted her lips slowly with his, needing more, and then deepened their kiss. Selenia wrapped her good arm around his neck, and he couldn't believe how right it felt, to have her like this, kissing him back.

Suddenly, guilt and self-hatred filled his belly and he pulled back, horrified by what he had done.

"Selenia, I'm so sorry. I don't know what came over me. You were scared and upset and I...I just needed to feel something good for a change. I don't know what possessed me to take advantage of you like that." He carefully lifted her off his lap and back down onto her sleeping roll. "Please don't hate me."

Confusion, and something else that he couldn't detect—lust, maybe?—burned brightly on her face. "It's okay," she said in a small voice. "We are both broken, both shells of who we used to be. Fate knows that we could both use a little pleasure."

"It can't happen again. Your brothers trust me with your life. I won't bring shame to your family and dishonor you. Please, forgive me. You should get some rest. I'm going to sleep outside."

Before she could respond, he swept out of the cave, positioning himself at the entrance. His dark skin protected him from the damage of the sun, and he lay there on the hot sand for over an hour, sleep eluding him, trying to get the memory of Selenia's lips against his out of his mind.

Chapter Twenty-Two

Selenia lay back on the sleeping roll, rubbing her fingers over her lips, still burning from Sion's kiss. Now that the initial shock wore off, she tried to grasp what she was feeling. Guilt, of course. Jurel hadn't even been gone a month and she already kissed another man. He kissed her first, to be fair...but she didn't try to stop it. Her lips moved with his, and something about it felt starkly different than it did with Jurel. She only kissed him a handful of times, and then they were mostly just chaste pecks on her lips. But this...this was sensual and seductive.

Her face burned hotly, and she felt like she was betraying Jurel. How could she kiss another man? Her head swirled in confusion, and pounded, both from the heat exhaustion and the contradicting feelings in her body. Sion was a childhood friend. He was older than her, closer to Grayden's age, whereas Jurel was closer to her in age. But her heart ached for Sion, hurt for the intense torture he endured. She shuddered, thinking of him bound and shackled to Cressida. The horror was almost too much to even comprehend.

The pain radiated from her shoulder all the way up into her neck. She refused to cry, refused to show any weakness. She was tired of crying, tired of her aching heart.

Selenia turned her head and tried to see Sion's

silhouette in the encroaching darkness. She could just make out his stronger shoulders. He faced away from her, guarding the mouth of the cave. He was resting, but she could tell he wasn't asleep. Any sudden sound forced him to lift up his head, scanning the desert in front of them.

She sighed, realizing that they both hardly got any rest. He was busy taking care of her after she foolishly allowed herself to get overheated, and her shoulder was throbbing.

"Sion," she called out softly. He raised his head immediately, and pushed himself upright and walked towards her.

"What is it, princess?"

Princess? He never addressed her that way before. She mustered up the angriest glare she could and looked up at him. "Do not call me that again."

Sion was flustered, unsure of where to look. Selenia watched his gaze land on the cave wall again. "I crossed a line. I won't cross it again." He folded his arms in front of his chest.

"Sion," she said again, trying to sit up. He saw her struggling, sighed and knelt down to help her. His touch was gentle, but she could tell that he was trying to keep his hands away from her as much as possible.

"You can touch me."

He looked at her, but shook his head no, and then moved towards the sleeping roll. "Are you ready to go?" he asked, rolling up her sleeping roll and throwing it over his shoulder.

"Yes, I want to get home as soon as possible," she said, cradling her arm.

Sion dropped the roll and walked back over to the

saddlebags on Damion. He fiddled around in them, and pulled out the golden robes he wore at Cressida's court.

"I was going to burn this when we got back home, but tearing it is good too."

He grabbed the sleeve of the garment and ripped it off, then threw the rest of it on the desert floor. She watched him spit on it, and saw the fire of hate in his eyes. But when he came back over to her, he wore a mask of calm on his face, but Selenia knew it was just for show.

"Give me your arm," he said, and wrapped the sleeve around her arm before securing it around her neck. "That's the best I can do out here."

Selenia dropped the hand supporting her arm, and felt relief. It still hurt, but at least she had better use of her other arm.

Sion finished packing up, refusing to allow Selenia to help at all. She came over and looked at Honor, wondering how she should attempt to hoist herself up on the mare's back. Before she could come up with a plan, Sion was beside her. With one swift motion, he grabbed her by the waist and settled her on Honor's back. "Thank you," she said. "That would have been difficult on my own."

She grabbed the reins with one hand, but before she could command Honor to go, she felt Sion's chest press into her back as he leapt on behind her.

"What are you doing?" she asked blankly.

"Do you really think you're in any condition to ride? Let alone in unfamiliar territory in challenging weather?" Sion grabbed Honor's reins from her hands and started the horse off at a steady pace. He whistled, and Necteria and Damion followed behind obediently.

Neither Sion or Selenia said anything for a long time. Selenia was wrapped up in her own thoughts, ashamed of her betrayal to Jurel's memory. Sion was equally engrossed in his own thoughts, and Selenia guessed he was feeling guilty as well.

Finally, she broke the tension. "So, are you going be cold and standoffish towards me forever?" She gave him a sweet grin, and he returned a small one.

"Probably," he said with a smirk.

"Well, we weren't that close anyway," she teased back. She felt his body relax slightly behind her and the tension dissolved between them.

"What do you miss most about the Snow Lands?" Selenia asked.

Sion looked thoughtful, taking time to consider his answer. "The way the foothills of the mountains look after the snow has settled. The smells of the town. The market always smells so wonderful."

"Except for the time you, Phillippe, Grayden and Jurel let all those cows into the village." She felt a small pang, remembering how much they all laughed as the cows wandered the cobblestone streets, harassing patrons and irritating vendors as they left their droppings everywhere.

"I thought your father was going to murder us. I'm pretty sure that was when he decided it was time for us boys to train with the armies."

"What was it like? Having so many friends?"

Sion looked at Selenia, not understanding her meaning. "You mean Jurel and your brothers?"

She nodded. "I really don't have any friends back home."

Selenia could feel Sion's chest expand and then

tighten. She felt his hand rest on top of hers, and looked down where their hands met. Her fair skin, his dark olive complexion on top.

"I'm your friend, Selenia."

Chapter Twenty-Three

R enya sat at the small vanity, a quill in her hand.
She'd been working on learning to write with it,
eager to record her thoughts. Margot found her a leather
bound journal with cream parchment pages. Renya
spent a lot of time alone in her room, so writing was her
sole companion most nights. Margot would visit her,
but she had other duties in the castle, so much of the
evenings were spent in solitude.

She posed the quill over the page, trying to get
used to the flow of the ink on the parchment. It was a
struggle to get used to, and she developed great respect
for anyone writing anything with a quill. While she
really didn't miss too much from the human realm, she
would have to ask Grayden if he found the ball-point
pens she left in her bag that he recovered from the
snowbank.

Grayden. They were apart for over five weeks
now. Almost the same amount of time that they were
together before Cressida took her to the Shadow Realm.
She absentmindedly grabbed for her ring, which was
tucked into her nightgown on a thin, silver chain that
Margot found for her.

Renya? Renya?

Grayden's voice sounded frantically in her head.
It was clearer than ever, as if he was standing right next
to her.

Grayden? I can hear you!

I'm on my way. I'll be there soon. Get ready.

Renya threw down the quill and ran to the window. She couldn't make out anything in the darkness of the realm, but her heart beat wildly. Grayden was coming for her.

She looked around the room, uncertain if there was anything she wanted to take with her. She grabbed the pillowcase from her bed and threw the notebook and quill inside. She recorded some of her deepest thoughts inside that journal, and it couldn't remain behind. She pulled out her dagger from where she hid it under the mattress, trying to decide how to carry it since she was in her nightgown, then found a blue ribbon and tied it tightly to her calf. Other than that, there was nothing from this room she desired to retain.

Renya rushed back to the window, squinting in the darkness, trying to see any sign of Grayden.

"Renya!"

She turned, and Grayden was behind her, holding the post of her bed as if he needed it to remain upright.

"Grayden!" She ran over to him, tears already gushing down her cheeks.

He pulled her into his arms, crushing her against his muscular chest. "My Little Fawn!"

Grayden held her so tightly she couldn't even look up to see his face, but she could feel his tears wet her hair. She sobbed into his tunic, her entire body shaking with relief. Her legs buckled under her, and she slid to the floor, taking Grayden with her. She could feel his chest shake, feel the relief in his body as he held her to him. He cupped her cheek gently with one hand, and then rubbed his thumb over her tears.

"Don't cry, my love. It's okay. We're okay."

"I know this reunion is long overdue, but sadly, we don't have time for it."

Renya lifted her head from Grayden's body and looked into her father's face. Cyrus's blue eyes sparkled, and she could just make out a bit of wetness leaking out of the corner.

"You came back for me," she said, looking between the two men. As her eyes moved between them, she saw another figure hovering in the background.

"Phillippe!" She made a move to go and embrace him, but Grayden growled and pulled her even tighter in his arms.

"I'll give you a hug later, Renya. Once my brother finally releases you."

"I'll never release her," he said, burrowing his head into Renya's hair. She felt his breath, hot against her neck, and then he inhaled deeply, as if familiarizing himself with her scent.

"Grayden, you need to let my daughter go," Cyrus said gently. "We don't have much time, and this kidnapping needs to go perfectly."

"What do you mean?" Renya asked, twisting a bit in Grayden's embrace to look at Cyrus.

"Do you know where Cressida's chambers are?" her father asked.

"No I don't, we've met in the throne room and sometimes in her study."

Cyrus nodded. "Sion told me where they were. They are across the sky bridge, to the right. You're going to have to run for it, and act like you're trying to get to her for help. It's the only way to keep up the appearance that you're loyal to her and that your mating bond is broken. Phillippe and Grayden will take out any guards that come to your aid, and I'll deal with Cressida. My magic isn't strong enough to defeat her after breaking the blood promises, but I can hopefully hold her off."

"Won't that be dangerous?" Renya looked at the three men, worry evident in her gaze.

"It's the only way. Let us catch up, and we'll grab you and I'll transport us towards the edge of the forest. My magic won't allow me to get us all the way back to the Snow Lands, so we'll have to run for it."

"She'll catch us," Renya warned. "Her dragon will hunt us down."

"Don't worry about that. I can cloak us until we get to the Spring Lands. They'll give us shelter." Cyrus looked confident, but Renya bit her lip. This plan was reckless, and she was horrified something would go wrong. Since the blood promise was broken, Cressida could hurt or kill Grayden. And once she saw Renya vanish with Cyrus, she would know that the magic binding her to Cressida was long gone.

"Don't worry, Little Fawn. I won't let anything happen to you." Grayden placed a soft kiss at her hairline, and she shivered from the small touch, her body coming to life in his arms. She took a deep breath, trying to suppress the feelings that came over her once she was near him.

"I'm not worried about myself, it's you three I'm concerned about. Cressida really thinks that I'm loyal to her, I don't think she would hurt me at this point."

Grayden's eyes widened in surprise. "That's... amazing Renya. We could definitely use that to our advantage."

"We can plan all this out later. Let's get going," Phillippe said, reaching for the broadsword on his back.

Renya opened the pillowcase and handed Grayden her journal, and he swiftly tucked it into his tunic. "It won't make sense if I'm running with that in my hands."

He gave her another kiss, this time on her forehead, and then turned to face Cyrus and Phillippe. "Are you ready?"

The men nodded, and Renya slipped out the door. The hall was deserted, the servants in their bed hours ago. "Let me get past the throne room, and then I'll start screaming."

Renya walked quietly through the empty halls, pausing whenever she thought she heard footsteps. They snuck into a few rooms here and there to avoid the guards on their night routes, but made it to the throne room without being detected.

"Ready, Renya?" Cyrus asked.

"I'm ready." She moved towards the sky bridge, taking one tentative step before screaming.

"Help! Someone help!"

Within seconds, three guards appeared behind Renya on the sky bridge. Phillippe and Grayden easily took them out, knocking them unconscious quickly and moving behind Renya.

"Help! Mother, help me!" More guards, but still no Cressida. The Shadow Queen's guards posed no threat for Grayden and Phillippe, and they were able to defeat them easily. Renya continued to scream, running down the hall to where Sion said Cressida's chambers were located.

Finally, at the end of the corridor, Cressida appeared. She was dressed in a black silk nightgown, and this time, she wasn't prepared enough to hide the gash festering on her leg. But Renya hardly had time to glance at it before Grayden tackled her.

"Mother!" she squealed from underneath him, looking up at Cressida, hoping her eyes showed anguish and adrenaline instead of the lust she felt from having Grayden holding her, even if he was pinning her to the floor.

"How dare you come to my palace! You foolish idiots. She's bound to me. You couldn't take her even if she wanted to go. And she doesn't. Isn't that right, Renya?"

"Mother, please, help me! Don't let them take me!"

Cressida sneered, enjoying Grayden's look of despair at Renya's words. "Oh, did you not realize? She's no longer fated to you. I'd kill you, but I made a promise that prevents me. But that doesn't mean I can't have someone else volunteer. Brandle!" she called.

Before he could appear, Cyrus moved into the corridor. Cressida hissed. "You!"

Before she could raise her fingers, Cyrus reached out with a golden web of rays and with a bright flash, they were gone.

∞

Renya swore she could hear Cressida's screams from the edge of the forest. She looked up from the ground, seeing Phillippe and Grayden next to her. Only Cyrus managed to stay upright, and the rest of them had tumbled to the ground. Grayden and Phillippe jumped to their feet, and before Renya could push herself up, she was swept into Grayden's arms.

"Put me down, Grayden," she said, squirming against him. "I can walk."

Instead of setting her back on her feet, he pressed his mouth to hers, giving her a searing kiss that should have embarrassed her, knowing her father was there to witness it. Instead, she melted into his arms, feeling weightless and worry-free for the first time in weeks. He supported her easily, cradling her close as his lips reacquainted themselves with hers. She sighed deeply against his mouth, and ran her fingers through his messy hair. It was longer than it had ever been, and he sported a full beard. She could feel it scratch the side of her face as he continued to move his mouth against hers, and she wondered how it would feel between her thighs before chiding herself for letting her thoughts get away from her.

"Okay, that's enough." Phillippe twirled his sword and then launched it into the ground right next to Grayden's feet. "We have to get moving, you two.

Grayden reluctantly set Renya down, but instantly grabbed her hand. She squeezed it, and he returned the small gesture of affection.

"We need to move quickly and quietly. I can use a cloaking spell, but I can't mask our voices or the environment around us. That means we watch every branch, every bush. We can't make any noise." Cyrus reached out his fingers and a golden web covered them all. They could still see each other, but everything around them took on a hazy, gauzy tone, as though they were looking at everything through a light mist.

"Which way?" Grayden asked Phillippe.

Phillippe looked around. Behind them, the dark forest was silent. In front of them, the darkness transitioned into a glow that illuminated another forest. "Northwest," he said, pulling his sword from the ground.

Phillippe led the way, relying on nothing more than the position of the moon and stars to guide him.

"How does he do that?" Renya asked Grayden.

"Shhhhh," Cyrus whispered gently.

I'm not sure, Little Fawn. I know he spent time with a master navigator at camp. His voice was clear in her head, and she could feel him again, that spot inside her heart once again full. She felt deliriously happy, almost not believing that they were once again together.

I'm happy too, Renya. I can't wait to be alone with you. Just you wait.

She blushed, hoping no one could see the redness that appeared on her cheeks and crept up her neck. She wanted him as bad as he wanted her, and it was so hard not to be able to hold one another. Instead, Grayden drew little circles against her palm with his fingers, and she shivered from head to toe.

A loud roar came from behind them, and Grayden grabbed Renya instantly, shielding her with his body. Phillippe pulled out his sword, and Cyrus held his fingers at the ready.

Brutus' scaled body was just distinguishable beyond the canopy of the trees. Renya could make out a figure on his back, and she knew it was Cressida.

Brutus darted in and out of the trees, sometimes dipping below the foliage line as Cressida scoured the forest floor, looking for any trace of them. They all stood incredibly still, hardly breathing. Renya's heart thumped so loud, she was sure that if Cressida flew anywhere near, she would be able to hear it.

Brutus took high into the sky, flying in larger and larger concentric circles, until he was almost directly overhead. As he came closer, Renya began shaking in fear. She hadn't come this far to be taken again. Grayden put his arm around her and kissed her hand.

You're alright, my love. Your father's magic will protect us.

She felt a pang of sadness from their bond, and she could feel his shame. She knew he hated relying on Cyrus to protect them.

Finally, Brutus and Cressida headed east towards the Sun Realm.

"She thinks that's the first place we'll go," whispered Cyrus. "It's the closest and where my power is the strongest."

"Plus it's abandoned," Renya said.

"Actually..." Phillippe began. "It's not."

Renya looked at all three of them. "It appears there's a lot I need to be caught up on."

∞

Renya's legs were killing her, but she refused to complain. She was cooped up in Cressida's palace for such a long time, and before that, in the Twilight Kingdom, without any type of strenuous exercise. She hiked abundantly when she lived in California, and in Seattle she didn't have a car and walked everywhere she needed to. Plus, she was still wearing the ridiculous satin slippers that were provided to her in the Shadow Realm.

"Are you doing okay, Renya?" Cyrus hung back to

walk next to her and Grayden. For most of the trek, he led the way with Phillippe, letting Grayden and Renya spend some time together.

"My feet hurt a little, but I'm fine," she said. The instant she uttered the words, Grayden hoisted her up in his arms. She tried to protest, but he just hugged her closer to him.

"Just for a few minutes," she acquiesced. She caught her father's eye watching their interaction, and she blushed.

"Renya, you don't need to be embarrassed for being in love. You're fate-bound, there's no shame in that at all. I happen to think highly of your mate, anyways."

"I'm sorry, I just...I don't know how to feel. I hardly know you, but you're my father, and I feel like I should remember more of you...since you were the first man in my life. But...Grayden has protected me since I came into this world, and I—"

"You don't have to explain," Cyrus said, holding back a branch for Grayden to pass by. "I'm glad you have someone to protect you now. I looked over you the best I could in the human realm. But I'm getting older. The human realm aged me significantly, and I won't always be around. When the time comes for me to join the Fates, I'll gladly go, knowing there is someone here who loves you so completely."

Renya felt her eyes water. After feeling alone for so long, she felt like she finally belonged. She had a father, Grayden's family, and her aunt.

"Did you find Aunt Agatha?" she asked, drying her tears on Grayden's shoulder.

"No, but Sion and I are going to go through the

portal as soon as you're delivered safely to the Snow Lands."

"Where is Sion?"

"He's taking Selenia home. I didn't want her anywhere near Cressida," Grayden said, his head resting on top of Renya's.

"That was wise. I don't want her around Cressida either."

"Did she hurt you, my love?" Renya could feel his heart race at the question, could feel the dread he felt while awaiting her answer.

"No. She was rough on me in the beginning, but I think she actually might care for me a bit."

"I felt—at times, you were happy, Renya. I was scared that you would want to stay there." He swallowed hard, obviously anxious.

"Oh Grayden, I was miserable! The only friend I had was Margot, the lady who attended me. Well, and Beauty."

Beauty. She left Beauty behind. She felt a pang of sadness in her soul.

"Who's Beauty?" Renya knew Grayden picked up on her emotional turmoil right away.

"She's...amazing. Cressida now has four dragons. But the youngest, Beauty...she bonded with me. She was—is—my friend. I know that sounds weird, but—"

"Not at all. I'm glad she provided you comfort." He lowered his head as another large branch hung low along their path.

Renya grabbed his neck and then swung her legs out of his arms. "I can walk, you don't need to carry me the rest of the way."

"Actually, we're here," Phillippe said.

Renya looked up, and just in front of her was a picturesque meadow, with flowers of all colors swaying in a gentle breeze. She stepped out of the shadows of her mother's land and into the fresh lands of spring.

Just beyond the meadow was a lake, and Renya could see several swans, in varying shades of pink, resting on the surface of the water. Cherry blossoms floated in the fresh breeze, and the air smelled of jasmine and honey.

"It's beautiful." Renya bent down and ran her fingers through the grass, and a ladybug landed on her arm. She held it up, noting that it was pink instead of the typical red she was used to. Before she could examine it in greater detail, it spread its wings and flew off.

"I think the Spring Land Acropolis is just on the other side of the meadow," Phillippe said, taking off his gloves and shoving them in the pocket of his trousers.

"Have you been here before?" Renya asked Grayden.

"I have. I met with Samatra and her husband, Thesand, last year. They are kind rulers, good to their people and cooperative neighbors."

A flight of butterflies flew by, their wings iridescent and sparkling under the soft light of the spring sun. Renya was entranced. After spending significant time in the Shadow Realm, she couldn't help but notice that everything here was bursting with new life and energy.

Renya grasped Grayden's hand, holding it tightly in her own. She was nervous about meeting another set of rulers. She got along well with King Tristan from the Tidal Kingdom, and became fast friends with his sister, Esmeralda. She also respected and admired Queen Kalora and her daughter, Julietta from the Twilight Kingdom. She only hoped that she made a good impression on these new rulers as well.

"You'll be magnificent, Renya."

She smiled at his encouragement. Sharing her thoughts with him was frightening before, but now, after being separated and watching him face his death, there wasn't anything she didn't want to share with this man.

Phillippe led them farther into the meadow, and Renya lifted her head up to the sun, basking in the warm rays.

"There's no doubt you belong to the Sun Realm, my daughter," Cyrus said, a smile on his face. "You blossom in the light."

Renya just smiled back, leaning into Grayden, smelling his masculine scent she missed so much.

They reached the pond, which was actually more the size of a small lake, Renya realized. She saw a school of rainbow colored fish circling, and the swans floated peacefully along the glassy surface of the water. She stood there for a few minutes, mesmerized by the idyllic scene, before Grayden gently grabbed her hand to lead her back towards the group. As he held her hand in his, Renya detected sadness and a frown appeared on his face. A picture flashed across her mind, and Renya knew exactly what was wrong. He was picturing his mother's ring, and how it looked on Renya's finger when he slipped it on in the hot springs. She pulled her hand out of his.

"It's okay, Grayden," she said, pulling out the necklace from the bodice of her dress and unclasping it.

She slid the ring off and placed it on her finger where it belonged.

Grayden's face still looked uncertain.

"Grayden, what is it?"

He looked away quickly, not answering her. She stopped in the dewy grass, and let Phillippe and Cyrus continue ahead.

"Grayden."

He finally turned to look at her, and Renya saw the fear in his eyes. "Honey, what's wrong?"

He took a shaky breath. "When we were apart, I woke up one night and I felt...I felt you."

"What?" Renya was completely confused by his meaning.

"You were...satisfied," he said, not meeting her gaze and instead, looking down at his worn boots.

"Oh my god!" she exclaimed, and her cheeks flushed as she realized his meaning.

"It's okay, Renya. If you sought comfort with someone else, I—I understand. I can't imagine what you must have been going through, alone in that palace with...her. I don't blame you at all. But you were not wearing your ring...and it scared me."

It was hard for Renya to witness his insecurity. She wondered if their separation took its toll on their bond. She comforted him the best way she knew how, and moved into his arms and placed a hot kiss on his throat.

"There was no one else, Grayden. There will never be anyone else. I had a—dream—about us." She flushed an even deeper red, and could feel the heat radiating from her face. "I only think of you, always. The only reason I wasn't wearing my ring was because

Cressida took it from me and flung it out into the forest. I found it while I was riding Beauty, and I tucked it away against my heart to keep it safe."

"But...your mating mark is also gone. Renya, what happened?"

She smiled at him, and held out her arm, rubbing the make-up off vigorously. "I was forced to hide it. Cressida tried to make Cyrus break our bond. She thought he was successful, so I had to cover it."

She heard him release another breath, and thought she detected a strangled sob. His panic tore at her chest, and she almost felt as if his sudden lack of trust was her own shortcoming.

"Thank the Fates," he said, swiftly pulling her to him. He cupped her chin and peppered her face with kisses. "I was so worried."

"Grayden, you don't ever need to feel insecure. We are bound for life. Nothing will ever change that."

He nodded, kissing her forehead before finally releasing her and pulling her along to catch up to Phillippe and Cyrus.

They scrambled up a slight hill after passing the lake, and the Spring Land Acropolis came into view.

Renya didn't know what to expect, but it wasn't this. She felt as if she had stepped into ancient Greece. Just ahead stood an enormous structure with huge, ivory columns towering overhead. In front of the palace, surrounded by twin columns supporting a large, burnt orange pitched roof, was an open-air market. Cinnamon and nutmeg, cloves and citrus marked the air. It was a feast for the eyes as much as the senses, Renya thought, taking everything in.

A large marble staircase led up to the acropolis,

with figures carved out of stone in between the handrails. Renya was shocked to find some figures she recognized. Diana the huntress was portrayed, with a quiver of arrows slung over her back. She saw Dionysus as well, his glass overflowing with wine. The appearance of the Greek gods made her wonder how intertwined the human and Fae worlds really were.

Continuing up the stairs, Renya could hear children laughing and residents bickering and bartering with the shopkeepers, in loud and boisterous voices. The stairs led directly into the marketplace, and Renya tried to look everywhere at once. There was a stall selling fresh fruit, and Renya recognized some, but not all of the exotic bounty. There were purple and green fruits resembling oranges, and star-shaped fruit in every color of the rainbow.

A silk merchant was set up across from the fruit stand, and Renya had never seen so many fine fabrics before. Gauzy light cottons, heavy brocades, velvet, satin...she knew if Selenia was here her mouth would be agape and her fingers digging into her purse for coins. There were also all kinds of hats, some with veils, and crowns weaved with flowers. She wished she could linger here, tasting the odd fruit and browsing at all the stalls, but she moved quickly to try and keep up with Grayden and Phillippe's large strides. Cyrus walked a bit slower, and Renya caught up to him easily.

"We have a similar market in the Sun Realm," he told her, glancing at a woman with a tray full of spun sugar pastries.

"Really?" she asked, her mouth almost watering as a turquoise, flower-shaped cake caught her eye. "Is it really just cloaked?"

"It is. It takes large amounts of my magic to keep it hidden, which is why I'm currently no match against Cressida. Luckily it held when I was trapped in the human realm, but the strain aged me greatly. Between cloaking the Sun Realm and the Snow Lands when we arrive, I'll pretty much be overextended. Even when and if we lower the cloaking, it will take some time to gain back my powers. That's why we desperately need your aunt. Between the two of you, I think you'll be able to take on your mother and her army."

Renya felt her stomach turn, nervous about what she would have to do. She was well aware that in the end, it would come down to her or Cressida. One would survive, one would not. The prophecy said that she would be her mother's downfall, but who really knew how things would play out? She thought that sacrificing herself to Cressida in the Twilight Kingdom was fulfilling her part in it, but she was wrong.

"Is something the matter, dear?" Her father looked down at her with his sparkling blue eyes scrunching in worry. She felt her chest tighten, felt herself growing warmer towards this man who was a stranger, but cared for her.

"I'm fine. Just nervous about what's to come."

He took her hand in his and patted the top. "All will be right."

His comforting touch brought tears to her eyes. Grayden was her protector, her confidant, best friend and lover. But to have a father...it was something Renya never truly realized was missing in her life.

Grayden looked back at Renya over his shoulder, and gave her a small smile. She knew he could feel the sudden rush of affection she had towards her father, and was happy for her.

Phillippe stopped, and two guards came out from their posts as they approached another set of columns. These pillars were even more intricate and impressive, the stone carved in spiraling circles, with miniature figures of animals, mythical and real (or, maybe all real, Renya thought) placed on every other level.

The guards were dressed in loose tunics with black leather trousers. Their boots were made of a buttery leather, and instead of swords, they were each armed with a bow and a quiver of arrows. Both men had long, flowing hair, one brown, one blond.

"We are here to see Queen Samatra and King Thesand," Grayden said. "I'm King Grayden of the Snow Lands."

"So you gave yourself a promotion, did you?" Phillippe teased, and Grayden elbowed him in the ribs and then glared.

"Please let them know we are here."

The guards both bowed low, and then rose. "We'll take you to the receiving room," the blond-haired guard said. He led them farther into the acropolis, which Renya guessed was the royal family's quarters. They moved into another building, which was closed off to the elements, but large windows and terraces let plenty of light in. The receiving room reminded Renya of a giant parlor, with chaises arranged around wooden tables. Flowers decorated every surface, and the smell was intense, but enchanting. Several of the flowers had blooms larger than her head, and some were almost four feet high. Renya resisted the urge to get closer to one of the arrangements, which caught her eye from across the room. It was a massive bloom, with every petal a different shade of blue, like a pantone rainbow arranged in a circle.

The guard led them to a low table with four chairs around it, and they each took a seat.

"They will be with you shortly," he said, and turned to rejoin the other guard out front.

Renya looked around the circular room, in awe. The ceiling was several stories tall, and every sound and noise echoed loudly. They all kept silent, not wanting their voices to travel.

Don't worry, everything will be fine.

Renya smiled at Grayden's reassuring tone in her mind.

"Renya!" A loud yell radiated throughout the entire room, and Renya stood up, recognizing the voice immediately.

"Esmeralda!" Renya exclaimed, surprised to see her friend. The pair rushed to each other and embraced warmly.

"I'm so glad to see you again," Esmeralda said in her sweet tone.

"You too. How long have you been here?" Renya asked.

"Three weeks. After you left the Tidal Kingdom, my brother and I finished up some business in our own territory, and then ventured here to discuss aligning our forces with the Spring Lands."

Grayden came up and squeezed Renya's waist. "Esmeralda, it's so good to see you again." He took her hand and kissed it respectfully, and Renya felt heat flare up along her body in jealousy. She tensed up, but then relaxed as soon as Grayden dropped her friend's hand.

Esmeralda caught the entirety of Renya's

reaction. But instead of being upset, she chuckled. "I take it you finally sealed your bond." Her eyes sparkled mischievously.

The heat in the back of Renya's neck migrated to her cheeks.

Phillippe strode over and inserted himself into the conversation. "Are you going to introduce me to this lovely lady?"

Renya watched the color appear in Esmeralda's cheeks, now matching her own.

"Brother, this is Princess Esmeralda from the Tidal Kingdom."

Phillippe grabbed Esmeralda's hand and placed a kiss on it, his dark eyes fixed on hers. "I've heard much about you, but your beauty was never mentioned. What a travesty."

Renya wanted to snort at the corny praise, but she looked at Esmeralda and saw how much she was enjoying it and held back. She didn't know Phillippe incredibly well; he was either sincere or a major lothario.

"Grayden!" A booming voice sounded from across the entrance hall. Renya took her eyes off of Phillippe and Esmeralda and saw King Tristan strolling towards them. He was wearing a pewter crown made of intertwined eels and a chartreuse tunic with dark boots. His face was relaxed, but his emotions were still guarded as usual. He did allow himself a slight grin when he shook hands with Grayden. Grayden clapped him on the back, and they immediately began discussing what transpired since their last correspondence.

Phillippe looked between Esmeralda and the

men, then sighed and quickly joined Grayden and Tristan in their talks of war.

Renya knew she should join them, but she was just so happy to see a familiar face.

"I see you are wearing your mate's ring," Esmeralda said, gesturing to the snowflake engagement ring. "I hope that we will be invited to the wedding if you've not already wed."

Renya rubbed the ring, glad it was resting back on her finger where it belonged. "Of course! I wouldn't dream of excluding you and your brother."

Esmeralda gently took Renya's hand and examined the ring more closely. "It's beautiful."

"It's because of you that I still have it."

Esmeralda looked at Renya, her face scrunching in confusion.

"I was taken hostage by the Shadow Queen—"

"Oh my goodness!"

"And she took my ring and flung it down into a ravine. The aragonite necklace you gave me led me to it."

Esmeralda beamed. "I had a feeling you would need it. But Renya, how did you escape from the Shadow Queen?"

Renya began her long tale, eliciting several gasps and looks of shock from Esmeralda.

"Oh my, Renya! What are you doing here now?"

Before Renya could answer, everyone in the receiving room went quiet. Renya turned her eyes to the doorway that Esmeralda and Tristan came through, and she saw a man and woman coming towards them.

Queen Samatra walked slightly in front of her husband, her lilac gown floating elegantly behind her. Delicate floral patterns, in darkening shades of purple adorned the fabric, with a fitted bodice that accentuated her small waist. The flowing skirt cascaded to the floor, creating a sense of ethereal movement with every step she took. Queen Samatra wore a floral headpiece with live flowers, carefully arranged to form a graceful crown composed of a cluster of blooms. Renya thought they might be violets; the flowers varied in shades of purple, ranging from deep indigo to a soft lavender.

Renya suddenly felt uncomfortable in her dirty white nightgown. Her braid was untidy and large pieces of hair had fallen out of it and hung messily in front of her eyes. She knew her skin was covered in sweat and her hands were filthy. She hid them behind her back, praying that no one asked to shake her hand.

Won't stop me from kissing every inch of you, my mate.

Renya suppressed a smile and stood a little taller. Grayden always praised her, always knew how to comfort her. She gave him a tiny nod from across the room.

King Thesand was not what Renya was expecting. He was dressed in black leather, a sword at his hip, and wore no crown to signify that he was a ruler. His black hair was cropped short, and his eyes darted around the room, taking in his new guests cautiously. He let his wife approach the group first, but it was clear he was ready to defend her at a moment's notice with the large bow in his hands and the full quiver of arrows at his back.

"Welcome," Queen Samatra said, looking over her visitors carefully. She shook Renya's hand,

Phillippe's and Cyrus's, but gave Grayden a slight nod of the head.

"I've heard from our guests that you two are fate-bonded. I'll try not to touch him in your presence, Renya. I've instructed my husband to do the same with Renya."

Renya immediately looked over at Esmeralda, and saw a crimson blush in her cheeks as she quickly looked down. It was obvious Esmeralda related the tale of Grayden's tyranny in the Tidal Kingdom.

"That's most considerate," Grayden said, trying to push aside the awkwardness. "I do get incredibly possessive when anyone touches my mate." He laughed heartily, and everyone in the room joined in.

Just like that, the tension broke and Queen Samatra invited everyone to sit around a large table farther into the receiving hall. Grayden didn't waste any time claiming a seat next to Renya, and Esmeralda sat on her other side. Renya suppressed a chuckle as Phillippe made a quick beeline for the other seat besides Esmeralda. She hadn't seen Phillippe in the company of other women before, so she wasn't sure if this was normal behavior for him or if he actually was interested in Esmeralda. Either way, it was good to see her friend enjoy the attention. She looked flattered when he asked her a few questions and complimented her appearance, and Renya thought back to the sadness Esmeralda exhibited in the Tidal Kingdom about not having a fated mate.

"What brings you to our lands?" Queen Samatra asked.

Cyrus answered before the others could speak. "We seek shelter and rest on our way back to the Snow

Lands. My daughter, Renya, was taken hostage by the Shadow Queen. While she was there, she was able to earn her trust, which could assist us later on."

Thesand nodded, stroking his chin. "We've been speaking with King Tristan about pooling our resources to make a final stand against her. We've agreed."

"That is wonderful news," Grayden said, grabbing Renya's hand under the table and squeezing it gently in his. "We'd like your input on where and how to take a stand," Grayden directed towards the other rulers.

Renya hesitated, then spoke up. "I have a suggestion."

All eyes turned towards her. She swallowed nervously before continuing. "While I was in the Shadow Realm, I learned that Cressida's magic is weakest in opposite power types. Since her magic is dark, it is weaker in areas of light, like the Sun Realm. I think that we should lure her there, using me."

Grayden grasped her hand harder, and she heard his voice resonate in her head.

I won't allow you to be bait. He laced his fingers with hers.

You don't have a choice, my love. This is how it has to be.

Renya thought he was going to protest, but his head gave a small shake of acceptance. She released a breath, glad the biggest hurdle of her plan was over.

"You'll only do that if I'm there too," Cyrus said, looking at Renya lovingly.

She closed her eyes quickly at the wave of emotion that came over her.

"I'm sorry, but who are you?" Thesand looked at

Cyrus, appraising him.

"I'm the King of the Sun Realm."

Gasps and mutters echoed around the table.

"That can't be—"

"It's not possible—"

"It must be a trick—"

Grayden stood tall and took command, like the natural leader he was. "I assure you, I've been to the Sun Realm. It's cloaked, but the entire city is active. More importantly, they have an army that is untouched. I've seen it personally."

More mumbles and side conversations. Finally, King Tristan spoke.

"Grayden, you've never given me a reason to doubt your word. You've been honest with me when the truth seemed unbelievable. If you say this is true, I believe you."

Grayden looked at Tristan appreciatively.

"Thank you, Grayden," Cyrus said. "We have much to plan, but I know my daughter and the rest of our party is exhausted from our travels. Would it be possible to continue this conversation tomorrow?"

There was no doubt her father was a true leader, Renya thought. He commanded the room and took charge as easily as Grayden did.

You get your strength and leadership from him, my princess. Another pulse of emotion tugged at her heart.

"I would definitely appreciate a soft and welcoming bed," Phillippe said, glancing at Esmeralda, who blushed deeply once again.

"Phillippe..." Grayden warned.

"What? I'm tired."

King Thesand ignored their banter. "We'll have

you shown to your rooms right away."

Renya stood up, and Grayden put his arm around her waist, touching her as often as he could. Several attendants appeared as if from nowhere, and led them to the guest wing.

Renya and Grayden walked through the hall, with Phillippe and Cyrus behind them. Esmeralda and Tristan also followed, and Renya guessed they were staying in the guest quarters as well.

The hall was long, and open to allow the sweet breeze to trickle through. They turned a corner, and off a large stairway leading outside were several miniature cottages. They all sported columns adorning the front, and red angled roofs. Esmeralda embraced Renya before heading towards a cottage on the far left, and Tristan entered the neighboring structure.

The attendant motioned to the building on the far right, and Renya followed behind Grayden as he pushed open the door. She looked around, seeing a large bed in the middle of the room, constructed from cherry wood. White linens covered the mattress, and frescoes depicting all kinds of flowers lined the walls. There were also a few more statues of Greek gods that Renya recognized from a mythology class she took in college.

The furnishings in the bedroom were minimal, with a small table with two chairs, a vanity and a trunk for storage. Renya brought nothing with her, so the trunk was useless. She walked over to the bathroom to peer inside, but before she made it to the door, Grayden's hand was on her shoulder, turning her around and pulling her against him.

He kissed her savagely, his lips hot and desperate against her mouth. His hands went to her waist and he backed her into the nearest wall, pressing his warm body into hers.

"Grayden, honey—" she started, but at that moment he pulled the thin nightgown she wore over her head. Before she could protest, he dragged his tongue in between the valley of her cleavage, and moaned loudly.

"I can't wait, Renya. I—I don't think I can be gentle." She could feel his lips move and his breath tickling between her breasts, and the sensation made every part of her body sing.

"I don't care," she gasped, tugging on his untidy hair so he would move his mouth back to hers. "Be with me. I just want to feel you." She tugged his shirt off and ran her hands down his chest.

When her fingers traced his side, a rough patch of skin caught her attention, and she pulled her mouth away from his and looked at the thick, raised scar that marked his flesh.

"I'm fine," he said, trying to kiss her again. Renya knelt before him, kissing every inch of his scar, the sorrow deep in her belly.

He moaned and pulled her upright, pressing against her. She couldn't believe how hard and tense he was.

He growled in his silky baritone, and then yanked her undergarments down. She clutched his shoulders as she stepped out of them, and then he was pressing his lips against her shoulder, nipping at her neck and collarbone.

She quickly fumbled with his pants, undoing the ties and pulling them down as quickly as she could. They fell around his ankles, and he didn't even bother removing them completely before wrapping her leg around his hip.

Renya bit down on her lip the second she felt him, straining against her folds. It was too long since she felt him this way, felt desirable and wanted.

Grayden grabbed her other leg and positioned it around his waist, and she locked her legs behind him as he supported her weight easily. He managed to stop for a split second, still pulsating against her, but he looked directly into her eyes. Deep pools of green glistened at her, and Renya felt her eyes mist as well.

"I swear to you, Renya. I will never, ever allow us to be parted again. Even in death. I pledge my soul to you. Fates be damned."

She shivered at the intensity of his words, spoken like an omen to ward off anything that tried to tear them asunder. She cupped his cheeks in her hands and kissed him again, feeling more and more desperate for his touch.

"Promise me," he said, pausing again.

She moved her hips, trying to get him to move, needing all of him.

"No, Little Fawn. Not until you promise me. No more sacrifices. From here on out, we do everything together."

"I promise," she whispered.

He thrust into her with one smooth motion, and they both lost themselves in the moment. She forgot how big he was, and how right she felt the second he was inside.

"Renya..." he groaned, a concentrated look on his face. "I can't go slow right now."

"I don't want you to go slow. I need you," she

pleaded, and he obliged, moving quickly inside her. It felt so good, so right, that it only took a few seconds for her to find her pleasure. She buried her face in the crook of his neck and mewed, trying to keep her voice low.

He moved even faster, eager to follow her. Then he released with a shudder and a cry that rang out through the room.

Grayden held her there, against the wall, for a few more seconds before collecting himself and carrying her to the bed, his trousers still around his ankles. He lowered her carefully on the soft mattress and then stripped off the rest of his clothing.

"Now that we got that first one out of the way, I can take my time with you." He leaned over and gave her another passionate kiss, and they started all over again.

Chapter Twenty-Four

S elenia leaned over Sion, looking at his face through the low light of the fire and making sure his breathing was even. Good, he was asleep. She had been waiting for hours for him to finally give in to the exhaustion she knew he was feeling. Selenia could tell he took his duty of protecting her very seriously, but after their long journey and a few sleepless nights, he finally let the relaxing pull of sleep take him.

She left the warmth of the campfire and crept silently towards the forest. She hoped she was in the right spot, but it was hard for her to keep track in the Twilight Kingdom. Every part of the forest looked the same, but she was sure this was the same pond they stopped at before.

Dry nettles crushed underfoot and she heard a bird take flight into the dusky air, frightened by her approach. She cradled her injured arm, trying to ignore the pain. Sion was able to find poppy plants that helped act as a pain reliever, but they were scarce and she was rationing the few plants they found. She took just enough of the bitter flowers in her morning tea to numb a bit of the pain, but it still lingered. She knew Sion was concerned about her arm, but Selenia was more concerned about the guilt she felt in her heart.

She walked for another ten minutes, and then began to feel panicky. What if this wasn't the way? She convinced Sion to seek out the pond for the horses, but what if it was the wrong one?

The smell of decay and rotten flesh hit her nose, and she spun around.

"I told you we would meet again, Selenia Snowden." The Murcurial circled, her body now wrapped in the cloak she took from Selenia during their prior meeting. "Did you bring me an offering?"

Selenia gulped. "How do you know what I'm here for?"

"I know everything, Selenia Snowden. The Fates whisper in my ear. When I was a babe, it drove me mad. But now I listen and enjoy the things I hear."

"So can you do it? Can you help me?" The desperation was evident in her tone.

"You know I require payment." The Murcurial's hollow eyes gleaned under the hood of the cloak.

Selenia undid the bow under her chin and removed the hat she purchased in the Sun Realm. The Murcurial's boney fingers reached out from underneath the cloak and snatched the hat away.

"Your payment is satisfactory," she said, circling Selenia once again.

"Then do it. Make me forget. Make me forget he ever existed."

"That I cannot do. Once in the memory, always in the memory. But...I can do something else."

"What?" Selenia cried, needing to forget his death, forget the betrayal she felt when Sion's lips were on hers.

"I cannot tell you before it is done. It will be painful at first. But in the end, you will be happier than you've ever been."

"Just do it." Selenia closed her eyes and waited. She could smell the Murcurial as she got closer, and she flinched when she felt the rotten fingers touching her forehead. A current of electricity went through her, then turned freezing cold. Her entire body shivered, and she felt like she'd never get warm again. But as soon as she felt the cold reach every extremity in her body, the warmth began. Heat radiated throughout her bloodstream, surging and burning every part of her until it reached her head. Pain erupted from behind her eyes, and then everything went black for a few seconds.

Selenia opened her eyes, but the Murcurial was gone. Before she could call out, asking her what she had done to her, her heart constricted.

An overwhelming, overpowering surge of lust went through her, causing her eyes to widen and her lips to part. She panted, unable to reconcile this feeling within her body with the thoughts going through her head. The need, the drive to find him was intense, unlike anything she ever experienced with Jurel. She still mourned him, mourned what could have been. But it was nothing like this. This soul-crushing, inconceivable notion that the rest of her life belonged to another.

She ran through the forest, her heart still pounding in her chest and her mind full of the images that ran through her head. How could she have not realized it? How could she be so blind?

Her skirt caught on a branch, but she didn't care. She just continued moving forward, letting her skirt rip, part of it still clinging to the tree as she pushed herself forward.

Selenia finally approached the campfire. She

looked down, and found him still asleep. She caressed his cheek, and he moaned softly, deep under. His dark face was smooth and warm under her hand, and she sighed deeply.

Her hands trembled as she resisted the urge to touch him, stroke him everywhere. Taste him.

Him.

Sion.

Her fated mate.

Chapter Twenty-Five

R enya lowered herself into the bath, sighing as the warm water encased her body and loosened her muscles. She didn't think there was a single spot on her body that didn't ache. Even her lips were swollen from Grayden's ardent kisses, and her scalp was sore from where he tugged on her hair a bit too hard in his desire to take her again and again.

She closed her eyes and sighed contentedly, happy to have a warm bath and get clean, thrilled to be back with her mate and reconnected. She could feel him again, much stronger than before. She wasn't sure if it was the nearness of him that enhanced their connection, or if it was the repeated rejoining of their bodies.

"What do you think you're doing?"

Without opening her eyes, she could envision the scene before her. A naked Grayden, towering over her, his muscled body still slightly damp with sweat. He'd worked his muscles hard, bringing them both to ecstasy again and again.

"Move," he commanded, and she opened her eyes and crossed her arms over her chest.

"No," she said, her eyes sparkling in amusement. "I'm going to relax in this tub all by myself."

Grayden threw his head back and groaned. "Why do you torture me, Little Fawn?"

Renya sat up, allowing the bubbles to drip down her chest and expose her cleavage to his searching eyes. She watched as his eyes darkened with arousal, and she felt the lust surging down their bond.

There was a knock on the door, and Grayden growled.

"Should I go get it?" Renya asked innocently, rising farther out of the water, allowing the droplets to run down her stomach.

"You are playing with fire, little one," he warned.

She smiled sweetly again, and he turned his back and left the bathroom to go answer the door, closing the bathroom door a little too hard. Renya smirked, enjoying the effect she had on him. She finished washing, taking particular care with her hair.

After a few minutes, Grayden returned, carrying a few different flowing gowns in his arms.

"Those aren't your colors, sweetie," she said, nodding towards the gowns.

He threw his head back and laughed. "These are from Esmeralda. She thought you might need to borrow some clothing."

"Oh god yes," she said, lifting herself out of the tub. Grayden grasped her arm, making sure she was steady on her feet as she stepped out of the slippery tub. He grabbed a towel and began drying her off.

"I can do that, Grayden."

"I know," he said simply, while continuing his ministrations.

Renya sighed and let him continue. She felt his guilt for their parting multiple times since they'd been back together, and if this helped ease that feeling, she'd let him take care of her.

She looked at the clothes Grayden set down on the counter. There were several different satin dresses, definitely in the style of the Tidal Kingdom, along with a pair of sandals and some undergarments. Renya felt immediate appreciation, she wasn't sure how she could put on that filthy nightgown after being clean. She didn't want any reminders of her time in the Shadow Realm, either.

Renya selected a bright yellow gown that was rather plain in front, with just a scoop neckline and cording around the waist. But the back of the dress was daring, with straps crossed in every direction, forming a net-like pattern across Renya's back. The length was shorter in front and then longer in the back, but since Renya was a bit shorter than Esmeralda it trailed behind her.

"Do you mind?" she asked, looking annoyed at Grayden. He watched her the entire time she dressed.

"Not at all. Although if truth be told, I'd rather you be undressing."

She bit her lip to fight the smile that was creeping up on her. "Hold that thought, mister. We were invited to dinner tonight."

A low growl was the only response she got. Sighing, she took her hand in his and led him out the door.

Esmeralda and Tristan met them outside.

"Renya, you look gorgeous," Esmeralda said, eyeing the borrowed gown. "I knew yellow was your color!"

Renya beamed, pleased by the compliment. "I appreciate you lending it to me."

"It looks much better on you than it ever did on

me. It fits you beautifully."

"I couldn't agree more," Grayden chimed in.

Renya blushed, feeling the heat surge up her neck.

Luckily, the arrival of Phillippe spared her any more uncomfortableness. He looked handsome, wearing a borrowed tunic from the Spring Lands like Grayden. As usual, his signature broadsword was slung across his back.

Instead of joining Grayden and Renya, he marched over to Esmeralda.

"You look radiant, Esmeralda." His eyes twinkled, and he brushed a kiss along her knuckles.

Renya watched Esmeralda enjoy his flirtatious behavior, glad for her friend. But, she was concerned about Phillippe's intentions. She'd have to ask Grayden about Phillippe's reputation with women.

Tristan, ignoring Phillippe's and Esmeralda's interaction, led the way back into the acropolis and into a large dining hall. Grecian in style, the dining room featured grand columns with intricate details and carved figures. The walls were painted an earthy brown, with gold accenting the carvings on the columns. In the middle of the room was a rich, polished wood table, complete with ornate chairs upholstered in luxurious velvet with a pattern of vines weaving up and down the fabric. Renya couldn't believe how beautiful the table setting was. Fine porcelain silverware and plates adorned a crisp white tablecloth. Olive branches and fresh roses made up the centerpieces. It was elegant enough for a wedding, in Renya's eyes. She rubbed her engagement ring as the thought entered her head, wondering if Grayden would bring up their wedding again. They hadn't talked about it since the night of their engagement.

Renya felt a soft breeze ruffle her hair, and saw large French doors allowing ample natural light to flood the space.

Renya was ravenous, ready for a warm meal and hopefully a peaceful nights' sleep. She sat down in one of the chairs, shivering slightly now that the sun had set and she was wearing a dress fit for the Tidal Kingdom.

Grayden plopped down next to her, grabbing her hand and placing it on his knee. Esmeralda sat on Renya's right, and unsurprisingly, Phillippe sat on the other side of her.

Samatra and Thesand entered, wearing the same clothes as earlier. They each took a seat at the head of the long table, and Renya felt their scrutiny upon herself and Grayden. She wondered if it was because they were fated, or if it was because of her parentage or the fact she'd spent considerable time in the Shadow Realm. She tried to ignore their stares and focused on the meal an attendant quickly placed in front of her.

A variety of fruits and vegetables were arranged on the plate, along with legumes and a seeded bread. There was also a bowl of steaming rice flavored with what Renya thought might be saffron. A tea with a brightly colored hibiscus flower floating in it and elderberry wine were brought out as well. Renya took a sip of the wine, and noticed how incredibly sweet it was. In fact, she mused, as she munched on a radish, everything was so flavorful and fresh.

Samatra must have noticed her facial expression. "Everything at the table was grown in our gardens."

"It's wonderful," Renya praised. Samatra smiled,

and Renya felt the ruler starting to warm to her. Grayden squeezed her hand again under the table. He had mastered one-handed eating and drinking, as it seemed his hand was always grasping hers.

"What are your plans now?" Tristan asked Grayden and Phillippe.

"I want to get Renya home to the Snow Lands as soon as possible. Once we're there, I need to speak with my advisors and retrieve my soldiers from the Twilight Kingdom. They've been helping with the rebuilding efforts there."

Renya tried not to feel guilty, but she was heartbroken over the damage in the Twilight Kingdom. She felt like it was all her fault.

Not your fault. You can't think like that, Renya. You never asked for any of this.

She glanced at Grayden, his green eyes full of compassion and assurance.

"At what point do you want to launch an attack?" Thesand looked at Grayden quizzically.

"Ideally within the next moon cycle. My fear is that Kalora will start to lose her powers soon. She's one of the few leaders left with an arsenal of magic, and I worry the longer we wait, the more likely she will start to lose them. However, we should also wait until Renya's aunt is located. She's Cressida's sister and incredibly powerful. Like Cyrus, her magic is still intact after spending significant time in the human realm."

"We can gather our men. Our archers never miss," Thesand said, rubbing his hands together as if the thought of going to war was enticing.

"My soldiers are ready too," Tristan said. He maintained his usual stoic appearance, but Renya could tell that Esmeralda was apprehensive about the coming battle. Her friend's eyes were downcast and she picked at her food.

Before anymore could be agreed on, a loud roar echoed through the air.

Bile rose up in Renya's throat as her body trembled in terror. Not again. She couldn't go back there.

Grayden pulled out his blade from its sheath and Phillippe was already standing with his large sword anchored to his shoulder. Thesand drew an arrow in his bow, and as if from nowhere, Tristan pulled out a small but pointy trident.

The roar continued, and Esmeralda stood, her eyes wide and panicky. Before she could do anything, a dragon appeared right outside of the open dining room. Phillippe pulled Esmeralda behind him, while Grayden lunged at the beast, blade held high.

"No!" Renya screamed, running in front of Grayden. An arrow buzzed by her head towards the dragon behind her, and she caught it in her golden strands of magic, stopping it in its path and shattering it into a million pieces.

Beauty sat on her hind legs and roared, then hit the ground hard with her clawed front feet.

"It's okay, girl. I'm here." Renya rushed over to the animal and stroked her head gently, and Beauty purred contentedly.

"Beauty, this is everyone. Everyone, meet Beauty. My...dragon."

Chapter Twenty-Six

S ion woke up, his senses on high alert. He couldn't believe he allowed himself to fall asleep. He was supposed to be guarding Selenia.

Selenia. Where was she? He frantically lifted his head as his eyes searched around the camp. There she was, sitting on a log and looking directly into the fire, a small blanket wrapped around her shoulders.

He walked over to her, and touched her lightly on her good arm. She jumped, startled by his presence.

"What are you doing up, Selenia? You were supposed to be resting. I'm worried about your arm."

She looked up at him, and something in her gaze was different. He wasn't sure what it was, but she seemed...off.

"Selenia, what's wrong?"

She looked at him and swallowed hard, grasping at her gown as if to still her hands.

"Nothing," she said, her voice wavering.

"Are you in pain?" he asked, frightened that her arm was getting worse or that she had lingering effects from her heat sickness.

"You could say that," she whispered.

Sion felt a rush of sympathy come over him, and he sat down next to her on the log, putting his arm around her waist. She flinched, almost as though his touch burned her.

"Selenia?" he questioned.

"It's nothing…you just…it's better if you don't touch me."

Sion felt a pit in his stomach. She must be angry about what transpired in the cave. He didn't know what came over him, and now she didn't even want him near.

"I promise, I won't touch you again," he said, removing his hand and inching to the far side of the log.

Selenia didn't respond and continued looking into the fire.

Sighing, Sion stood up. It was near morning, and if they made good time they could be in the Snow Lands by tomorrow, or even late this evening.

"Let's get packed up," he said, grabbing some dirt and throwing it over the fire to put it out.

Selenia said nothing, but moved to gather up her belongings, not even looking at Sion.

∞

Sion had never seen Selenia so forlorn. He assumed it was Jurel's death, hitting her all over again. Perhaps the kiss they shared sparked old memories for her. He wished he could do something to assuage his guilt, but she didn't even want to talk to him. When they stopped midday to water the horses, she scarcely glanced at him, and hardly said two words. It was worse than he feared. Would she say something to Grayden about his indiscretion? He tried to think back, find out what possessed him to make a move on his best friend's sister, but he couldn't fathom why he acted the way he did. Maybe he was just so lonely, starving for any type of touch that wasn't cruel or hurtful. She was so sweet and innocent, the opposite of Cressida.

And her lips. So soft and warm...

Fates, what was wrong with him? He needed to get away from her, and fast. He started counting down the hours, eager to be off their shared horse, so the temptation would leave him.

When they finally crossed over into the Snow Lands, there was no gradual shift in the terrain and weather like usual. The second they passed the boundary line, snow, thick and viscous, whipped around them.

"Sion, what's going on?" Selenia asked, trying to pull her small blanket around her shoulders, her nose already pink in the few minutes they'd appeared in their lands.

"I'm not sure, but I think it's some kind of blizzard," he said, amazed. Their lands had been losing their magic and becoming warmer and warmer, so they hadn't seen weather like this in quite some time.

"What should we do?" she asked, her teeth chattering.

Sion looked at the sky, trying to gauge how fast moving the storm was.

"Selenia, I was hoping to get back to the lodge by this evening, but I'm afraid this storm isn't safe for us to travel through. The visibility is horrendous, and I'm concerned that we'll go in circles and run out of provisions. I think we ought to stay the night."

"You're probably right," she said, pulling her blanket up around her shoulders even tighter.

"What happened to your hat?" Sion asked, looking at her pink ears and her hair whipping around in the wind.

"It must have blown away," she said.

An odd sensation down his spine hinted that she was lying, but it seemed such an odd, insignificant thing to lie about that he ignored his suspicions.

He scanned the horizon, looking for something to help shelter them from the wind. An outcropping of rocks caught his eye, and he directed Honor towards them.

He dismounted and then helped Selenia down. When he put his hands on her waist, she flinched, and he felt guilty all over again. She tried to keep her body away from him the entire time they rode, and the slightest touch caused her to tense everywhere.

"I'm afraid we'll have to share a tent," he said, his eyes searching hers. For a split second, he thought he detected a look of excitement, but it was so fleeting he was sure he imagined it.

"Alright," was her only reply.

They worked together, albeit silently, to set up a makeshift campsite. Once the tent was pitched and a fire flickering in front of the rocks, he motioned for Selenia to get inside.

She paused at the tent flap, watching him arrange himself in front of the fire.

"Sion, you'll freeze to death. I know you're adapted to the cold, but there's no way you could survive the night out here in a blizzard. Come inside."

He looked down at the snow covering his boots, and then back at the tent. He watched Selenia crawl in, and then headed in behind her.

She sat on the sleeping mat, shivering in her gown. Her clothes were soaked, and his were too. The snow was wet and damp, unlike the sweetly falling snow they were used to.

He sat down on the opposite side, trying to keep as much distance between them as he could. He watched as Selenia blew on her trembling fingers, trying to bring warmth into them. He struggled for a second, then moved over to her and took her hands in his. She looked like she might protest for a second, but then she held still and watched as he rubbed her pale hands in his.

"You have to keep your fingers moving, keep the blood circulating," he said, rubbing her fingers and then moving to her palms. "I refuse to allow you to lose a limb."

She trembled while he continued to caress her hands, and he worried that she was going to get hypothermia in her wet clothes.

"Selenia, I think you need to remove anything that's wet. The tent can keep us warm enough, but it won't do much good if you're in soaked clothing."

Wordlessly, she began to unbutton her blouse with her good arm, her fingers shaking. Sion wasn't sure if it was from the cold or if she was scared to be undressing in front of him. He turned towards the side of the tent, giving her privacy.

"Once you're finished, get into your sleeping roll and then I'll do the same."

Sion heard her struggle with her injured arm, but he didn't want to offer to help her undress. He'd already crossed far too many lines on this journey.

After a few minutes, her voice came quietly. "I'm finished."

He turned around, and saw her white shoulders, bare against the blankets and a sudden burst of desire surged throughout his body. He swallowed hard, reminding himself that she was off-limits. Sion turned again and began removing his soaked clothing. Once he got to his trousers, he remembered that he wasn't given any undergarments at the Sun Realm. He considered sleeping in his bottoms, but the wind howled outside and shook the tent slightly, and he decided against it.

"Selenia, close your eyes," he said, turning back to strip. The cool air hit his body, and he was glad to be getting out of his wet clothes.

He quickly shucked his pants and then crawled into his own furs. He glanced back over at her, and saw her eyes widen. Was she embarrassed at the thought that he was completely naked? Or the fact that they were sharing a tent? He wondered if he should say something, apologize for the conditions, but instead he just blew out the small candle he lit and closed his eyes, the situation completely confusing him.

∞

He was hovering near sleep when the sound of thrashing and crying caught his attention. He looked around in the dark, squinting to see what was happening. He could barely make out Selenia's silhouette, shaking and seizing. Without thinking he reached out to her, and pulled her close. She sat on his lap, stunned for a moment before she wrapped her good arm around his neck, sobbing into his shoulder.

"Shhhhh...I'm here," he said, rubbing her bare back. She continued to cry, unable to form words. Her chest was flushed against his, and he sighed, enjoying the warmth their bodies made together. The storm dropped the temperature significantly, and Sion couldn't ever remember being this cold. The wind howled around them, masking the sound of her sobs. He continued to hold her, and her scent enveloped him. She smelled like clean cotton and roses, and he was surprised, unsure how she could smell so amazing considering they had been traveling. He shuddered as he suppressed a sudden desire to run his fingers through her soft hair.

Slowly, she stopped shaking but continued to cling to him, like a newborn to its mother.

"I'm here for you, darling." The endearment rolled off his tongue so naturally that it surprised him. He expected her to pull away, but if anything, she grabbed him more tightly. Sion became very aware of the fact that she was completely bare from the waist up, and he could feel her soft breasts against his chest. Her nipples were hard and cold, and he took a shaky breath, trying not to give into the arousal he felt stirring in his groin. Her skin was supple and velvety, pale and inviting. He never thought he'd ever see another woman besides Cressida, and the longer he held her, the more enchanting she became to him.

He knew he should push her away, move her off his lap and back to her own furs. But he was drawn to her in a way he never experienced before. Sion knew she was a pretty girl, but he'd never felt desire for her.

"Sion?" she questioned, as if finally realizing she was in his lap. She let go of him quickly and then covered her chest with her arms, suddenly embarrassed.

He couldn't fathom why she would be embarrassed. Her body was the most alluring he'd ever seen before.

"Selenia, I..." he trailed off, looking for an excuse

for his attraction to her, but none came. Instead Sion just stared at her lips, remembering how sweet they tasted against his.

As if sensing his thoughts, she moved forward, hands still covering her chest. She dipped her eyelashes and looked up at him, and his heart skipped a beat.

"Beautiful," he whispered, reaching up to stroke her cheek. "So beautiful..."

Selenia continued to watch him, unmoving. He wondered if she could feel the same pull of desire that he felt.

Throwing caution into the wind, he moaned and leaned forward to press his lips to hers.

Electricity jolted through him, and the second his lips met hers, he fell. There was no turning back, no way to climb out of this hole he dug for himself, as he quickly fell in love with his best friend's sister.

Chapter Twenty-Seven

"**N**o, Beauty."

The dragon looked up at Renya, ears back and stomping slightly at the ground.

Renya sighed, trying to coax the dragon into the stall in the stables. It was the third time she'd tied up the dragon, and she tied the knots even tighter, hoping they'd hold this time. Renya knew that Samatra and Thesand were incredibly uncomfortable with Beauty in their lands, so Renya promised to restrain her until they were ready to leave tomorrow. But Beauty managed to break free twice, terrorizing the village trying to seek out Renya. Grayden already made reparations to several market stall owners after Beauty went on a eating spree and ate an entire stall clean of fish, and another of deer meat. The second time she got out, she managed to tear into the wall of the guest house Renya and Grayden were staying at, and Renya woke up to her nudging her awake, growling slightly at Grayden for being too close to her. Rubble scattered across the room, and Grayden promised to send funds to replace the walls of the guest house, too.

All in all, Renya knew they needed to return home to the Snow Lands and find a permanent solution for Beauty. It was clear that she wouldn't be separated from Renya, and the larger she got, the more problematic it was going to become.

"Should we try chains?" Grayden came up behind Renya, putting his arms around her waist and resting his chin on her shoulder.

At the suggestion, a low growl started in Beauty's throat, as if she understood exactly what Grayden was proposing.

"No, I'll just tie them tighter and add more ropes. I'm not sure what to do with her."

"It's clear that she's bonded to you," Grayden said, eyeing the dragon. She was growing bigger every day. "Did Cressida bond to any of the other dragons?"

"The adult male one," Renya said, scratching Beauty affectionately on the snout. "But it's not like it is with Beauty. She seems incredibly determined to be by my side at all times."

Beauty circled the stall before finally collapsing in the hay. She closed one eye lazily, but kept the other partially open, watching Renya's every move.

"I can't believe you have a pet dragon, Little Fawn."

"Not exactly what I was expecting either," Renya said, as Beauty's watchful eye started to droop.

"Do you think she's big enough to ride?"

"I could ride her, but she doesn't have any kind of harness or saddle. When I left the Shadow Realm, she couldn't fly with me on her back, but could carry me on the ground. Her wings are growing larger each day, though." Already her wing span had doubled in size since Renya last rode her.

Beauty's eye finally closed, and the soft sounds of a snoring dragon sounded through the barn. Renya walked towards the barn door, Grayden following. She latched it securely and then bolted it with an extra lock that was installed just to try and contain the troublemaker of a dragon.

"Are you excited to be going back to the Snow Lands?" Renya asked, wiping her hands on her borrowed dress. This one was a pale blue silk, with tulle sleeves that went down to her wrists.

"I'm more eager to get you home and back into my furs," he said, stopping her on her path back to the acropolis. He stood in front of her, trailing his fingers up her arm, and then tenderly cupping her cheek. Renya looked into his eyes, and saw love and affection pouring out.

"I love you," she said, snuggling down into his hard chest.

"Oh Little Fawn. There are no words to describe what you mean to me. I'm completely and utterly yours, for all time. The moment you came for me, I ceased being just me. It's now us, forever."

Grayden kissed the top of her head as Esmeralda walked by, with Phillippe following behind. Renya noticed that Esmeralda was holding a bouquet of fresh flowers, and she had no doubt that Phillippe picked them from the meadow.

"Did you finally get that rabid beast back in her stall?" Phillippe asked, catching up to Esmeralda as she made her way over to Renya and Grayden.

Renya untangled herself from Grayden and lightly pushed Phillippe on the shoulder. "She's not rabid, and she's not a beast." She put her hands on her hips and stared him down. "She's my friend."

"A friend that could eat us all," Phillippe mumbled.

"She won't hurt anyone as long as I tell her not

to."

Grayden glanced at the barn and then back at Renya. "Do you mean that? Can you control her?"

"I don't control her. We're just...friends."

Phillippe snorted. "Right...friends with a deadly dragon. Grayden, your mate is crazy."

"No crazier than you are, thinking you have a chance with Esmeralda," he retorted, and Renya watched as Esmeralda blushed again.

"What are you doing over here, Phillippe?" Renya asked, wanting to get back inside with Grayden as soon as she could. Although they were together multiple times per day, they had a lot of catching up to do.

"Thesand invited us to inspect his army with him," Phillippe said.

"Then let us go," Grayden said, motioning to Renya.

"Actually," Esmeralda said, "I was wondering if I could speak with Renya. You are leaving tomorrow, and I don't know when we'll have a chance to catch up."

Renya was torn, glancing between Grayden and Esmeralda.

You should go, Little Fawn. Go enjoy some time with your friend.

She nodded, but remembered that only she could hear what Grayden said. "I'll stay with you, Esmeralda."

Esmeralda looked thrilled. "Great! I packed some lunch for us if you'd like to relax by the lake."

"That sounds wonderful." Renya gave Grayden a quick peck on the cheek, but he turned her back towards him for a heated kiss.

Phillippe made gagging noises, and Grayden pulled away. "You're just jealous," he said to his brother.

Phillippe looked at Esmeralda wistfully, and Renya realized that Grayden was right. Phillippe was incredibly jealous that Grayden had someone.

Grayden patted Phillippe on the back, as if he understood his feelings, and then they headed off in the direction of the acropolis.

"Come," Esmeralda said, leading them away from the barn to a stone pathway lined with roses. They walked for a little while, the sun shining down on them. Renya felt peaceful, but she knew that the feeling wouldn't last.

They stopped under a cherry tree right next to the lake. Esmeralda spread out a teal colored blanket and they both sat down.

Renya looked off into the distance, barely making out the mountain range that stood behind Snowden Lodge. She was enjoying her time at the Spring Lands, but she couldn't wait to be home again.

Esmeralda uncorked a bottle of elderberry wine and handed Renya a small glass. She continued to unpack the basket, pulling out little raspberry cakes with a thick icing and several different types of cheeses.

"This was so sweet of you," Renya said, grabbing one of the cakes.

"It was no trouble. Besides...I wanted to talk to you about something."

Renya knew what she was going to say before she opened her mouth.

"It's about Phillippe, yes?"

"Fates, am I so transparent?" Esmeralda groaned, putting her hand to her forehead.

Renya chuckled. "No, not at all. But he certainly is."

Esmeralda looked pleased. "I like him," she admitted, quickly looking down at the soft grass lining the bank of the lake.

"I don't blame you. He's quite charming," Renya confessed.

"This might be awkward, but when we were children, my father hoped for me to marry Grayden. But his father refused."

Renya felt a tiny stab of jealousy but moved on quickly. Grayden was hers and hers alone.

Esmeralda continued, "but I'm so glad for it. Grayden is sweet and kind, but..."

"Broody?" Renya guessed, a coy smile on her face.

"Yes. But Phillippe...he's so funny and carefree. I know he has his own burdens, but he makes me feel like I'm the only thing that matters."

"I'm happy for you, Esmeralda. But to be honest, I don't know a great deal about him, so I don't know how much help I can be."

"That's not it at all. I wanted to know...before your bond, did you feel something for Grayden? I think I'm falling for Phillippe, but a part of me still hopes that there's a fated mate out there for me."

Renya chewed the inside of her lip thoughtfully. "Yes, I suppose I did. Honestly, I was attracted to him the second I met him. He was handsome and noble, and I did feel drawn to him. I even loved him before our bond came. We had a solid friendship, and we tried to downplay our physical relationship, but looking back, I think I always knew he was for me."

Esmeralda looked deep in thought. "I'm definitely attracted to Phillippe, and the timeframe for me to develop a bond has passed. But...it's hard to let go of the dream, you know?"

Renya didn't know, but she didn't want to tell Esmeralda that. The last thing she was thinking of was developing a fated bond when she stumbled into this world.

"Esmeralda, I think that if you like Phillippe, you should go for it. You can't live life waiting for something to happen to you. This could be your chance for love and happiness. I loved Grayden before we became mates, and even if I had never been fated to him, I knew we belonged to each other."

"Thank you, Renya. That was exactly what I was hoping to understand."

"Of course. For what it's worth, I think you look really happy with him."

Another sweet smile from Esmeralda. "Well, enough about that! Tell me how Grayden proposed!"

∞

"Renya...my Little Fawn..."

She closed her eyes as she felt him enter her, desperately seeking the connection they shared.

"Grayden..." she moaned, unable to believe that she was really here, pinned beneath him. Renya couldn't stop herself from constantly running her fingers all over his body, just to make sure he wasn't a dream. Which in turn, led to more couplings. She wasn't complaining though. She needed him as much as he needed her. They used each other's bodies to convince themselves that they could never be parted again, desperately clinging to each other.

"Gods, Renya..." Grayden continued, his eyes fixated on hers. A shiver went down her spine at the intensity in which he claimed her. "I can't ever live without you. Never leave me again."

She tried to reassure him, tried to say something, but at that point he angled his hips and she shook, pleasure coursing through her bloodstream.

Grayden followed behind her, relief shuddering throughout his body. He collapsed on the bed next to her, pulling her on top of him and keeping himself within her.

Renya sighed contentedly as he caressed her arms and placed a soft kiss along her neck. Her head against his chest, she listened to his heart pound, and then slow as he recovered from their exertions.

"I love you," he whispered, running his fingers through her now tangled hair.

She lifted up her head and planted a kiss along his jawline, feeling the thick hair that now covered part of his face.

"You should shave soon," she said absentmindedly, rubbing her palm along his chin and cupping his cheek.

"I'll do it tomorrow morning," he replied, his eyes closing.

"Wait," she whispered. "There's something I want you to do first."

He opened his eyes, staring deeply into hers. "Whatever it is, I'm happy to do it."

She struggled with the request, suddenly embarrassed as she pictured his scratchy face between her thighs.

You should never feel ashamed to ask me for anything that makes you feel good.

Renya blushed, knowing that he must have seen

what she was thinking, but she didn't stop him as he kissed a trail down her stomach. Her breathing hitched as he moved between her thighs, his rough stubble tickling against her.

"Is this what you desire?" he breathed, blowing gently against her folds. She nodded, squirming as he continued worshiping her body.

Chapter Twenty-Eight

S elenia felt peaceful for the first time since Jurel's death. With Sion's arms wrapped around her, she felt safe and protected. Loved, even. She knew he wasn't aware that they were fated, she could feel it in her soul that he didn't realize it. It was cruel to allow her this gift but to not allow Sion to reciprocate. He obviously felt something for her, but she knew it wasn't the desperation and gnawing desire that flooded her senses.

The Murcurial said it would hurt, at first, but she would be happy in the end. That was something, wasn't it?

She sighed and tilted her head back towards Sion. He held her tightly, his arms around her waist and his warm breath hot against her neck.

Her nightmare brought them closer together. Selenia dreamt that Sion was in Cressida's court, and she was forced to watch as Cressida cut him over and over again, marring his beautiful skin. With a devilish look in her eye, the Shadow Queen carved out Sion's heart right in front of her. That was when she woke up, with Sion's chest pressed against her own. It took her a while to realize that he was safe, and not locked away to do Cressida's bidding. When he told her what happened to him there, it upset her. But once he became hers, the revelation was absolutely horrifying. She'd stab Cressida in the heart for hurting her mate.

Her mate. Fates, how could this be so? Sion was well past the age for it. But then again, Grayden was too when he discovered he was fated to Renya. Was her mating bond somehow locked like Renya's? Or did the Murcurial create it? If she had somehow, when would Sion feel it?

Her head felt dizzy, trying to piece out this strange, yet exhilarating revelation. Selenia debated telling Sion, but it made no sense, and she didn't think he would believe her. No, she needed to figure out exactly what happened before she confessed.

Her face brightened. They were in the Snow Lands, and they should be home today. Surely Almory would know what to do. Perhaps he would be able to force Sion's bond to her, so they could be deliriously happy together.

She traced her fingers lightly over his hand on her stomach, thinking about the kiss they shared last night. After a few minutes, Sion pulled away, and the loss of his body against hers was so substantial that she began to cry again. He held her then, pulling her to his furs, wrapping her in his muscular arms and placing tender kisses along her back. Even now, his chest was pressed to her back and she could feel the warmth radiating from him. Her bottom rested against him, and she could feel his hardness against her backside.

She was horribly naive when it came to men, and the only knowledge she possessed about sex had come from romance novels hidden deep in the false bottom of her wardrobe. From what she read, the hardness she felt indicated that he wanted her. Relief flooded her. Perhaps he sensed their connection, even without his side of the bond activated.

Sion shifted in his sleep, and Selenia felt herself being pulled to his body even tighter. She could scarcely breathe, but she didn't care.

Finally, Sion began to wake up. Selenia dreaded the moment, knowing that when he woke up and realized how close they were, he would undoubtedly push her away again. But for just a little bit, she could pretend.

She could tell the instant Sion remembered the previous night. He tensed behind her, a shaky breath escaping him.

He started to pull away, but Selenia turned towards him and touched his face with her palm. He blinked rapidly, and she watched him swallow hard.

"None of that," she said, looking deeply into his eyes. "You aren't going to pull away."

He closed his eyes, and Selenia could feel the pulse of desire tug at them both.

"Selenia, this can't happen…"

"What did I just say?"

Sion pushed himself up, untangling his limbs from hers. "I took advantage of the situation. You're sad because of Jurel, and I'm preying on that." He held the fur over his body as he tried to pull his trousers on, nearly falling over in the confined space of the tent.

"You did no such thing. If you must know, my nightmare last night was about the horrors you endured at the hands of the Shadow Queen."

Sion paled, his hands pausing on the laces of his pants.

"Why would you dream about that?"

Selenia bit her lip. She wanted to tell him, make him understand that what was happening between them was inevitable. But she knew it would be hard for him to believe.

"It just...bothered me," she finished lamely.

They both looked anywhere but each other.

Sion broke the palpable tension first.

"We should get going." He turned his back to her, indicating that she should dress.

She rolled her eyes, even though she knew he couldn't see it. He held her all throughout the night, her half-naked body pressed against his, but in the light of the day, he was concerned for her modesty. She struggled getting her arm into her sleeve, the pain worse than ever. The weather was so poor that they didn't even eat dinner, and Selenia was desperately overdue for the pain relief that the poppy concoction provided.

Sion heard her grunts of pain and turned. She was mostly dressed, but her bad arm hung out of the sleeve, her blouse still open. Selenia could see his concern, his pity for her condition.

"I'm fine," she grumbled, leaving her injured arm outside of the blouse and shrugging on her cloak.

"Selenia."

All it took was her name on his tongue, his voice thick, causing a shiver down her spine. He moved towards her and her breathing hitched, watching his hands reach out to hers.

The second his hand made contact with her skin, she felt a jolt of electricity trail through her body. From the widening of his eyes, Selenia knew he felt it too, although he didn't comment on it, but instead focused on helping her into the rest of her clothing.

Once her borrowed cape from the Sun Realm was

clasped around her neck, Sion opened up the tent flap and crawled out.

When she looked outside, her mouth dropped. At least three feet of snow settled around the camp, completely covering the terrain.

"Whoa."

"We haven't seen snow like this in ages," Sion agreed, heading towards the horses, his feet sinking deep in the wet snow.

Selenia followed him, teeth chattering. The horses were tethered under a tree, their thick coats protecting them from the cold.

"Can I help pack up the tent?" she asked.

Sion shook his head. "It's too wet to take back. We'll leave it and just take what we need."

∞

Selenia had never been so excited to see Wesalie again. The town was quiet, everyone hunkered down for the evening, but the low glow from the streetlights was like a beacon, leading them up the gravel path to Snowden Lodge.

She could feel Sion's excitement as well, his body practically humming once they reached the outskirts of the town.

"How long have you been gone?"

"Almost a full year. Before I went to the Shadow Realm, I was up in the mountain training camp."

"Will you stay at the lodge or go back home?" Selenia tried not to sound too hopeful at the prospect of being under the same roof.

"I'll stay here until Grayden is back. Then I'll head out towards the foothills."

Selenia nodded. "Has your house been abandoned all this time?"

"No, my grandmother is living there. As soon as my father died, I moved her there. It's bigger than her old house and closer to the town."

"That was good of you." She leaned back into his arms, the scent of him too strong to ignore. She felt him tense against her, but then he relaxed as Honor continued up the path to the lodge.

Two grooms were waiting for them, no doubt spotting them as they came up the long hill. Sion dismounted first, and then pulled Selenia off and carefully lowered her to the ground.

"Selenia!"

She whipped around to see Tumwalt rushing towards her, Almory a few paces behind. Tumwalt had grown grayer in the weeks they'd been gone, and his hairline receded even more. He looked thinner, as if their absence caused him a great deal of stress. Almory looked the same, although his eyes twinkled even more, as if he was pleased to see them.

"Selenia is hurt," Sion said immediately, looking at Almory.

"I'll see to her at once—" Almory started, but was cut off by a woman who appeared quickly, racing across the yard with speed that didn't match her age.

The woman looked at Selenia and Sion, sizing them up quickly. She wore several strange pieces of clothing, layered as if to keep her warm in the Snow Lands.

"Where is Renya?" the elderly woman asked, eyes darting quickly around the courtyard and behind them, as if she expected more guests to appear.

Selenia understood immediately who this was, even though she hadn't met her the last time she barged into the lodge.

It was Renya's aunt, Agatha.

Selenia's jaw fell the second she realized that Renya's aunt was here, not only in their world, but here at the lodge.

"She's not with us," Sion said, clearly baffled by the woman's appearance. "You're Renya's aunt? I met you briefly in the Sunset Land. You hit me with some falling rubble."

"Ah, the spy, is it? Hopefully I just knocked some common sense into your brain. If my Renya isn't with you, where is she? That boyfriend of hers better be taking care of her. He's far too handsome for my liking, but he does seem to care about her."

Selenia tried to piece together the timeline in her mind. Based on her speech, she guessed that Agatha didn't know Renya was fated to Grayden. She glanced at Sion, and he shook his head slightly while Agatha looked behind them again, as if Renya would pop out from behind the horses.

Sion was right. It wasn't their place to tell her of Renya and Grayden's bond.

"If everything went to plan, Renya, Cyrus, Grayden, and his brother Phillippe should be on their way here as we speak." Sion looked at Tumwalt next. "Have you had any communication with them?"

"None since they left the Twilight Kingdom. We've been in the dark here."

"You all better hope my Renya's in one piece. What has happened since Renya came back through the portal?"

Selenia spoke up. "Renya's powers were unlocked by the Shadow Queen. We went to the Twilight Kingdom so Renya could be trained by Queen Kalora—"

"That old bird is still alive? Hmph. She stole my beau from me when we were younger and I've never forgiven her for it."

"—and then the Shadow Queen came there and took Renya—"

Agatha gasped at this revelation.

"But Renya was able to get on her good side. Cyrus, Grayden, and Phillippe went to the Shadow Realm to get her back."

"What's being done to end this threat for good?" Agatha looked at them all, hostility rolling off of her in waves. Selenia wasn't sure if she was hostile towards them, or if this was just her personality.

Sion cleared his throat. "Grayden has a plan."

Agatha snorted. "I'm sure Pretty Boy does. Hopefully it's better than the plans he's had so far."

Selenia wanted to argue, but she was tired and cold. She shivered, and then felt Sion's eyes on her.

"We can talk about this later. Selenia is in pain and needs to be seen to."

Sion gave her a gentle nudge forward and Almory beckoned for her to follow him. She turned her back and marched away from the courtyard, towards Almory's workshop. Just before the doors closed behind her, she could hear Sion trying to reassure Agatha.

"Grayden is the best leader I've ever known. He also loves Renya. She's safe as long as she's with him."

Chapter Twenty-Nine

R enya worried for the borrowed horse she rode on. Not only were the Snow Lands much too cold for the creature, bred for the Spring Lands, but every time Beauty swooped down to check on Renya, the poor thing reared up and almost threw Renya. Grayden begged her to ride with him, but she refused, knowing they had an audience and also knew what usually happened when they rode together.

She looked over at Phillippe, who had been unusually quiet since they left the Spring Lands. Renya had a feeling that it had to do with leaving a certain Tidal Princess behind. She caught Grayden's eye, and he slowed to ride next to her.

"Has Phillippe said anything to you?"

"About what?" Grayden asked, looking puzzled as he tightened his hand on the reins of his horse.

Honestly, men could be so dense, Renya thought.

"You didn't notice? He's been quiet the entire way home."

Grayden glanced at Phillippe, then back at Renya. "I guess he has…"

"He has a thing for Esmeralda."

"Really? That surprises me."

"Why would it surprise you?"

"Well, he's never been one to spend time with just a single woman, if you know what I mean."

Renya frowned, trying to decide what to do with that information.

"Do you think he could be serious about her? I don't want my friend to get hurt."

"Honestly, I don't know. I'd hoped he would have settled down by now, especially since he's older than I am and not bound by duty like I was before. But he never showed much interest."

"Well, maybe this is a good thing for him," Renya said. "It would be a great match."

"I would like to see him happy," Grayden admitted.

"Esmeralda said they would join us at the lodge soon. Her brother wanted to spend a few more days practicing with their soldiers in archery."

"That reminds me, Little Fawn," Grayden said, stopping his horse in the snow. "Now that you're back... do you still want to get married?"

"Of course, why wouldn't I?"

"I actually meant, would you like to get married before we go to battle? I can't stand the fact that you don't belong to me on paper."

Renya snorted. "I think what we have means much more than a piece of paper does."

"I also want to be married in the eyes of the Gods," he continued, looking at Renya hopefully. "And I was thinking, since Esmeralda will be here in a few days, perhaps we could do it then?"

Renya's heart sank. A look of panic crossed Grayden's face, and she quickly sought to explain. "It's just that...I don't want to get married without Aunt Agatha there. Since my father is going to try and find her after we are settled in the lodge, I'd like to wait until he comes back, if you don't mind."

"Of course, Little Fawn. I've waited an eternity for you. What's another week?"

Renya smiled, thankful he understood.

"What are you two conspiring about back there?" Phillippe called over his shoulder, slowing his horse down when he noticed that the pair fell behind.

"You," Grayden retorted, and Phillippe cracked a small grin.

Renya decided to broach the subject. "Soooo... Esmeralda?"

Phillippe's grin widened. "Did she say anything about me?"

"Just that you're an idiot..." Grayden mumbled.

"You better not hurt her, Phillippe Snowden. She's an amazing friend and a sweet person."

Phillippe's eyes looked wistful. "Trust me, Renya," he said, turning to look forward once again. "She's far more likely to hurt me."

∞

It was almost morning by the time they arrived in the village. Grayden insisted that they ride through the night, worried that by this point, Cressida would have been to the Sun Realm and learned that Renya wasn't there. The Snow Lands was the next logical place he would take her. There had been a blizzard while they were in the Spring Lands, and the thick snow at least covered their tracks.

Once they reached the village, Cyrus began looking around excitedly. "I haven't been here since I was a young man," he said. "Hardly anything has changed."

Renya was thrilled to see the village was indeed the same as she left it. After the destruction that occurred in the Twilight Kingdom, she was fearful for the little town of Wesalie, but it was the same as the last time she saw it, the night of the Sky Lights Festival. Was it really that long ago? So much had changed since she and Grayden watched the twinkling lights dance across the dark sky.

"Do you think Selenia and Sion have arrived already?" she asked Grayden, eager to see both of them. She missed Selenia terribly, and she was still so worried about the young girl, especially after Jurel's death.

"I'm hopeful that they are. As long as they didn't encounter any significant delays, they should have arrived a couple of days ago."

They approached the courtyard, and everything was as Renya remembered. The air still smelled of pine, a smell that permeated from Grayden at all times no matter how far away from his lands he was.

Grayden entered first, Renya behind him and Cyrus and Phillippe taking up the rear. From her view, she could see Tumwalt racing towards Grayden. Renya figured he had much to talk to Grayden about, but she was still hesitant on how to act around him after he accused her of bewitching Grayden. A woman was walking directly behind him, shouting at him, but Renya couldn't make out the words she was saying, but that didn't matter.

It was her aunt.

"Renya!" Aunt Agatha cried, running past Tumwalt and Grayden to the horse carrying Renya.

Renya's heart nearly burst at seeing her aunt. Although she still hadn't completely forgiven her for concealing Renya's identity for so long, she was still the first family Renya ever knew. Plus, she now understood that Aunt Agatha gave up her entire life in this world to keep Renya safe.

Renya half-fell off of her mount, eager to hold her aunt in her arms, as if to reassure herself that this was all real. The second her feet hit the cobblestones, she was pressed into a giant hug, tears streaming down her face as her aunt cooed in her ear.

"Sunshine! Oh, my dear! I never thought I'd see you again!"

Renya sobbed, unable to contain her relief. She could feel Grayden's relief too, down through their bond.

Oh god. She would have to tell her aunt she was engaged. And fated to Grayden. She gulped and tried to hide her ring, wanting to wait until the time was right to tell her aunt.

Aunt Agatha let her go and held her at arm's length while Grayden dismounted and handed over their horses to a waiting groom. Phillippe and Cyrus did the same.

"Sunshine, I can feel your power radiating from you! I'm sorry we locked your magic, it was the only way to keep you safe—"

"It's okay. Really, I understand why you and my father did what you did."

Renya watched Agatha swallow hard and then look at Cyrus.

"You told her?"

Cyrus chuckled. "It's good to see you again too, Agatha."

Agatha ignored his greeting. "She knows you're

234

her father...and her mother—"

"Is Cressida," Renya finished. "Yes, unfortunately I know."

Renya could see Tumwalt greet Grayden while she was talking to her aunt.

"Sunshine, I—"

Before Agatha could finish, a thunderous roar ripped through the courtyard and Beauty landed right behind the horses, who reared up and ran out of the courtyard, the young grooms following behind, their cries echoing off of the stone walls of the courtyard.

Aunt Agatha looked surprised, but not stunned. Tumwalt, on the other hand, fainted.

Renya looked around sheepishly. "Oh yeah, I have a dragon now."

Agatha raised her eyebrows as Beauty pranced over to Renya's side, nudging her arm for a pat.

"Well, I think you have quite a bit to fill me in on, Sunshine."

∞

Renya sat opposite Aunt Agatha in the library, with a fire roaring in front of them and crimling tea steaming in mugs on a small side table.

"So I was stuck in that blasted rocky land for weeks! I forgot how awful the coastal worlds are, nothing but water and rocks. I finally found a broken portal, and it took forever to fix it."

"I'm just so glad you're here!" Renya looked down at her skirt, smoothing it absentmindedly.

"Out with it, Renya."

"What?" Renya asked, sipping the contents of her mug carefully.

"You have something to tell me, and you don't want to. You've been in my care since you were a babe, you don't think I know when you're uncomfortable?"

Renya set her drink down and steadied her breath, staring at the fire. "So, Grayden and I—"

"Are fated."

Renya jerked her head up from looking at the fire. "You know?"

"Of course I know. You're mated and engaged."

"Who told you?"

Agatha laughed, her shoulders shaking slightly. She looked at Renya and then picked at the hem of her shirt. She wore a man's tunic and leggings, clearly loaned from someone in the Snow Lands.

"I'm not blind, Sunshine. You're wearing his ring and your mating mark shines clearer than the moon in the Twilight Kingdom."

Renya looked down at her wrist, where the corner of the snowflake peaked out from her sleeve.

"You never seemed very interested in tattoos, and that ring has Snowden written all over it. It wasn't exactly a secret."

"Are you disappointed?" Renya's stomach churned as she waited for her aunt to answer.

"Fates, no child. Of course not. You think I would be upset over something fate decided? No, Sunshine. I raised you to be a strong woman, to not depend on any man. Are you that woman? At any time in the Sun Realm did you need Grayden to come and rescue you? Or did you manage on your own?"

"He did rescue me," she said hesitantly.

"Did he now? Sion said you stayed voluntarily after he and Cyrus left."

"When did you hear that?"

"I was speaking with Tumwalt."

There. It was no longer than a split second, but the tips of her aunt's ears turned red like she was embarrassed. Was it Tumwalt? Did her aunt have a thing for Grayden's advisor? Renya chose to ignore what she saw, and moved on.

"Yes, I stayed. I needed Grayden there though. I was miserable without him."

"Of course you were, Sunshine. He's your mate. Your other half. You needed him to comfort you. But that's no different than me missing you when you were gone. In my eyes, you set out to do the impossible and succeeded. Your mother must trust you if you've won the heart of one of her prized dragons. Obsessed with them as a child, she was."

"What was she like?" Renya winced and rubbed the bridge of her nose after she asked the question. Did she really want to know what her mother was like? Would it humanize her? Make it harder for Renya to do what she must?

Agatha pondered the question. "She was younger than me, of course. Independent. It seems to be a Shadow Realm trait that we all share." She looked at Renya with a knowing grin. "But thoughtful too. She was interested in the history of our people, wanting to know where we came from and why. I thought she might end up being close to the Gods, like Almory is. Some people seem to have a connection to them, almost spiritual. She seemed like she might have possessed that. Once our parents died, I had taken over the leadership of the Shadow Realm, and I thought she might train under a seer or healer. But then she met your father."

Renya closed her eyes tightly. She didn't want to hear anymore. Everything Aunt Agatha was saying resonated deep in her bones, and she kept trying to reconcile the version of Cressida that she knew with the one that Aunt Agatha grew up with.

The fire popped and hissed, and Renya watched as the flames licked the wood. Agatha sighed.

"It's not easy for me, Renya. I should have ended her in the Sunset Land. I had her, powerless and friendless, right within my grasp. But instead I fled, leaving her to lick her wounds. I couldn't do it then. I'm not sure if I would ever be able to do it."

Renya reached out and squeezed her aunt's hand. "It has to be me, anyways."

Agatha didn't respond, just continued to gaze into the fire.

"So, tell me about the wedding. How did he propose? Am I invited?"

Renya laughed, and then proceeded to relay the story to her aunt.

∞

Renya crossed her arms and pouted. "She'll just destroy your home to get to me."

"Our home, Little Fawn," Grayden gently reminded her. "And yes, we will find a permanent solution. But right now I think she needs to be locked up."

"What about the balcony outside of your room?"

"Our room, Renya," he said, and then sighed. "I guess that's as good a space as any. But she can't come into the bedroom. She's already larger than a horse and the lodge is old."

Renya grinned. "Deal." She opened the wardrobe and pulled out the first dress she could find, eager to get downstairs and join everyone for dinner. The gown she haphazardly threw on was midnight blue, reminiscent of the starry night sky, and was made of luxurious silk, draping gracefully to the floor. Adorning the gown were delicate snowflakes, intricately embroidered with shimmering silver thread, scattered across the bodice and trailing down the skirt. Every step she took in the gown resulted in a rustling noise, almost as if the gown itself was whispering a tale of winter magic.

Grayden stopped, his tunic only halfway on, and drank Renya in. "That gown is gorgeous on you, my Little Fawn."

Renya beamed, running her fingers along the material of the gown. "Doria must have made it for me after we left. I don't recognize it."

He finished pulling on his shirt and walked over to her, placing a kiss along her temple. "Remind me to thank her for taking such good care of my mate."

"I missed her so much, and she was certainly happy to see us again," Renya replied. The second they appeared on the landing outside of their room a few hours earlier, Doria was there, shaking with excitement. She fussed over the state of Grayden's hair, demanding that she allow her to cut it before he left their chambers again, and then worried about Renya's weight, proceeding to force feed her a tray of sweet pastries.

Grayden held out his arm to Renya, and they left the room.

"You've finally cut that mop on your head," came

a teasing voice from down the hall. Selenia ran towards them, embracing Renya then giving her brother a playful slug. "Renya, you look beautiful. I'm so happy you're safe and back where you belong."

"Me too. You look amazing, as always, Selenia." Her gown was a tad short for her, hinting that she'd grown taller since she last wore it, but it was beautiful nonetheless. The buttercup yellow dress displayed delicate dragonflies dancing across the fabric, their wings shimmering in iridescent hues. The dragonflies, meticulously embroidered with golden thread, were so realistic that Renya thought they might take flight at any moment.

Sion came out of the room on Selenia's left, looking slightly startled at seeing them all huddled outside in the hall.

Renya noticed Selenia shift uncomfortably when Sion joined them. She frowned, perplexed by Selenia's reaction to Sion. Renya watched Grayden, to see if he noticed it, but like usual, he didn't pick up on the things that Renya seemed to. She'd have to ask Selenia about it later.

They all walked towards the stairs, and Phillippe joined them from the far side of the hall.

"You weren't even going to wait for me?" he teased.

"I assumed you were already stuffing your face," Grayden said playfully.

Renya watched Selenia again. Not even a hint of amusement sparkled in her eyes. Something was definitely up with her. It was a joke that she should have made, not Grayden.

They continued to the dining room, and when

Renya walked in, she saw her aunt was already there, sitting next to Tumwalt. Renya watched the pair hard, trying to discern if there was something going on there, but didn't see any tell-tale signs.

She moved towards the far end of the table and sat beside her aunt, with Grayden sitting down right next to her.

"You look radiant, Sunshine."

"Thanks, Auntie. You do too." Someone provided Agatha with an upgrade in her borrowed clothing, which Renya suspected was the work of Doria. Her aunt donned a simple gray dress with tiny beaded roses all over the skirt. Renya had never seen her aunt in anything but pants and a shirt. Her hair was braided and wrapped elegantly around her head.

Almory was also there, sitting next to Tumwalt. Cyrus was on Almory's left, and they chatted animatedly and Renya wondered if they previously knew each other. They had never all dined together before, so Renya assumed this must be a special occasion so they could all discuss the upcoming plans and tactics for their stand against Cressida.

Phillippe and Selenia sat across from Renya, and she thought she detected a slight uptick in Selenia's expression as Sion glided into the seat beside her, taking up the last available chair.

Grayden stood up and clicked his knife against his glass of wine. A hush fell over the chit chatter as all eyes turned to him and Renya.

"Now that we're all together, I think it's important to fill everyone in on what has happened over the past six weeks."

Nods came from all across the table. Renya even

had trouble remembering who knew what.

"Renya now possesses her full powers, and has trained underneath Cressida. Cressida believes that Renya is on her side, and loyal to her. She is under the illusion that she is being held against her will. Cyrus, Renya's father, who is also the King of the Sun Realm, worked with Almory this afternoon to place a protection spell over the lodge and the town. As long as we reside here, it's cloaked and Cressida cannot find anyone in the village. It's the same spell that has kept the Sun Realm safe for all these years."

Only Tumwalt looked surprised by that knowledge. Grayden continued, "with the help of the Tidal and Twilight Kingdoms, as well as the Spring—"

Beauty's roar came from outside, shaking the ornate snowflake chandelier in the ceiling.

Renya's eyes widened. "Something's wrong," she said, rising from her chair and quickly running out of the dining hall towards the garden. Her dress trailed behind, and Grayden and the others were on her heels.

She threw open the solid oak doors and saw Beauty, just behind the boundaries of the lodge, pinning something to the ground. Or, rather, someone. A cry of pain echoed through the area, and Renya raced to see who Beauty had trapped under her talons.

Brandle, face white as snow, was screaming, his arms and shoulders pinched down by the juvenile dragon. Beauty's teeth were bared, and Renya could see her hot saliva dripping onto Brandle's cheek.

"Help me!" Brandle screeched, wispy magic floating from his fingertips, but nothing substantial coming forth.

Renya moved forward, unsure of what to do.

Before she could decide, Cyrus stepped forward and bound Brandle with his golden strands, holding him in place.

"Renya, call off Beauty. He's no good to us if she rips him to shreds.

"Beauty, come here."

The dragon picked up her head, and looked at Renya, and then back at Brandle. A low, guttural growl came from the back of her throat as she continued to stare down Brandle.

"Beauty!"

Reluctantly, Beauty moved aside and sauntered over to Renya, where she sat on her hind legs and looked at Renya expectedly. She sighed, then gave her a pat on her head. "Good girl, Beauty." The dragon purred and swished her large tail before glaring back at Brandle.

"How did he get in here?" Phillippe asked, staring at Brandle and then at Beauty.

Before anyone could answer, Renya saw a blur move past her at full speed.

Grayden was on the snow-covered ground, a knife raised to Brandle's throat.

"I warned you, if you touched one hair on my mate's head, I would slit your throat. And now I'm going to fulfill that promise." He raised his hand, but Renya quickly reached out with her magic and froze him in place.

Beauty let out a large bleat, as if she was disappointed that the carnage was stopped.

"Grayden, you can't kill him. Not yet. He could be useful to us." Renya looked at Brandle, his clothes torn and tattered and multiple scratches adorning his arms, no doubt from Beauty's razor sharp talons.

Renya released Grayden, and the second he was free, he growled and moved to attack Brandle once more.

"Grayden!"

He got up angrily and threw the knife into a nearby tree, planting it several inches into the bark. Without looking at Renya, he stormed off back inside the lodge.

"That was intense," Selenia said, approaching Renya cautiously. "And you have a dragon now? When was that fact going to come out?"

"Sorry, everyone. I know she's a handful—"

At this, Beauty snorted and laid down near Renya's feet.

"—but I don't know what else to do with her."

"She's a great asset to us, Renya," Phillippe said. "But how did Brandle end up here?"

Cyrus cleared his throat. "I'm guessing she found him outside of the perimeter of the spell boundary line. Since she was within the boundary when I cast the spell, she's able to bring people in. From the looks of him, she must have dragged him around a bit."

Beauty purred again, looking pleased with herself. Brandle continued to squirm in his bonds, his eyes darting around.

"What should we do with him?" Sion asked, looking at Brandle with intense hatred.

Tumwalt spoke up. "We have chains in Almory's workshop that prevent magic from being used. We can lock him up and interrogate him."

"Make sure they work," Sion said. "He's an oily asshole." He spit on Brandle's body as Cyrus hoisted Brandle up with his magic.

"Let's take him to the weapons room," Almory said, and Tumwalt and Phillippe left, with Cyrus maneuvering Brandle across the snowy garden.

Selenia looked frightened, and Renya watched a conflicted look cross Sion's face, almost as though he wanted to comfort her.

Yes, there was definitely something going on there.

"So, a dragon?" Selenia asked, watching Beauty snore at Renya's feet. "Is she a baby?"

"I think she's definitely more in the adolescent phase. She behaves like an irate teenager lately."

"I guess I've missed a lot." Selenia looked a bit hurt.

"Don't worry, Selenia. I'll fill you in on everything after I calm your brother down. I think you have some things to share with me too," Renya said, pitching the last part of her sentence lower so only Selenia could hear.

Selenia shrunk down a bit, flustered, then nodded.

"Sion, could you put Beauty back in the stables? Tell the groomsman that they need to restrain her with iron only. She breaks through everything else."

Sion sheepishly approached the slumbering dragon.

"Beauty." Renya nudged her with her toe. The dragon opened a lazy eye and glanced at Renya. "This is Sion. He's a friend. Go with him."

Like a reluctant teenager, Beauty ambled along behind Sion, swishing her tail irritatedly and looking over her shoulder at Renya with what Renya thought was a scowl on her face.

She gave Selenia an apologetic smile and went back inside the lodge, heading straight for the staircase. She was sure Grayden would be sulking in their room.

Sure enough, she opened the door to their chambers and there he was, sitting on a chair by the fireplace with his head in his hands. She tried to enter quietly, but her dress rustled as she approached the back of the chair. He tensed, but she threw her arms around him from behind and rested her head against his neck, placing a light kiss there.

He put his hands on top of hers, which were hugging his chest. She could feel his rapid breathing under her palms, feel his chest rise and fall quickly.

"Honey, you can't tear apart every single person who's wronged me."

A deep, soul crushing sigh escaped his lips.

"I can't think straight when it comes to you, Renya. I used to give Phillippe such a hard time about his impulsivity and inability to control his emotions. Now I'm ten times worse than he ever was."

"Grayden, you can't blame yourself. This bond is a part of us, and I think we are meant to feel this way for each other. There is so much good that comes with being fated, but there are things that we will struggle with too. But we'll do it together."

He closed his eyes before looking back at her.

"You're right, of course. I just—I couldn't even look at him, knowing he took you from me here in the forest and then all the grief I'm sure he caused you at the Shadow Realm."

"He mostly left me alone after Cressida started to favor me."

"I need to kill him."

Renya suppressed the slight smile that threatened to appear on her face. Men. They were all the same sometimes. "I promise, when the time comes, you can make him pay. But not now. We can use him for information, perhaps use him as a bargaining chip. We don't even know why he's here. I'm sure he's following orders from Cressida to get me back—and we need to know what those are."

"I know, all that makes sense. But it's like I'm possessed. I can't handle him being alive when he dared to touch what's mine." He practically growled the word *mine*, and Renya couldn't believe how primitive, yet sensual it was.

"I am yours," she responded, turning his head and planting a searing kiss on his lips. He moaned, tugging at her until she was perched on his lap, her legs over the arm of the chair, her head cradled in his arms.

"My Renya," he growled, licking the seam of her lips until she allowed his tongue access. "My everything."

She felt dizzy, swept up into his passionate embrace. He unlaced the back of her dress and then slid his fingers across the front of her chest, groping and exploring as she gasped. His other hand pushed aside her skirts, and she shivered as he reached her core.

"This is mine too. Only mine."

She instantly was lost, swimming in the deep pools of her desire. This was the last thing she thought would happen when she came up here to console him, but sometimes their bodies spoke more deeply than their words could.

Grayden rose from the chair, easily cradling her body against his as he took her to their bed. He set her on her feet, helping her out of the elaborate gown before shucking his own tunic and pants quickly. He groaned when he saw her, and Renya knew it was partly due to the seductive underclothing that she put on. He fiddled with the strap of her bralette, rubbing the soft lace between his fingers.

"You will be my undoing, sweetling." He rested his forehead against hers and exhaled, his breath shaky. Renya felt her core tighten with pleasure, pleased to garner such a sexual response in him.

His fingers found the lace of her bottoms, and he slowly traced a line around her thigh, while caressing her face with his other hand.

"You don't know what you do to me, Renya." He backed her carefully towards the bed until her knees bent, and then leaned over to cover her mouth with his.

She whimpered as he kissed her, needing more but unable to vocalize it as all of her senses became overwhelmed.

"I mean it, Little Fawn. From the moment I carried your unconscious body to my tent, that was it for me. Everything I ever want is right here in this bed with me. Now lie back, my sweet girl, and let me love you like you deserve."

At that moment, he placed his hand within the hollow of her back and moved her up the bed, making sure she was comfortable, and then covered her body with his. She invited his touch, and he gave a wicked grin as he felt how ready she was for him.

"You were made for me to love, Renya."

She pulled his face to hers, and kissed him deeply as he moved between her legs. The second he entered her, she was connected to him so deeply that she felt robbed during the hours of the day where they couldn't be together like this.

Grayden shuddered as he reached her end, but moved slowly, and Renya could tell he was determined to make this time slow and sensual. Their long parting took a toll on his restraint, and she knew he struggled to take things slowly. She didn't mind the quick pace he usually set, but for tonight, his languid love making was exactly what she needed. She was back where their story started, back here in the lodge where they fell in love.

Chapter Thirty

Selenia watched Sion lead Beauty towards the stables, and debated going after him. Finally, the pull towards him got the better of her, and she ran after him, her satin shoes slipping in the slick snow.

He stopped as he heard her coming, turning around. Beauty stopped as well, obeying Renya's orders to go with Sion even though she wasn't there to enforce them.

"Selenia, you're going to freeze out here!" He took off his tunic and pulled it roughly over her head. Instantly she was enveloped in his warm scent, reminding her of the sweet breeze off the summer sea.

"Sion, take your shirt back. You'll freeze now." She tried hard not to fixate on his bare chest. He was completely smooth there, without a single stray hair. She'd seen other men with their shirts off before, but they didn't compare to the sight of his olive skin against the crisp white snow. She gulped, trying to pull his shirt back over her head. Sion gave her a stern look, and she dropped the hem and let it fall to her thighs.

He marched ahead, Beauty once again following. They reached the barn, and both young grooms looked at Beauty with fear in their eyes.

"She won't hurt you," Sion said, trying to assuage their fears.

Even Selenia looked skeptical. "How did Renya

end up with a dragon?"

"I'm guessing she bonded with the newest offspring. You know Renya, she's something special."

Selenia pressed her nails into her palms, trying to calm the rough sea of jealousy about to drown her. She loved Renya. Renya was like a sister, fated to her brother. There was no need to be jealous. It was just their bond. Selenia now understood Grayden's insane behavior since Renya came into his life.

Sion passed by the grooms, who looked anywhere but at the dragon meandering past them. He moved to the enclosure at the very end, and led Beauty inside. She obeyed, but gave him an irritated look as he locked the stall door shut.

"That won't hold her for long," he said to the older of the two boys. "Tomas, that's your name, right?"

The boy nodded nervously, obviously concerned that he was going to be asked to attend to Beauty.

"Tomas, I want you to go to the blacksmith and have him fasten some iron chains for the dragon. I also want this stall reinforced with iron bars on the outside. Have him come up here and take the measurements."

Tomas looked relieved that his chore was taking him away from the dragon, who was eyeing him curiously. He scampered away, not even looking over his shoulder.

The smaller boy approached Sion. "His Lordship's horse is also foaling."

"Starlia? Finally!" Selenia squeaked. "I'll let my brother know right away. He'll want to be here for this."

"This is great news, hopefully that will put him in a better mood. I could tell he was frustrated that Renya wouldn't let him kill Brandle."

Selenia chuckled, and Sion smiled at her. She felt the stirring and longing in her stomach and quickly looked away. She was thankful for the cold, which helped mask the heat rising in her cheeks.

Sion quickly looked away from her, and she tried not to sob at the rejection and instead, followed him back up to the lodge. When they got to the top of the stairs, he started walking back down the opposite hall, no doubt to fill Grayden in on Starlia's condition.

"Sion, wait," she said, opening the door to her room. "Let me give you back your tunic."

He followed her to her bedroom door, and she tried to pull the shirt over her head, getting one of the buttons caught in her hair.

"Ouch," she said, tugging on it.

"Hold on, I'll help you. You're just pulling out your hair."

The second his hand made contact with her head, she couldn't help but lean into the palm of his hand, her cheek resting there comfortably. The slightest moan escaped her lips, wanting his touch so badly that she was practically burning.

He looked into her eyes, and she could see the lust there, and it gave her a bit of relief to know she wasn't alone in her attraction. She watched his eyes move to her lips as she parted them, trying to calm her rapid breathing.

He untangled the button from her hair, not taking his eyes off of her lips, and then he held his shirt in his hand, still watching her.

And then he was kissing her, his hand cradling the back of her head and pulling her towards him, and her stomach was suddenly fluttering, like she'd swallowed the dragonflies adorning her dress. Selenia wrapped her arms around his torso, and he groaned into her mouth.

Spurred on by his response, she stood on her tiptoes and moved her fingers along his collarbone, dancing along his strong shoulders. He grabbed her roughly, pressing her body close to his, and her eyes widened as she felt him harden against her abdomen.

She backed into her room, needing him in a way she had never needed anyone or anything before.

"What is going on here?" Phillippe's voice thundered and Selenia opened her eyes, and saw the panic in Sion's.

Phillippe's fist made contact with Sion's jaw, and he spun back away from Selenia and hit the wall.

"What do you think you're doing to my sister?" Phillippe roared, cocking his fist back to hit Sion again.

"Phillippe, stop!" Selenia screamed, trying to grab his arm before he could take another swing at Sion.

Sion's lip was bleeding, and he was trying to tug his tunic back on as quickly as he could.

"What's happening?"

Selenia groaned as Grayden joined them in the hall, the door to his own chambers wide open. Selenia could tell from his hair and the way his own tunic was on backwards that he had been busy with his own romantic encounter.

"Sion took advantage of our sister!" Phillippe fumed, pushing Selenia aside as he rounded on Sion again.

Sion stood still and quiet, awaiting his punishment.

"Please, Brother, stop!" Selenia shouted, once

again stepping in between the two men.

"Phillippe, I'm just as angry as you, but you need to control yourself," Grayden said, touching his brother on the shoulder. "Sion, explain yourself. Now." His words came out as a growl, and Selenia wasn't sure what was worse, Phillippe's fists or Grayden's tone.

"I'm sorry," Sion said quietly, his face looking pained. "I have no excuse for my behavior. I don't know what has come over me. There is no explanation I can give, no action to take other than to accept whatever punishment you see fit to bestow." He hung his head low, refusing to look at any of them.

Grayden looked at Phillippe, who nodded. "Sion, you are one of my best friends and a trusted confidant. Normally an offense like this would be banishment, exile from our homelands. But given your loyalty up until now, I won't force you to leave the Snow Lands. Instead, I'm reassigning you to the mountain camp."

"No! Don't take him away from me!" Selenia couldn't believe the pitch of her own voice, the anguish strangled in her throat.

"He's taken advantage of you, Selenia. You were feeling depressed and unsettled from Jurel's death, and he preyed upon you," Phillippe spat.

"That's not true at all," she said, looking at Sion. He refused to meet her eye, and looked at the runner under his feet.

"My decision is final," Grayden said. "Sion, leave now."

Sion turned and headed for the stairs, his head still lowered like a dog being punished by its master. Selenia felt physically ill with every step Sion took, and she panicked, not knowing how she could handle his absence.

"You can't send him away!" she yelled desperately. "He's my fated mate!"

A hush fell over the hallway, and Sion stopped, his shoulders hunched as he faced the stairs. He slowly turned around, his jaw hanging.

"What do you mean, Selenia?" Renya's voice carried down the hall as she walked towards them, her hair messy and a silk nightgown hugging her frame.

Selenia gulped and felt the tears burn in her eyes. "I'm fated to be with him."

"That's impossible," Grayden said, instantly dismissing her words. "He's too old for you."

Sion finally spoke. "Selenia, it's sweet of you to try and lie for me, but you know we are not fated. I feel affection for you, and I took advantage of your friendship. But I'm not your mate."

Selenia started sobbing, unable to control the flow of emotion that came over her. "It's true," she begged, looking at her brothers.

Renya spoke. "Grayden, you of all people should know that exceptions occur with fated bonds." Her voice was firm, but gentle, and she looked at Selenia with concern. "Selenia, tell us why you believe you're fate-bound to Sion." Renya walked over and put her arm around her, and Selenia felt a rush of affection towards her soon-to-be sister.

"When Sion and I came back from the Sun Realm, we stopped in the forest that borders the Twilight Kingdom. I was hurting, aching for Jurel—"

"See! It's grief that's driven her to these actions —"

"Phillippe." One warning word from Renya was

enough to make him shut his mouth. Renya squeezed Selenia's shoulder, encouraging her to continue.

"And I just wanted to make it stop. So, I tricked Sion into taking me to the pond where the Murcurial appeared."

Hurt flashed in Sion's eyes, and Selenia looked away, embarrassed by her sudden guilt.

Renya looked baffled. "What's a Murcurial?"

"Almost like a soothsayer," Grayden answered. "They are akin to witches and are said to know the future."

"That's elkten crap," Phillippe argued. "They are just no good pranksters."

"Anyways," Selenia continued. "I sought her out and asked her to help me forget about Jurel. She said she could make the pain lessen, but not in the way I thought. And that it would hurt at first, but I would be happy for it in the end. She touched my forehead, and then...I knew. Sion is my mate."

Selenia looked at Sion, not caring about anyone's reaction but his. He looked confused, and disbelief was evident in his dark eyes.

"I know it's unbelievable, but I think somehow the lack of magic has masked our bonds. I think the Murcurial broke through whatever was blocking me from feeling the bond. But it's true. I know in my heart that I am fated for Sion."

Grayden looked torn, like he wanted to believe her, but Phillippe looked skeptical. Renya gave her shoulders another squeeze, as if to let Selenia know she was on her side.

Selenia's eyes darted to Sion again, and he met hers, walking slowly towards her. He stopped right in front of her, and Renya let go of her shoulders and moved back to Grayden's side. Sion fell to his knees, looking up at her.

"If you are truly my mate, Selenia Snowden, then I am the lucky one." He kissed her knuckles, his brown eyes piercing hers. "But I must confess, I don't feel the certainty that you do. I admire you, care for you...lust after you," he whispered the last line, "but I don't know that I'm fated to you."

She touched his cheek. "I understand, Sion. I'm sorry you had to find out this way, but I couldn't have you sent away. Being around you hurts me, knowing you don't feel our bond, but having you gone —I wouldn't survive it." The words rushed out, and she normally would have been embarrassed at such a confession, but she'd already opened herself up wide and let the raw truth tumble out.

"Grayden. You can't possibly send him away and subject your sister to more pain." Renya looked expectantly at Grayden.

"Yes he can!" Phillippe thundered.

"Phillippe Snowden! If you don't stop acting like a world-class asshole, I'm going to write to Esmeralda and tell her what a hot-headed, idiotic dick you are!"

Selenia suppressed a smile, and even Grayden looked impressed at Renya's threat.

"I don't know what half of those things you said mean," Phillippe retorted. "But I get the gist of it. I don't like it, but I won't interfere." He turned his back and headed down the stairs.

"Thank you," Selenia mouthed at Renya, and she returned a small smile.

"It's getting late," Grayden said, looking at the

wooden clock hanging behind him. "I say we finish talking about this in the morning."

"Oh! Grayden!" Selenia exclaimed. "I forgot to tell you, Starlia is having her foal!"

His eyes lit up, and he grabbed Renya's hand excitedly. "Come, my sweet Little Fawn. I've been waiting for this for a long time."

As Grayden pulled Renya away, Sion looked down at Selenia. She tried to read his expression, but it was hard for her to tell what he was thinking. She hoped that once his side of the bond was awoken, things would become easier for them. Instead, they stood there and looked at each other awkwardly, until Sion kissed her hand and left for his own room. Selenia sunk down onto the floor, her back against the wall, and cried.

Chapter Thirty-One

T he little filly wobbled on her legs, trying to nurse as Starlia looked on proudly. Renya was so grateful to see Starlia, and her heart was overjoyed at the birth of her daughter. Grayden was insanely proud as well, boasting at how easy the delivery was and how good his mare was with her filly.

"What are you going to call her?" Renya asked, watching the foal attempt to gallop around the pen.

"Whatever you'd like, Little Fawn. She's yours."

Renya felt her heart flutter. She dearly loved Starlia, and the thought of having her own horse, graceful and majestic, excited her.

But then the little filly tripped and landed head-first in a pile of droppings and that vision went right out the window. Renya laughed at the pony as she stood up, shaking her head as if confused about what just happened.

"So, what's her name, Little Fawn?"

Renya thought for a second, her eyes drawn to the sweet little creature. "Talia."

"Talia," Grayden repeated. "I like that."

They watched the mother and foal bond for a few more minutes, and then Grayden put his arm around Renya. "Should we go to bed?"

"Go to bed...or go to sleep?" Renya teased.

"Both," Grayden responded, laughing heartily.

The sound made Renya's chest tighten and her mood lighten. There was nothing better sounding than Grayden's laughter.

Grayden fed Starlia a few arctic pears and then patted Talia on the head, then Renya headed down to the far side of the stables to check on Beauty before they left.

The dragon purred the second Renya was near, swishing her long tail excitedly. She had almost doubled in size since Renya met her, and her wings were now over four feet wide. She was growing too quickly, Renya thought with a pang. She wasn't sure how she could possibly keep a full-grown dragon in this world long term. Maybe Almory or Cyrus would have some ideas.

Beauty began ramming the door of the stall and Renya sighed. As much as she loved Beauty, it wasn't good for her to be restrained and locked up like this. She was no better than Cressida, keeping her pets in her glass cage.

"Can you ride her, Little Fawn?"

Renya looked at Beauty, her tail switching back and forth and her eyes on Renya's every move. "I did a few times in the Shadow Realm, in the forest."

"Why don't you try here? She's obviously annoyed at being cooped up, and I can feel your tension." He moved behind Renya, and she felt his strong hands press into her shoulders.

"Mmmmm," she moaned, arching like a waking cat into his arms. "That feels nice."

"Careful, Little Fawn," he warned, his hands wandering down to her waist before he wrapped them around her. "Or neither of us will get any sleep tonight."

Renya felt some of the tension in her body leave

as she chuckled. "No matter what I do, that's usually the case."

"Has your insatiable appetite finally got the better of you?" he asked, eyes sparkling mischievously.

Renya elbowed him in the ribs and danced just outside of his grasp. "Do we have a saddle or reins I could try with her?"

She followed Grayden to the tack room, and he sorted through the bridles and saddles before tying a few together.

"I think this might work," he said, pulling at the leather to test it.

Renya nodded, nervous but eager to ride Beauty again. She waltzed back to the stall and unbolted the door.

"Be careful," Grayden warned, but Renya just stuck her tongue out at him. He laughed again, and Renya could feel his eyes on her as she worked to arrange the makeshift saddle and bridle on Beauty. The dragon protested a bit, stomping around and nudging at Renya while she adjusted the reins, but then sat patiently when she realized she was going to get to leave the stall.

"I'd recommend taking her out the back entrance of the stables," Grayden commented, as he stepped back to allow Renya to coax Beauty away from the other horses and towards the back.

Renya attempted to swing her leg over Beauty's back, but the dragon had grown so much that she could no longer hoist herself up. Grayden came over and clasped his hands together and gave her a boost up. She settled herself in the saddle, feeling a bit uneasy. Beauty was even taller than the last time she rode her, and she seemed more excited than usual. Renya was afraid that she'd take off running and throw her.

"Calm, Beauty," Renya murmured, stroking the dragon's neck. Beauty purred and then started walking towards the open door. Renya turned briefly and saw Grayden behind her, encouraging them.

"Okay Beauty, let's do this." She pulled on the reins, and Beauty took off, careening through the snow with ease.

Renya was thrown back for a moment, unbalanced, before she righted herself in the saddle and held on tightly.

Laughing, she threw her head back, enjoying the snow whipping around her and the cool wind rushing through her hair. The air stung a bit, but the cold was nothing compared to the exhilarating pace that Beauty set.

Be careful, my love. I just got you back.

Renya grinned, her chest light. Grayden was by her side again, her aunt was safe, and she was momentarily protected from Cressida by her father's magic. Giddy, she urged Beauty faster, her worries seeming to roll off of her with every step Beauty took. Beauty ran faster, and turned her direction back towards the lodge.

"Careful, Beauty," Renya said, as the dragon continued a grueling pace towards the gardens. Beauty continued forward, and Renya grasped the reins, pulling back. "Beauty, no! We're going to crash!"

But the dragon continued forward, and Renya closed her eyes, preparing to smash into the brick wall surrounding the garden.

But then, a feeling of weightlessness stirred in

her belly, and she could feel the air from Beauty's wings flapping. Renya heard a giant 'whoop!' from Grayden below. Wait, below?

She opened her eyes, and clung to the reins. Beauty soared over the garden, circling and gaining more and more altitude.

"Beauty! You're doing it, girl!"

The dragon purred again and switched directions, heading back towards the village. Renya could see the shocked look of the few villagers left on the streets, and they began pointing and waving.

Renya could feel Grayden's panic and worry through their bond, and she tried to urge Beauty back towards the stables, but the dragon had a mind of her own. She flew past the village, and soared over the snow-covered foothills leading to the mountain range. Renya's stomach dropped as Beauty suddenly started to descend. Renya watched in amazement as Beauty finally reached the ground, her wings fluttering softly until she landed delicately, right in front of a small stream. The water flowed freely here, and Beauty dipped her head and drank.

"Thirsty girl, huh Beauty?" Renya cooed at the dragon, trying to remain calm even though her heart was racing from the excitement of flying on Beauty and the anxiety she felt radiate from her bond.

Beauty drank for a few more seconds, then started running again, then gliding, then flew high up into the air. The higher she went, the more Renya shivered.

Almost as though she sensed her discomfort, Beauty croaked a strange throaty sound, and then headed back towards the stables. A few minutes later, the lodge came into view and she could feel Grayden's relief. Beauty gracefully landed in front of the stables, and Grayden rushed over to help Renya off.

"I can't believe it, Renya! You flew! On a dragon!"

"Way to state the obvious," she said, grinning at Grayden. He helped her off, and her feet hit the ground. She swayed a bit, off balance from the sudden descent and the adrenaline coursing through her system. Grayden's protective arms instantly steadied her, and she let herself be taken into his embrace.

"Have I told you how magnificent you are, my mate?" he asked, nuzzling her neck and then kissing the spot right behind her ear.

"Daily," she teased, enjoying his affection.

Beauty purred, watching the pair, and then circled them both before heading back into the stable.

Chapter Thirty-Two

G rayden held his dagger right at Brandle's throat. "I should slit you from ear to ear for touching my mate," he growled, his voice thunderous and echoing off of the walls of the room.

The chamber was once a dungeon, but they hadn't used it as such for many years. Grayden's father converted it to a weapons storage, but the chains still remained. Brandle was in the center of the room, chained to a chair, pale and cowering as Grayden continued to threaten his life.

"Do you not have words for me?" Grayden continued, jerking Brandle up by the collar of his robes. "Did you think there would be no consequences for touching what is mine?"

Brandle sputtered, eyes wide and darting. Grayden released his hold and Brandle fell back into the chair, which creaked and shifted with the impact. Grayden roared and threw the dagger at Brandle, feeling a bit of satisfaction as it just grazed his neck before impaling the chair he was sitting on.

"Grayden," Cyrus warned. Grayden continued pacing the chamber, fisting his hair in his hands. "Do we need to do this without you?"

Grayden sighed, trembling and clenching his knuckles. He promised Renya he wouldn't kill Brandle... yet.

Phillippe moved in, standing in front of Brandle. "Tell us why you are here, or else I'm going to let my brother gut you like a fish."

Brandle shook again, and Grayden rolled his eyes as he saw a gleam of a tear in Brandle's eye. Weak. He was weak, hiding behind his powerful cousin and his magic.

"Fine, I'll tell you everything. Just please, don't hurt me," he whined, staring at Grayden. Grayden grinned, relieved that his presence was enough to frighten Brandle.

"Then speak, you disgusting coward," Phillippe said, his arms crossed in front of his chest.

"She's coming here to the Snow Lands. She might be on her way now already. She wants her daughter back."

Grayden growled again, and this time Cyrus came over and put a gentle hand on Grayden's shoulder. "She's not going to take her again, son. I've made sure of that. I'll protect her with my life."

"I will too," Grayden replied, grinding his teeth. He hated relying on Cyrus's magic for everything. He wanted to protect Renya himself, protect his lands and people.

"Is she bringing her army?" Cyrus asked Brandle. He shook his head no, and Grayden felt a bit of the tension leave his body.

"She must think she can come in and grab Renya and leave," Phillippe said, still eyeing Brandle carefully. "Are you sure your magic will hold up?"

"It should," Cyrus said. "It's weaker than it's ever been, cloaking two separate areas, but it should hold for a little longer. We need to start making plans, though. I can feel myself weakening."

"Just in case, I think we need to restrict everyone in the village and have them shelter inside, and I want everyone in the lodge to wait her out in the sublevels." Grayden looked at Phillippe, and he nodded his agreement.

Just then, a loud roar echoed throughout the lodge, terrifying and deep. Grayden's heart sank. She was already here.

"Stay with Brandle," he ordered Sion. "And don't kill him," he added, knowing Sion wanted him dead just as much as he did.

"Grayden, go to my daughter," Cyrus instructed. "Don't let Renya anywhere near Cressida, and don't let her out of your sight. You know how she is, she'll want to sacrifice herself."

Grayden nodded, but hoped in his heart that Renya's last promise to him was enough to deter her from that. "Phillippe, I want you to go outside and protect the village. If Cyrus's magic holds, she shouldn't be able to see anyone."

Phillippe left without saying a word, and Grayden headed in the direction of the stables. Renya was often there during the day, stroking her new filly and talking to Beauty. Grayden was almost certain that the dragon understood every word and command Renya gave her.

He rushed up the stairs to the main floor, issuing orders to every servant he met to stay inside the lodge, before leaving through the back door. He trudged towards the stables, the heavy snow making it difficult to move quickly.

Another roar, followed by deafening silence.

Grayden looked up, and saw Cressida on the back of one of her dragons, only a few yards away from the lodge, circling in the sky. He stopped, feeling exposed in the middle of the snowy field. But Cyrus's magic held, and she circled around and around, irritation easy to read in her posture.

He heard a loud roar from inside the barn, and knew Beauty was agitated. Ignoring Cressida above him, he ran for the stable, throwing open the door and closing it against the cold air.

"Grayden!" Renya exclaimed, and quickly ran to his side, fear in her eyes. "She's here!"

"Shhhh, it's okay. She can't find you. Everything looks abandoned. Cyrus told me that she doesn't know of this type of magic, so she won't even suspect that we are hiding in plain sight."

Renya nodded, her fear preventing her from speaking. Grayden grabbed her hand, holding it in his. Her hand was cold, and she was shaking. He wasn't sure if it was from the temperature or fear.

"She won't take you from me again, Renya."

Her bottom lip trembled, and Grayden knew she was trying so hard to be strong. He understood her fear, because it was the same as his. His dreams kept him up at night, horrible nightmares where she was ripped from his arms. He often awoke, covered in sweat, breathing unevenly until he found Renya next to him. He held her tight in those moments, not wanting to wake her, but needing the comfort her warm body provided him.

He did that again now, covering her body with his, feeling her tremble beneath him. He kissed her hairline, trying to comfort her the best way he knew, and in turn, comforting himself as well.

Beauty continued roaring, but it was a panicky, throaty roar. Grayden wasn't sure if she was picking up on Renya's nervous energy, or if she could sense the other dragon.

Renya sighed from inside the protective cocoon of Grayden's arms and then carefully untangled herself. Grayden watched her walk towards the stall that held Beauty, and undo the iron latch keeping her contained. She comforted Beauty, making soft crooning noises, and the dragon began to settle.

"Do you think she's gone yet?" Renya asked him, her eyes moist with unshed tears.

"I'll go check," Grayden said, walking towards the door. He opened it, and peered outside. The snowstorm had picked up, and visibility from the barn to the lodge was poor, but he didn't see any sign of her. He stood at the door for a few more minutes, making sure she was really gone before heading back to Beauty's stall.

"I think she's left, Little Fawn."

Renya exhaled, looking at Grayden, and then ran over to him. He pulled her into his arms again, and held her for a long time, listening to her heartbeat against the howling wind outside.

∞

"I think we need to make our move now," Renya said, her voice strong and steady. Grayden watched on with pride, glad she was asserting herself and becoming the leader she was meant to be. "She'll only keep searching, and next time, I imagine she'll bring her entire army."

Tumwalt, Almory, Phillippe, Agatha and Sion all joined them in the cabinet room. After Grayden and Renya left the stables, they immediately called a meeting. It was time for them to stop planning and start acting.

"How will we draw her to the Sun Realm?" Agatha asked.

"Brandle," Grayden said. "We'll force him to send her a falcon stating that Renya will be there, held against her will."

"Then what do we do with him?" Sion asked, and Grayden knew he wished the answer to be death.

"We bring him with us," Renya said, looking at Sion. "I know that's not what you want, Sion, and it's not what I want either. But if something goes wrong, perhaps we can use him as a bargaining chip. But I do promise you this, Sion. He won't be allowed to go free. Even if Cressida bargains for his life, we will track him down."

"Do you promise?" Sion asked.

"I promise, Sion," Renya said.

"So, what next?" Phillippe asked.

"We coordinate with our allies: the Spring Lands, the Twilight and the Tidal Kingdoms. I need to let them know immediately, since Tristan was going to come here next and will need to change directions," Grayden said. The second he mentioned the Tidal Kingdom, his brother sat up a bit straighter. Renya must be right, Grayden thought. Phillippe was very interested in Esmeralda.

"And we're all meeting in the Sun Realm?" Tumwalt asked quietly. He was still cautious around Grayden, not wishing to invoke his wrath. Tumwalt was also careful to be respectful to Renya. Grayden was glad that his advisor finally understood her importance in their world, and in his life.

"Correct," Grayden said. "This evening, I'll send a falcon to Tristan, Kalora, Samatra and Thesand. We'll march under Cyrus's cloaking spell, and the Tidal Kingdom will travel along the river with the Spring Lands to avoid detection. Kalora's army will stay close to the trees in the Twilight forest and then move at night in the desert. Hopefully we can all get there undetected. When we arrive, that's when we'll force Brandle to write to his queen."

"Does anyone foresee any problems with what we've proposed?" Renya asked.

Almory shook his head, pleased with the plan. Tumwalt stroked his chin, and then voiced his agreement. Phillippe and Sion both agreed.

"It's a good plan, daughter," Cyrus said, looking at Renya with the same pride that Grayden shared. "Let's put everything into motion."

∞

The next few days flew by, with everyone working furiously to prepare. Renya trained with Cyrus, picking up some additional pointers on how to wield the magic of the sun. Grayden watched, pleased to see his mate bond with her father and grow even stronger in her magic. For his part, Grayden trained hard with Phillippe, Charly, and Sion, working their muscles until they bulged from the blood flow.

Tumwalt and Almory oversaw the village, ensuring every resident knew to go to the lodge as soon as any sign of trouble came. Almory and Tumwalt would both stay behind, at Grayden's insistence. If something happened, they would be in charge of securing the Snow Lands. Dimitri would come to the Sun Realm, and provide assistance to those injured in battle.

They all worked incredibly hard, right up until the night before. Grayden spent several hours that night in the cabinet room, reiterating their strategy and preparing for any unforeseen circumstances or problems they might encounter. Only when he saw Renya yawn, did he finally decide to dismiss everyone.

"Go get some rest. We leave at first light," he said, and watched everyone file out of the room, leaving him and Renya alone.

"Come with me, Little Fawn. I have a surprise for you," he said, grabbing her hand and leading her out of the room and up the stairs to their chambers.

They entered their room, and Renya looked around, her forehead wrinkled. "What's the surprise?" she asked. "Or was this just your attempt to get me in your bed so you can seduce me?"

"You'll see," he teased. "Wait here for a few minutes." He went into the bathroom, getting to work.

"The bathroom? What kind of surprise could you possibly have in there?" He could hear her mocking him through the closed bathroom door.

After a few minutes, he called her in.

Grayden looked around the room, pleased with how it turned out.

While they were all concentrating on the battle ahead, Grayden reached out to the best stone cutters in the village and had them replace the bathtub in their chambers. The tub was made of a beautiful piece of carved marble, smooth and warm colored in the light of the candles that he lit on every surface of the bathroom.

Lotus petals floated in the water, and Grayden knew the lavender bath salts he put in would delight Renya.

"It's...amazing, Grayden!" she beamed, happiness shining in her eyes. "How did you pull this off?"

"I have my ways, Little Fawn. I must admit, it was hard to keep it a secret. I tried so hard not to think about it so you wouldn't find out."

"Well, I didn't suspect a thing," she said, quickly disrobing. He watched her remove her clothing, excited but also worried. He wanted nothing more than to spend the rest of his life here, in his home, with her by his side. He wasn't sure if this would be their last night together, or if they'd have an entire lifetime of moments like these. Trying not to dwell on it, he brought his mind back to the present, watching Renya slip into the tub, giving him an encouraging look.

Grayden breathed deeply, as Renya dunked underneath the water, lotus petals floating around her. He stripped down and then crawled in behind her, dragging her across his lap and against his chest.

"I thought we got a bigger tub so we could have our own space?" she teased.

Grayden growled, and then playfully bit her earlobe. She sighed, and he kissed her neck, slowly making his way down to her collar bone. He placed another nip along her shoulder, and she began to squirm in his arms.

"Hold still, or I'll stop," he warned, and she giggled and splashed water back at him.

"I'm never going to do what you tell me to do," she threatened.

"You will right now," he replied darkly, dipping

his hands under the water to stroke the inside of her thigh. She shivered under his touch, creating ripples on the surface of the water, and he knew he had won.

"That's my good girl," he whispered huskily against her ear, his hands moving closer and closer to her center. "My sweet Renya. Hold still and let me love you."

He moved his fingers to her folds, and she jerked back against his touch. The second she moved, he stopped what he was doing.

"What did I say, Little Fawn?"

She didn't answer, but he could see the red creep down her neck and he knew it wasn't the temperature of the water causing her to flush. He continued gently kissing her along her neck, then replaced his fingers.

"Grayden," she whispered, as he began teasing her again, just enough to make her tremble but nothing more than that.

"Do you need me, my love?"

"Yes," she whimpered, leaning back farther into his muscular chest.

"I think we need to get clean first," he said, grabbing a tiny bottle and lathering up his hands. She whined the second he moved his hands away from her flesh, but he just grinned. She'd teased and taunted him enough during their time together, and he was enjoying the erotic game he was playing.

He ran his fingers through her hair, cleaning the strands and humming lightly as he worked the soap through.

"You're a tease!" she accused.

"It takes one to know one. Now hush. You're distracting me." But in truth, he was the one hoping to distract her. He knew tomorrow they would leave the protection of the lodge, and they wouldn't be able to be together again until it was over. He wanted to give her this one night, these few hours, to relax and try to forget what was coming.

She sighed impatiently, and then he gasped as he felt her fingers circle around him.

"You were saying?" she asked sweetly, and he growled a low growl.

"Keep playing with fire and you're going to get burned," he warned.

She slid her hand up and down his length and then turned her face towards him, a defiant smile evident.

"That's it, you've done it now." He stood up and stepped out of the tub before she could react, and then scooped her up in his arms. He carried her to the bed, dripping wet, while she protested.

"We're going to ruin the bedding," she complained.

"I don't care." He laid her on the bed, sweeping her wet hair off of her face before kissing her. He joined her on the bed, and rolled on top of her. She reached out to stroke his chest, but he grabbed her hands and held them above her head.

"Now you're going to pay for not listening to your mate," he said.

Her eyes flashed with desire, and he was glad. He leaned back in and kissed her, swallowing the smart remark that he was sure she was about to give him. He deepened the kiss, and he felt all the resistance leave her body as she melted into the furs under her.

He gave her one last kiss on her swollen lips

before beginning a trail of kisses down her body. He lapped up every drop of water that clung to her skin, and every drop that dripped down on her from his wet hair.

"What have you learned?" he growled.

"Absolutely nothing," she said, eyes sparkling. He groaned, loving the fire she possessed. She was truly of the Sun Realm. She burned so brightly for him; she was a beacon of hope for everything in his life.

"I love you," he said, now in the mood for tenderness.

"I love you too. Forever.

"Always," he agreed.

Chapter Thirty-Three

S ion's back ached. He'd been sitting against the wall for hours. Phillippe and Charly offered to guard Brandle, but Sion refused. He would be the one to ensure that Brandle didn't escape or slink off into the night. Cyrus enforced the room with magic, but Sion still felt like it needed to be constantly monitored.

He stretched his legs, his boots scraping against the stone floor. He was glad to be back in his normal clothing, thankful to be back in his home lands. He scratched his head, pondering all that happened since he had been back. His mind instantly went to Selenia. Was it possible? Was he actually fated to her? It would certainly explain the feelings he'd been having towards her. From the very little he knew about fated matings, they usually appeared past the teenage years, but before middle age. Certainly he hadn't had feelings towards her the last time he saw her, but that must have been two years ago by now. Grayden had feelings for Renya before they were fated, didn't he? He wished he could ask Grayden, but he had the feeling that a conversation around Selenia wouldn't be well-received.

The patter of quiet footsteps drew his attention away from his thoughts. He recoiled into the shadows, trying to discern who would have business down here.

Her slight frame came into view as she turned the corner, her auburn hair free and flowing down her back. She was wearing a white nightdress, with a crimson robe cinched around her narrow waist.

Sion watched Selenia approach the door to the weapons room, trying to figure out what she was doing down here. When she turned, he saw the glint from Grayden's dagger gleam in the torch light. She tried to open the door quietly, but it wouldn't budge.

"It's locked by magic, Selenia."

She jumped and dropped the dagger, the sound of clattering metal hitting stone bounced off the walls.

"Sion!" she squealed, her face red and flushed. He picked himself up off the ground and walked over to her, picking up the dagger and inspecting it.

"How did you manage to steal your brother's dagger?"

She bit her lip. "It's not his. It's Renya's. He had a copy made for her. I knew they would most likely be —preoccupied this evening, so I swiped it from their room."

"Why? Why kill Brandle?" Sion rubbed his jaw, looking down at her. He fought the desire to run his fingers through her ringlets. She looked so beautiful, pale in the light of the torches, her hair wild and free.

"You know why," she said, looking down at her silk slippers.

Sion frowned. "For me? Selenia, I'm not worth killing for. I wouldn't want your soul muddled and darkened with murder."

She didn't say anything and continued to look down. Sighing, he gently turned her chin up to look at him. He was startled to see her expression, her eyes moist and her lips curled as if she was in pain. He longed to pull her against him, to comfort her in his arms.

"You can't kill him, Selenia. We need him right now to feed information to Cressida."

Her face fell. "Was no one going to tell me this?"

Sion chuckled. "In all fairness, I don't think anyone anticipated you coming down here to murder him."

When he said the word 'murder', she flinched. Sion wondered if she would have been able to do it had she gotten through the magically enforced door. The Selenia he knew from childhood wouldn't have been able to. But this grown-up version of her, this fierce woman with passion in her heart and fire in her eyes could do anything.

"I don't know what came over me," she sobbed, tears streaming down her face.

Sion melted. "Hush, my darling. Come here." He held out his arms and she ran into them, sobbing against his chest. He felt himself respond to her nearness, and he pushed away the instinct, trying so hard to resist this woman that he was now starting to think he was destined to be with.

"Oh Sion, I don't know what I'm doing. I never wanted you to find out we are fated. I'm so confused, but I also couldn't have you sent away. I'm so sorry."

"Shhhhhh...dry your eyes, Selenia. You did nothing wrong. I'm just sorry that I don't feel the certainty you do. But I won't lie, I do desire you."

She looked up at him, heat flushing in her cheeks and down her neck. "Really?"

Sion swallowed hard. "Selenia, I'd have to be struck dumb not to want a woman like you."

She trembled in his arms, and he could no longer resist her. He didn't want her to feel rejection, because there was no part in him that could ever reject her. He brought his mouth to hers, kissing her gently and thoroughly. He felt her warmth under his mouth, felt her eagerness and her sweetness. May the Fates strike him down, he thought, but he was seriously becoming addicted to Selenia Snowden.

∞

The second they crossed into the desert, Sion's eyes instantly became focused on Selenia. She was dressed more appropriately this time, wearing a thin, silk top with only tiny straps to hold it up, and a light skirt that stopped at her knees. He gulped, trying to peel his eyes away from her exposed legs. She looked pale under the harsh light of the desert, but it gave her an ethereal quality.

How could he be bound to her and not know it? What did that creature—a Murcurial?—do to her? And more importantly, could she do it to him, too? If he managed to live past this war, he would seek the creature out, and pay whatever price he could to free his side of the bond so he could be with her fully.

"Are you okay?" Grayden hung back, looking at Sion carefully.

"Honestly, I don't know."

"I know I said some things back at the lodge—"

"Don't worry about it, Grayden. If I had a sister, I'm sure I would act the same way."

His friend nodded, his eyes up ahead on Renya. He noticed Grayden's eyes never strayed from her for long, and he envied how sure they both were in their love for each other. Sion never thought of love, never thought he'd live long enough to have it. He was broken;

irreparable damage was done to him at the Shadow Realm, but for the first time in his life, he felt a sense of hope. Perhaps there was a happily ever after for him as well.

Sion watched Grayden gallop ahead on his horse, eager to ride next to Renya, especially as they approached the Sun Realm. They all stood in front of the gate, waiting.

"How did you get in last time?" Cyrus asked.

"We crawled through a drain," Phillippe said. "Not quite the warm welcome I was looking for."

Cyrus laughed, and then lifted his fingers as a golden gush of air flew out, and the gate opened.

"Once all the soldiers are here from the other kingdoms, I'll cloak it again."

"What do we do with him?" Charly asked, nodding towards Brandle, who was chained and bound on a horse, tethered behind Charly.

"We have an inescapable dungeon," Cyrus replied.

"Tell me about it," Phillippe mumbled. "I got stuck in the passageway."

They filed into the city, and it was bustling with people in every corner. The citizens waved and gasped as they saw Cyrus.

"I guess I should have let everyone know I was back," he said absentmindedly.

They rode along the golden streets, people stopping and staring as their entourage passed by. Phillippe waved and winked at everyone they passed until Grayden smacked him on the back of his head. Sion heard Selenia giggle from behind him, amused by her brother's antics. He slowed down, riding beside her.

"A bit different than the last time you rode through here?"

"Yes," she replied. "It's quite beautiful. I'm envious that Renya has a place where she belongs."

"Selenia. You belong in the Snow Lands. Who knows, Cyrus might eventually want Renya to lead here, and I know Grayden will follow her anywhere. You could be in charge of the Snow Lands."

"I don't have usable magic," she said.

"If everything works out right, you might."

"Do you have any magic left?"

He frowned, thinking. "Perhaps a little. Cressida —" he cringed at even saying the name aloud—"would grant me little bits of power to do her errands. I haven't used magic since. It feels—tainted to me."

Understanding shone on Selenia's face as she gave him a sympathetic smile. "I know the feeling."

"Of course you do. I'm sorry my dar—Selenia."

She waved away his apology.

"Maybe you're right, maybe one day we'll have our full powers back—and I'll be able to control mine and yours will be pure again."

Before he could respond, Phillippe let out a loud whoop from behind them. Sion turned, and saw hundreds of soldiers marching towards the gates. The first group entering the city were wearing breastplates with shiny scales that seemed to catch on the light from the sun. They all carried large tridents made of pewter. Leading them was King Tristan, Sion guessed. He wore the same style of armor, but his helmet had the figure of an eel carved into it. Riding next to him was a woman in a periwinkle flowing gown, a pearl crown perched upon her long hair. Sion watched as Phillippe flicked his horse's reins and raced towards the pair. As soon as Phillippe approached, the woman's face lit up. Sion's jaw dropped slightly as Phillippe pulled a little trinket out of his pocket and handed it to her. He wasn't close enough to see what it was, but the woman looked incredibly pleased and tucked it carefully in the woven bag she wore.

"Wow. Phillippe has a crush," Selenia said, her eyes on her brother. "Never thought I'd ever see him try and woo a woman."

"Who is she exactly? I know she's obviously from the Tidal Kingdom..."

"Esmeralda, King Tristan's sister. She's pretty good friends with Renya now."

The Tidal soldiers continued to march into the city, Tristan riding ahead to speak with Grayden, and his sister siding up to talk to Renya. It was apparent that the Tidal princess wasn't a sure rider, and Phillippe trailed after her, watching her carefully.

Behind the Tidal soldiers came the Spring Land army. Dressed in dark green and with daggers at their hips and a bow slung over their shoulders, they moved quickly in cadence. Sion had never met Samatra or Thesand, but they rode ahead of their army, greeting Renya and Grayden as if they were old friends. Sion felt a burst of pride in his chest, proud that his friend assumed his role as leader so well. He'd come a long way from that scared teenage boy whose head Sion had to dunk in the trough to sober him up. Sion knew Grayden and Renya would make fine rulers, and he would help them however he could.

More and more soldiers entered the city, heading for the barracks on the east side of the palace. Sion hung back, letting the leaders talk. After being away for so long, he wasn't sure what his place was anymore. No longer a spy, but not quite a member of Grayden's family.

Selenia stayed by his side, and he was grateful for her presence. Somehow, she grounded him, made him feel less alone. They watched together as the final wave of soldiers, this group from the Twilight Kingdom, shuffled past. Selenia let out an excited sigh as they marched past.

"What is it?" he asked.

"Queen Kalora brought Julietta. I was hoping to see her again. She's been a good friend to me." She gestured towards a blonde haired girl wearing a bright orange dress.

"I'm glad you have someone your age to talk with."

She scowled. "Age doesn't matter, Sion."

Chapter Thirty-Four

Selenia sat in her borrowed room, with Julietta rifling through the trunk Selenia brought with her. The sun shined in through the open window, and Selenia could hear birds chirping. The room was decorated richly, with gold trim and velvet everywhere. The woodwork was all a dark mahogany, from the four-poster bed to the wardrobe cabinet.

"What's this large package in here?" Julietta pulled out a wrapped parcel.

"I completely forgot about that!" Selenia said, taking the package from Julietta. She unwrapped the corner of the gown, showing it to her friend. "I got it at the market in the city, actually. It's for Renya. A wedding dress."

"Selenia, that was so sweet of you! It's gorgeous," Julietta said wistfully, carefully inspecting the fabric.

"I'll give it to her tonight. With everything that happened back at the lodge it slipped my mind."

"This is the second time you've alluded to something big happening at your home. You can trust me, Selenia."

"I know. It's just...unbelievable." Selenia now understood what Grayden and Renya went through. Fated mates were so unusual, and hers was unorthodox as well.

"Well, I suppose the story actually begins in the

285

forest near your castle…"

Julietta's eyes widened as Selenia told her all about her first visit with the Murcurial, and then her second.

"What did she do, Selenia? To make you forget Jurel?"

Selenia stared out the window, watching the chiffon curtains flutter in the wind. "I haven't forgotten, exactly. But it's less painful…"

"What happened?"

"She…she unlocked my fated bond."

"What?" Julietta's voice raised higher than Selenia had ever heard it.

"Yes…I'm—I'm fated to Sion."

"Sion? That good-looking man you were riding with?"

Again, jealousy pooled in Selenia's stomach and she had to breathe deeply, calming her involuntary reaction to Julietta's comments about her mate.

"Yes. It's awkward because it's only one-sided. Whatever that witch did, it was only on my end. He doesn't feel the bond like I do."

"Selenia, that must be so difficult, to love someone who doesn't love you."

Selenia bit her lip. Did she love Sion? She certainly felt attracted to him, wanted him, cared for him…was this love? And did he love her? She knew he desired her, and there were those tender moments when they traveled together…

There was a knock on the door, and Selenia rose to her feet and opened it.

"Renya! I thought you'd be busy preparing."

Renya walked in, smiling at Julietta. "It's so nice

to see you again, Julietta." Renya turned back towards Selenia. "No, I don't think at this point there's much left to do. Sion and Grayden are forcing Brandle to summon Cressida as we speak. I just wanted to check on you and see how you're doing." She gave Selenia a pointed look.

"I'm doing okay. Really," she added, as Renya's face scrunched up in disbelief.

"If you need someone to talk to, I'm always here. And probably someone who understands the most."

"I appreciate you so much, Renya. I'm so glad we're going to be sisters. Speaking of, I have something I've been meaning to give you."

Selenia walked back over to the trunk and retrieved the wrapped dress.

"Selenia, what's this—" Renya gasped as she unwrapped the gown. "Selenia, this is incredible." Renya's fingers danced along the rosettes and then smoothed the fabric. "But surely, you'll want to keep such a magnificent gown for yourself—"

"It's a Sun Realm wedding dress."

Renya's jaw dropped, and Selenia saw the slightest bit of moisture coat her eyes.

"Selenia, this is so thoughtful, I can't believe it."

"I wanted you to feel like the princess you are on your wedding day. Here in our world, it's tradition for the bride's mother to make her wedding gown. I knew that wasn't going to be the case for you, but I still wanted you to have something special from your first home."

A few tears trickled down Renya's cheek. Selenia looked over and saw that Julietta's eyes were misty as well.

"This is the sweetest gift I've ever gotten," Renya

said, crushing Selenia in a tight hug.

"I know my brother is quite the gift-giver where you're concerned, so I doubt that. But I'm glad you like it."

∞

Selenia paced the halls, unable to sleep. She was nervous that something would go wrong tomorrow, worried that the people she cared about would be taken from her. She still remembered how she felt when Jurel was slain right in front of her, and she envisioned the same thing happening to Grayden, or Renya, or...Sion. The thought of him lying on the ground, a pool of blood underneath his body, drove her out of her room in a panic. She didn't know where Sion was staying in the palace, but she knew she couldn't sit still in her room any longer, so she found herself aimlessly wandering. She thought about waking up Julietta, but she was sharing a room with Kalora and Selenia didn't want to take any chances of messing up the much-needed rest those participating in tomorrow's battle would need.

After combing through a little reading room at the end of the hall, she decided to go back to her room, a book tucked under her arm.

Selenia saw his shadow first, rounding the corner. Before she could see his face, she knew it was him. Selenia watched as Sion walked to her bedroom, made a notion to knock on the door, and then walked away again before actually knocking.

"Sion!" she whispered loudly, rushing down the hall, her bare feet hitting the stone floor.

"Selenia? What are you doing out here?" He turned to face her. He was just in a loose pair of trousers, with no shirt. He had dark circles under his eyes, as if he hadn't had a good night's sleep in days.

"I'm—I'm just scared for tomorrow," she confessed, closing the distance between them until he was just a couple of feet away. "I'm worried for everyone."

He reached out his hand as if to stroke her cheek, but quickly drew it back. "You don't need to worry, Selenia. Our plan will work."

She turned her face up to him, studying his handsome features in the darkness.

"What are you doing outside of my room?"

Sion lowered his eyes towards the floor, shuffling his bare feet slightly.

"Sion?" she asked again, waiting for him to answer.

"Honestly, I'm not sure, Selenia. I was worried that this might be my last night in this world, and I couldn't stop thinking of you, and how much I regret that I can't feel our bond."

Selenia took a step closer, their foreheads practically touching. "How I wish you could," she murmured, looking into his dark eyes.

"Believe me, Selenia. I know I might not feel fate-bound to you, but I definitely want you." His voice was husky, filled with desire. Selenia swallowed hard, looking at the man before her. She'd never felt so desirable before, never felt so wanted or needed. Her knees felt weak, and she actually thought she might collapse from the wanting she felt within.

Sion reached out and stroked her cheek, and her skin tingled as her body responded. Her insides felt like they were on fire, like she would die if he stopped touching her. She stood on her tiptoes, and pressed her lips to his.

Unlike their hurried and lustful kisses before, this was gentle and tender. She felt Sion explore her mouth, his hands circling her and pulling her hips towards his. She felt his length hard against her, and she moaned slightly, knowing she was playing a dangerous game with this man who desired her.

She pulled away. "Do you want to come into my room?" she asked shyly. She wasn't sure she was ready for this next step, but she also knew she couldn't say goodbye to him like this.

A pained look crossed his face, and then he ran the back of his fingers along her jawline before tracing her bottom lip with his thumb. "Selenia—I won't take your innocence. Not like this. Not when I can't guarantee that I'll still be alive tomorrow night."

Tears stung in her eyes from his rejection. She turned her back to retreat to her room, mortified that she'd thrown herself at him.

Before she could shut the door, he softly grabbed her arm, pulling her back towards him, into his warm embrace. "But that doesn't mean I can't be with you tonight in other ways," he said darkly, moving into her room and closing the door behind them.

The second the door closed, he moved towards her, kissing her hungrily.

"Fates, you possess me, Selenia Snowden."

He began kissing a warm trail from her lips down her neck. He breathed in deeply, and Selenia sighed, needing the lavish attention he gave her.

"You are incredible, my darling," he cooed, slipping her nightgown off her shoulder and kissing her collarbone. "So sweet, so innocent. Pure and good, like the snow in the meadow."

She felt her body respond, felt the want and desire between her thighs. She let him move her towards the bed, and felt herself fall gently backwards. Sion adjusted her so she was resting comfortably on the pillow, and he leaned over her, his lips moving along her hairline.

"Sion, I need—I need—"

"What do you need, my darling girl?"

"You," she gasped, trying to pull him on top of her.

He moved between her thighs, still in his trousers. "I won't take from you, my Selenia. But I can certainly give."

She met his eyes as he gently began caressing her thigh. She felt her entire body clench with need as she whimpered his name.

"Hush, my darling. My sweet one."

He brought his mouth back down to hers, and deepened their kiss, exploring her with exquisite precision. Selenia had never been kissed so purposefully before.

She gasped as she felt his fingers trace the outline of her undergarment, and then she lifted her hips up, giving him access to remove them.

"No, my Little Fox. I won't claim you. Yet."

She shivered at his phrasing, heat rising as she imagined giving herself to him completely.

He continued to tease her, stroking her lightly, before moving up to caress her breasts. She moaned into his mouth, and she felt him smile against her. "Is this what you need?

She nodded, her voice lost to her. He raised himself above her, and then without warning, pushed his hips against hers. She could feel him, feel his hardness, pressing against her center.

"Sion, what are you doing?" she gasped.

"Shhhhh...tell me if you want me to stop, Selenia." He tilted his hips slightly and pressed again, and she felt his length hit her in just the right spot.

"Don't leave me. Please don't leave me." Selenia knew her plea meant more than just asking him to continue, and hoped he understood her meaning as well.

"I never want to leave this bed, Selenia."

He gave her another scorching kiss, and then thrust against her, this time a bit harder and then he circled her nipple with his fingertip.

Suddenly, she felt her entire body seize, and pleasure radiated throughout her. She trembled, not fully understanding what was happening, but knowing it was the start of something amazing. She let the sensation course through her, making her toes curl and her fingers tingle.

Sion stopped kissing her. "Open your eyes, Selenia."

She opened them, not realizing they were closed. Her eyes met Sion's, and she knew, knew with all of her heart...He might not feel their fated bond, but she knew deep down that she was loved.

Chapter Thirty-Five

R enya sat on the chair in her childhood nursery, her stomach in knots. The knife Grayden gifted her was tucked within the bodice of her gown, and she gazed out at the room, taking in the care that had gone into decorating it.

Cyrus walked over to her and patted her shoulder gently. "It'll all be over soon, my Sunshine. If you'd rather, I can be the one to end it."

Renya was tempted by the offer, but it was personal. Cressida threatened the people she loved too many times to count, and she knew it must be her. The prophecy even dictated it.

"Thanks Father, but I should be the one to do it."

Cyrus's eyes watered as he looked at her, and she felt tears spring into hers as well. It was the first time she'd called him father. It seemed right, looking around the nursery where she was loved and cared for as a baby. She struggled initially, feeling abandonment and hurt, but she knew it was done to protect her.

Her father kneeled down on the floor and looked up at her. "I've always loved you, my Renya."

Renya sank down off the chair and into her father's awaiting arms.

"Shhh…it's okay, my daughter. We have a lot of time to make up, but I'm not going anywhere and neither are you."

She wanted to disappear, hand over this burden to her father. He would do it, with no hesitation. She wanted to be a child again, protected and loved, safe in a nursery. But then she looked around the room, furniture broken and rubble littering the ground. There was no freedom. This destruction, this mess was from her own mother, determined to end her daughter in order to keep and enhance her own magic. Despite Cressida's softening towards her, it must be done.

Are you in place, Little Fawn?

Yes. How is Beauty behaving?

She knows you're in the tower and if I don't keep on her she tries to get to you, but other than that, she's been great.

"Are you talking to your mate?" Cyrus looked down at Renya and then helped her to her feet.

"How did you know?"

"You get a peaceful look on your face. I could do that with your mother before I broke our bond."

"Do you ever miss her?" Renya couldn't fathom breaking her bond with Grayden. It was as much of a part of her as her arms or her face.

He sighed deeply. "I miss what we had before she found out about the prophecy. We were happy. You, me and your mother. But on her quest for power, she lost sight of the most important thing."

She's here, Renya. Be careful, my love. I'll find you when it's all over.

"She's here," Renya announced, moving to what was left of the window. Sure enough, she saw Cressida riding towards them on Brutus. Behind her, thousands of soldiers marched towards the gates of the city. Renya gulped, fearful for all of the soldiers on their side, including the ones that were her family.

It'll be okay. Deep breath. She felt a sudden sense of calmness, and knew Grayden was trying to steady her nerves. She felt guilty, knowing that he was the one about to face a large army. She just had to kill her mother.

Another painful knot grew in her stomach and she swallowed down her fear, trying to push it aside.

Cyrus stood behind her, fingers out. His eyes scanned the horizon carefully, watching as Cressida landed right in front of the gate of the city. Unbeknownst to her, the combined strength of the Twilight and Tidal Kingdoms, Snow and Spring Lands, were waiting on the other side.

The Shadow Queen raised her fingers, seeming to swipe through the air.

"What's she doing?" Renya whispered, even though she knew she couldn't be heard from up here in the tower.

"She's looking for the residue of my magic. Once the Snow Lands appeared abandoned, she must have realized that I'd cloaked it."

"Can she break it?"

"No," her father said a bit proudly. "But I'm going to allow her to think she can."

Cyrus waited until a burst of dark magic flew from Cressida's fingers, and then he shuddered and held out his hands. Renya watched as waves of golden power radiated back into him.

"She'll know where I am now," he said, almost glowing as his power settled back within him. "But if I was successful, she won't know she's walking into a trap. She must have expected something, and that's why she marched here with her army, but hopefully we will catch her off guard."

Renya watched as the Shadow Realm soldiers waited for a command. Cressida raised her right hand, and they all got into marching formation.

"It's begun." Cyrus said, his eyes focused on Cressida as she blasted through the gate with her magic. The soldiers began entering the city, and Renya felt like she was going to be sick.

"He'll be fine. I've watched your prince, observed him ever since I found out he was your mate. He's strong and capable, and more importantly, if he promises to come back to you, he will. I never dreamed I'd meet a man who loves my daughter as much as I do, but I'm so thankful that I have. And I hope to have grandchildren someday," he added, blue eyes dazzling and sparkling. "No pressure, though. You do things in your own time," he added.

Renya put her hand to her stomach unconsciously. She wasn't one hundred percent certain, but she was starting to suspect that she might be carrying Grayden's child. Prior to coming through the portal, her cycles were irregular, which she chalked up to the stress of dealing with the scandal. She'd also felt nauseous on and off, but she attributed that to her fears and the uncertainty. But now...she was starting to notice subtle changes in her body that left her wondering. She never wished for a 24-hour pharmacy so bad, with their aisle of endless pregnancy tests. She dismissed the thought quickly, hoping that Grayden was so preoccupied that he hadn't peered into her thoughts. Anytime her emotions were strong, he had the tendency to check in with her. She didn't feel the familiar pull of him in her mind, so he must have attributed her apprehension around the potential pregnancy to the current situation at hand. Once she was sure, she would tell him. Renya didn't want to be mistaken in this, and she also knew that revealing news like this could distract him during the battle, and she couldn't have him unfocused. Not only that, but she knew Grayden wouldn't allow her to do anything remotely dangerous if there was a chance she was carrying their son or daughter.

She watched, her anxiety mounting, as the first of the Shadow Queen's soldiers entered the city. As they planned, Grayden swooped in on Beauty, landing in front of them. Renya didn't want any deaths, and she asked Grayden to offer the soldiers a chance to retreat. She couldn't hear what he said, but she watched as he pleaded with the army.

Cressida appeared, and shot a blast of magic towards Grayden, and he ducked. Beauty quickly lifted him up and away to safety, and Renya grimaced as the soldiers marched on.

"I knew she wouldn't allow for a peaceful solution," Renya said, twirling her engagement ring on her finger. "But I really hoped she would."

The carnage started as the two forces clashed. Even up in the tower, she could hear the cacophony of banging metal, confounded with occasional shouting and battle cries. Armor met armor, creating a deep, reverberating sound that hung in the air. Renya shuddered, knowing there would be many deaths in the next few hours.

Cressida weaved above the city on Brutus, shouting orders and commanding the troops, slowly making her way towards the tower. Renya couldn't make out any specific soldiers, but it terrified her knowing that Phillippe, Tristan, Charly, Thesand and Sion were all down there. Kalora and her aunt were also there, and she couldn't see them but could see the tell-tale sign of their magic. She imagined Selenia, hunkered down and terrified in the library of scrolls, sick with worry over Sion. She knew Julietta, as well as Esmeralda would be comforting Selenia, but that Esmeralda would worry about Phillippe too. But if all went well, Renya was hoping with Cressida's death, Sion would be able to feel his bond to Selenia. That thought helped to resolve her feelings and her fear about ending Cressida's life.

"Can you tell at all who's winning?" Renya asked Cyrus.

"No, they are holding steady," he replied. "Our side hasn't fought her army back yet, but they haven't gotten deeper into the city." He looked sad, and Renya realized that he loved his lands as much as Grayden loved the Snow Lands. With a pang, she realized this was her realm as well, and she felt the horror her father felt as the darkly-clad soldiers tried to infiltrate the streets.

She watched as a group of soldiers broke past several Tidal Kingdom warriors, and instantly set the grass ablaze near the communal garden. Her fingers clenched and she ground her teeth as she took in the destruction.

"It won't be long now," Cyrus said, peering out the window. Brutus was getting close enough that Renya could see his eyes gleam and his scales reflect under the scorching sun. She saw Cressida, wearing a black skin-tight leather suit, cape trailing behind her.

Brutus circled the dilapidated tower a few times before leveling towards the window.

"Renya, get back," Cyrus gritted through his teeth.

A second later, Cressida appeared in the large stone window, stepping into the room. Renya shivered as dread overcame her.

"Well isn't this fitting," she crooned, looking at the destroyed room. "It's right that we should end it here, where it all began."

"It began before this, Cressy. The second you found those scrolls, you set in motion this whole cycle of events."

"Don't. Call. Me. That."

Renya watched as her mother's face turned ashen and her body tensed up. Her hair was coiled into the elaborate braids she liked to wear, and her makeup was dark and threatening, giving Renya a sense of foreboding.

"Why not? It's what I called you before."

"Before you deceived me and broke our bond." Cressida's eyes were bulging, her nostrils reduced to small slits.

Cyrus chuckled, arms crossed lazily against his chest. "Well, are you here to make the trade? Your cousin for all the magic you've siphoned out of this world?"

"You fool," she cackled. "Like I would go to any trouble to save my idiot cousin. Keep him, kill him, it matters not. I'm here to reclaim *my* daughter." Cressida made a motion with her fingers, as if to summon Renya to her, but Cyrus was faster. He bound Cressida with the golden strands of his magic.

She easily broke free, laughing at the broken attempt. "Your magic is no match for mine."

This time, she moved quickly and froze Cyrus where he stood. From the look in his eyes, Renya knew he was surprised. He tried to break free, only managing to move his head a bit.

"I have a few more tricks up my sleeve since we last met. Did you ever wonder why Brandle was captured so easily?" The cruel smile she flashed made Renya step back.

"You took Brandle's magic?" Renya asked, finally addressing her.

Cressida ignored her question. "Daughter, come to me. Let's destroy your father once and for all. We'll take his magic, and then move on to even bigger things."

"Yes, mother," she replied obediently, moving towards Cressida. Before she could take more than a few steps, she was suddenly paralyzed.

Confusion swirled over Renya as Cressida moved in. What happened? Why was she frozen?

Cressida stood before her, and grabbed Renya's arm roughly, pushing up her sleeve. "You thought you could fool me?" She dropped Renya's arm and started pacing in the tower. Horror rose up in Renya's throat as she realized what her mother saw on her arm. Her mating mark was there, sparkling in the light peeking through the gaps in the ceiling.

"Your bond was never broken," she accused, grabbing a broken picture frame off the dresser and slamming it on the floor so the glass shattered everywhere. She looked at Cyrus. "You deceived me!"

Cyrus was silent, unable to move. Renya could

see his eyes darting quickly, trying to find a way out of the hold his former mate had on him.

While Cressida's attention was on Cyrus, Renya took a deep breath, her lungs expanding as she tried to calm herself and get out of this situation.

Little Fawn? What's wrong?

Grayden! She reached for his mind. *I need you to help me like you did at the Twilight Kingdom. Calm me, help me center my magic.*

He didn't ask why, which surprised her, but she instantly felt him, in that special place inside her, helping to regulate her breathing and calm her palpating heart.

You can do this, Renya. Do this, and then we'll get married.

The image of her, walking towards him and pledging her soul to him came into her mind, and the jolt of emotion caused her magic to lash out, and free her from her mother's hold. Cressida's eyes bulged as Renya's magic wrapped around her, immediately releasing Cressida's hold on Cyrus.

"Renya! You did it!" His chin was held high, eyes gleaming. He came over and embraced her, but kept his eyes on Cressida. He smoothed Renya's hair and placed a fatherly kiss on the top of her head.

"It's time," he said, nodding towards Cressida, who was struggling within the searing bonds of Renya's magic. She sputtered, freeing her mouth.

"Renya! You are my daughter! Don't listen to him! Assist me! Release me!"

Renya pulled the dagger out of her bodice, and for the first time ever, she saw the look of horror on Cressida's face.

"Don't do this, Renya. I love you in my own way. Let me go, and let me be a mother to you."

"Stop it, Cressy," Cyrus warned, coming to stand behind Renya, silently supporting her. "Don't listen to her, Sunshine."

Renya took a deep breath and stood directly in front of Cressida. She looked at her mother, who was a bit taller due to the high heeled boots she wore. She positioned the knife, ready to end her mother's tyranny.

"Killing me won't bring the magic back," Cressida hissed as Renya brought the knife down. She stopped, centimeters from Cressida's chest.

"Ending your rule will restore our world." Cyrus glared at his former mate.

Cressida chortled. "I admit, I've been siphoning off magic from all corners of our world. But killing me won't restore the balance."

Renya looked at her father, her fingers sweaty and struggling to keep the dagger in her hand.

"It's a trick, Renya."

Renya fixed her grip on the handle of the dagger and brought it to Cressida's throat. "What do you mean?" She pushed the tip in a little, causing the blood to pool beneath Cressida's white flesh.

"You're a fool, Cyrus. You've only believed what you've wanted to believe. I haven't been destroying our world—I've been trying to save it."

Chapter Thirty-Six

"**G**rayden, behind you!" Phillippe's voice rang out, and Grayden swerved on Beauty just fast enough to avoid the flaming arrow that zoomed by his ear.

He didn't even have time to thank his brother before he saw Tristan, fighting hand to hand with a group of five Shadow Realm soldiers. He pulled on Beauty's harness, and directed her towards Tristan. The second Beauty's feet hit the ground, Grayden jumped off her back and she took off, charging another group of fighters. They ran as soon as she came hurtling towards them.

Grayden pulled out his sword and took out the three men on Tristan's right, while he took the other two.

"What happened to your sword?" Grayden asked Tristan, whirling around to take on another soldier, making quick work of him.

"I made the mistake of trying to take on the smaller dragon," he said, rubbing his shoulder. "It's lodged in the beast and I had to retreat." He jabbed his thumb just beyond the city gates, where Grayden saw the other dragon snarling and clawing at the wall surrounding the city.

Grayden put his fingers in his mouth to whistle for Beauty, but he stopped when he saw Agatha approach the dragon attacking the wall, her magic crackling in the air. A shadow, darker than the darkest night, enveloped both Agatha and the dragon, and Grayden couldn't see anything that was happening. He turned, heading back towards the palace, worried about Renya.

"Grayden!"

He turned around, looking for the voice. He saw Sion on the ground, a deep gouge in his side. He was laying in the middle of the street, bleeding against the golden tiles. Grayden didn't waste any time before hauling his friend up, and hoisting him on Beauty's back. He knew Beauty couldn't carry both of them, and he promised Renya he'd stay with Beauty so she could protect him, but this was the only way to get Sion help. He knew Renya would understand. He clenched his fingers, praying to the Fates that Sion would survive. Not only to assuage his guilty conscience for the way he treated his friend when he found out about his relationship with Selenia, but also because he couldn't put Selenia through the heartbreak. She finally had started to push aside the dark cloud that seemed to follow her, and he refused to let his sister's mate die.

"Beauty, quickly! Take him to the palace, to Dimitri!" He gave Beauty a pat on the rump, and she took to the sky, Sion draped over her back.

He ran back towards the palace, trying not to look at the fallen soldiers that lay on the ground. He took a deep, pained breath but continued moving forward. War always brought casualties, but he valued all life. It was what he hated most about being a ruler, knowing that he sentenced these men to die when he directed them to join in this fight.

He tried to push the thought out of his mind as he continued down the street, dodging soldiers and looking out for any civilians who might still be lingering around, unable to make it to the palace.

He reached the courtyard, and his eyes instantly darted up to the tower. Golden light could be seen radiating from the room, and his stomach loosened and he unclenched his jaw a bit when he didn't see a trace of black mist.

Something wet nudged his hand, and he looked over to see Beauty, attempting to get a pat. He shook his head, knowing if the situation was different he would be chuckling over the behavior of the dragon. It was clear that Renya had done a number on the beast, just as she had him. He gave Beauty a pat, but his breath burst out of his chest when he saw how much blood was on her back.

He wanted to run straight to Renya, to make sure she was okay, but he knew her father would protect her. Right now, he needed to look after Selenia, which meant ensuring Sion's safety. He moved towards the main hall, which was set up as a temporary infirmary. His eyes widened as he looked across one of the tables and saw Selenia, hair pulled back and an apron over her dress, assisting a man with a broken leg. Julietta was wrapping it, and Selenia helped to hold the man still, whispering words of comfort. Grayden wanted to shout at her, scold her for not obeying him, but he stopped. Selenia's heart was wonderfully pure, and if she wanted to help nurse the injured, he wouldn't get in the way. From the look on her face, he surmised that she didn't know about Sion. He knew the agony he would feel if Renya was hurt, and Selenia's calm demeanor told him more than he needed.

Grayden caught sight of Dimitri, and instantly knew that he was working diligently to save Sion. Bloody linens surrounded the table, and he appeared to be rubbing a poultice on the wound, while Samatra handed him a clean bandage. Grayden sprinted over, catching Dimitri's eye.

"He'll survive, provided there's no infection," Dimitri said, dark circles under his eyes and his lips pressed thin.

"Thank you. Twice now you've performed miracles to save my kin and friends, and you shall be rewarded."

"No reward needed," Dimitri said, patting Sion's unconscious body on the shoulder and heading to the next table to tend to another patient.

Now that Sion was seen to, he reached out for Renya, and felt uncertainty and confusion through their bond. Puzzled, he made his way over to the stairs and took them two at a time, needing to see that she was okay.

He reached the landing and threw open the door, sword drawn in caution. He saw Cressida, bound in the corner, with Renya standing before her, her dagger hanging loosely by her side. The air was tense, and unease hit him and made him shiver.

"What's going on?" he asked, looking at Cyrus and Renya.

"Ah, if it isn't my daughter's mate!" Cressida squealed, as if she was truly enjoying this reunion.

"Renya, do what you came here to do," he encouraged, ignoring the Shadow Queen. He marched to Renya's side to show his support.

Instead, Renya dropped her dagger, and Cressida sighed in relief. "I knew you couldn't do it, daughter."

Daughter. The second Cressida echoed that word, his entire body clenched and his fists curled inward. How dare she call Renya that! This was the woman who tried to kill her as a child, kidnapped her twice, tried to take her magic, and nearly killed him. If it was too hard for Renya to do it, Grayden would be more than happy to. He moved and raised his sword, but he was suddenly frozen in the heat of Renya's golden bonds.

"Renya, what are you doing?" he asked, eyes darting, looking at her for some kind of understanding.

"We can't kill her, Grayden. Killing her won't fix our world."

"What do you mean? Of course it will! She's been stealing magic!"

Cyrus exhaled. "Renya's right, son. The balance was already broken before she began empowering herself."

"So? Either way, it doesn't matter." He struggled against the confines of the magic, and Renya looked guilty.

"I'll release you, but you have to promise me you won't touch her until we figure out what to do with her."

"Oh, touch me, please," Cressida said mockingly, and if he had been free Grayden would have murdered her with his bare hands right then and there.

He took a measured breath, slowing his heartbeat. "I promise you, Renya."

She studied him for a second, and then the magic holding him captive broke.

"We need to restrain her, permanently." Renya said, eyeing Cressida. "I don't trust her."

"I don't either. There's a spell we can use, but I can't do it alone. I'll need your help to make any kind of permanent bindings."

"She needs to call off her soldiers, too."

"Will someone please explain to me what's going on?" Grayden looked at Renya, arms crossed in front of his chest.

"Renya, I'll take her down to the library. There's a secure room there that should hold her for a while. I'll make sure she puts a stop to her troops first."

Grayden snorted. "I remember that blasted room."

Cyrus wrapped his magic around Cressida and then disappeared.

"Now please explain why your dagger isn't down that witch's throat."

"I went to do it, and she said something that stopped me. Remember Kalora's tales about the first Fae? And how the magic faded as the Gods left? She said she knows how to bring them back, how to restore the world to what it once was. That's why she's been gathering magic, why she was so obsessed with the Sun Realm scrolls. It makes sense, Grayden. When I looked at the histories of the houses, the fated bonds and lack of powers started way before I was born."

"This is true, Little Fawn, but there's nothing we can do about that. We need to kill Cressida, and then the magic she took will return to wherever it came from."

She sighed. "Are you willing to live in a world where fated bonds have died out? Think of what we share. Can you deny that experience to others? What if there's a way to restore everything? What if we could restore your magic completely? Allow Esmeralda to find

308

her fated mate? Allow Sion's bond to your sister to materialize? For Julietta to regain her powers? For the snow in your lands to cover the ground completely? The glaciers to stop melting? Are you willing to ignore the possibility that we could make it right?"

"Renya, I'd love to believe that's true. But the prophecy says that—"

"Yes, I know. That the sun betrays. But that's already happened. My father betrayed my mother when he broke their bond and hid me away. What if this entire time, the prophecy had nothing to do with Cressida? What if it was all about bringing back what's been lost to our world? Grayden, please."

He looked into her eyes, seeing the desperation there. The desire to fix a broken world. To save everyone in it. His Renya and her pure heart. Her generosity of spirit. The ferocity she wore as a cape. He didn't trust Cressida, but he trusted Renya with his life.

"If this is what you need to do, Little Fawn, I support you. I'll be there with you each step of the way. I just have one demand before we go galavanting off on another adventure."

"What's that?" she asked cautiously.

"For Fates' sake, would you marry me already?"

Epilogue

Renya looked ahead, seeing Grayden smile at her. His tunic was pressed, and for once his hair was tidy. He almost didn't look like himself. She would have plenty of time tonight to mess it up, she thought, as she glided towards him.

Her father walked beside her, prepared to give her away to Grayden. The tradition made no sense to either male, but Renya insisted her father walk her to the altar. Cyrus agreed immediately, giving Renya whatever she wanted. It was obvious to her that he felt guilty about the time he lost with her, and he was every bit the doting father she never knew she was missing.

She felt deliriously happy, knowing she didn't have to look over her shoulder anymore, or fear that Cressida would take her away from Grayden. Cressida was currently bound in the depths of the Sun Realm, unable to use her magic for anything. She'd been forced to give up all the magic she acquired over the past twenty-five years, and little by little, Fae around their world regained some of their powers. But, disappointingly, nothing else seemed to change. No new fated bonds came forward, and Grayden's lands still warmed.

The only surprise was Julietta. Her full powers returned the second Cressida released them. Apparently she had taken them while Julietta was an infant. Renya enjoyed watching her test them out, watching her bond with Kalora as she trained her daughter. She saw both women sitting next to one another on the far side of the forest, and smiled happily to see them there.

They continued down the long pathway, lined by their friends and family. Even Samatra and Thesand had arrived, and Margot from the Shadow Realm was there with her son, who had fled rather than go to war on Cressida's behalf.

She passed Esmeralda and Phillippe, who were standing next to each other. Esmeralda wore a gorgeous headpiece of flowers pinned in her hair, and Renya knew that she didn't bring it with her. Combined with the fact that she saw Phillippe down in the garden earlier, she had a suspicion that he was actively courting her friend.

When she passed Sion, he gave her a respectful bow. His side was still bandaged, but Selenia had become his full-time caretaker. She never left his side, and Sion seemed happier than Renya had ever seen him. He had taken the news of Cressida's survival hard, needing her dead to erase the scars she caused him. Selenia was angry as well, perhaps even more so than Sion. But today, they both looked happy.

Renya heard a sniffle, and she saw Doria on the left side of the path, gently crying into a handkerchief.

Cyrus continued guiding her down the rose-lined path, passing her aunt and Tumwalt, only stopping when she got to the altar. Before her, Grayden stood with Almory, who was dressed in ceremonial robes. Almory looked like a cross between the Pope and a circus performer, and Renya held in her giggle the best she could.

I don't know what a pope or a circus is, Little Fawn, but I trust you'll tell me later.

Hush, we need to pay attention, she scolded lightly, and turned to face Almory.

The ceremony was quick, less than five minutes, which was fine with Renya. She knew it was important to Grayden to be married in the same spot as his parents, but she felt like she'd been married to him almost since she came through the portal.

As Almory pronounced them man and wife, a hush suddenly fell around the snowy forest, and everyone's gaze turned towards the left of the altar. Renya looked, and her breath hitched in her throat.

Three elkten stood there, as if invited guests to the wedding.

Grayden grasped her hand, looking as the elkten watched over them.

"Our union has been ordained since the beginning," he whispered in Renya's ear. "and it will last until the end."

Renya smiled, and closed her eyes as his lips brushed hers in a kiss, sealing their marriage and strengthening their bond.

The End

...for now...

Author's Note

I know, I know. I said that book three was the conclusion. And it is–in a sense. It's the end of Renya and Grayden's love story–they will never be separated again, and their happily ever after is set in stone. As an author, I'm done wreaking havoc on their lives.

When writing book three, I hoped to wrap up all loose threads and end it in a nice and tidy package. But the more that the side characters came to life for me, the more and more I felt that it was a disservice to them to rush their stories for the sake of the trilogy. Especially Selenia–oh how I love her character. She was never supposed to have her own point of view, but the more and more she talked in my head, the more I wanted to see things from her perspective and watch her grow and evolve.

Yes, the threat of Cressida is gone. She's not going to cause much more trouble, except for her snide retorts and embarrassingly flirtatious comments to her daughter's husband. But magic still needs to be fixed, and our next cast of characters–Selenia, Sion, Esmeralda, Phillippe, and Tristan are going to take a starring role in this quest. Of course, Renya and Grayden will be there–and yes, we are going to get to see their wedding night and find out what happens when Renya tells him her news. But their relationship is done with its tribulations. Nothing left for them to do but relax in their giant bathtub after questing.

And omg, yes. At some point I will kill off Brandle in a grand fashion. Just trying to decide who gets to do the lucky honors.

So, prepare yourself for three more books! We'll have one with Selenia and Sion, one with Esmeralda and Phillippe, and one with Tristan and his leading lady (I can't personally wait to see him show some emotion.) And yes–Renya will be there, and of course Grayden goes wherever she does.

I do have one book that I'm currently working on, called *The Collector*, which is a dark contemporary romance. I'm slated to finish that, and then I will return to A World of Sun and Shadow.

So, stay tuned, follow me on Instagram and Facebook, and keep reading!

-Rachel

Made in the USA
Monee, IL
05 August 2024

63324306R00187